Emma Page

A Fortnight by the Sea

Penguin Books

Penguin Books Ltd,
Harmondsworth, Middlesex, England
Penguin Books,
625 Madison Avenue, New York, New York 10022, U.S.A.
Penguin Books Australia Ltd,
Ringwood, Victoria, Australia
Penguin Books Canada Ltd,
41 Steelcase Road West, Markham, Ontario, Canada
Penguin Books (N.Z.) Ltd,
182–190 Wairau Road, Auckland 10, New Zealand

First published by
William Collins & Co. in their Crime Club 1973
Published in Penguin Books 1976

Made and printed in Great Britain by
Hunt Barnard Printing Ltd, Aylesbury, Bucks
Set in Linotype Pilgrim

For D.S.P. with love

Chapter 1

A sunny July morning with a salty stir of breeze among the tall green spears of montbretia in the narrow border under the kitchen window. Pauline Barratt looked up from her notebook with its jotted reminders, menus, dates and names; she gave a resigned sigh as her gaze came to rest on the narrow leaves. By the time the scarlet flowerheads broke from their sheaths the summer would be over. It was racing past her as it had raced for the last few years, in a whirl of bookings and cancellations, arrivals and departures, beds to be made up, lunches to be thought of.

Footsteps along the passage, the slightly ponderous steps of someone well into middle age, carrying with them a strong suggestion of purpose.

'There you are, madam,' Bessie Meacham said as she came into the kitchen. 'I'll get the packed lunches out of the way and then I can start on the cooking. Just the one couple for sandwiches today?' Saturdays in the busy season might be pretty hectic early and late, but at least they offered a relatively calm spell in the middle.

Pauline turned from the window. 'Yes. And just one person in for lunch.' She frowned. 'I'm not sure yet about the numbers for dinner.'

'Probably best all round then if I make a good large beef or chicken casserole,' Bessie said with decision. 'And I can roast a nice leg of lamb as well. A big potato salad and a couple of cold sweets, should be enough late strawberries to make a flan.'

Pauline felt a touch of the old sense of inadequacy that still visited her fifteen years after she had walked through the front door of Oakfield as a bride of eighteen, not altogether able to credit her good fortune in actually marrying Godfrey Barratt. Bessie had stood waiting in the hall to welcome her – of course she hadn't been Bessie Meacham then, but Bessie Forrest. She was twenty years older than her young mistress; she had

7

worked at Oakfield ever since she'd left the village school at fourteen.

Pauline had never been able to rid herself totally of the notion that Bessie regarded the house – and the domestic quarters in particular – as her own property. Her impersonally pleasant manner always seemed to imply that Pauline was a temporary interloper to be casually humoured until she saw fit to drift off elsewhere.

'I don't think there'll be any strawberries left.' Pauline was determined to find some point on which she could assert authority. 'The beds were picked over pretty thoroughly a couple of days ago. Better make it a raspberry flan.'

Bessie took a loaf from the bin. 'Mr Meacham'll find some strawberries for me,' she said comfortably. 'Don't you worry about that.' She liked to refer by this formal title to the man she had met and married during her holiday in the spring. She had gone off to Torquay with no special thought of romance, nothing beyond what any seaside holiday might be expected to offer – she had been Miss Bessie Forrest for fifty-three years, but that didn't mean she didn't have her fancies and inclinations like everyone else even if she'd never previously got as far as the altar.

A piercing ring sounded from the back door. Bessie glanced at the clock. 'That'll be the butcher.' Tradesmen in the near-by town of Chilford still found it worth while to send their mobile shops the four or five miles inland to the prosperous village of Westerhill.

'Let me see.' Pauline wrinkled her brow. 'A chicken, stewing beef – '

'I've got it all in my head,' Bessie said amiably. 'No need for you to trouble yourself, madam.' She went unhurriedly out into the passage.

The flowers, Pauline thought, I suppose I ought to go and see what Meacham has cut. All those vases to be arranged and herself the only person who could be relied on not to make a hash of the job.

From somewhere in the upper regions she caught the drone of a vacuum cleaner. Better go up and run her eye over the bedrooms, make sure everything was being done properly. A small squad of daily women assisted in a piecemeal fashion with the running of Oakfield, each with her own methods, duties, schedule of hours.

In the doorway Pauline turned and surveyed the room with its high ceiling and long windows. One day when there was money to spare – if ever such a day should dawn – it could be transformed into a glitteringly modern kitchen. In the meantime it would benefit considerably from rather more thorough cleaning and tidying than it was getting at present. Or was likely to get before the pace slackened in October.

Ah well – she smiled fleetingly – just as well there wasn't any question of giving the room a good turn-out just yet; she wouldn't in the least have relished raising the matter with Bessie. Like many people with an easy-going surface and slightly slapdash ways, Mrs Meacham was capable of fierce resentment at the suggestion that other methods might have something superior to offer.

Pauline made a dismissing movement with her shoulders, stepped into the passage and set off at a brisk pace towards the stairs.

The study at Oakfield was a comfortable room facing south. The furnishings – leather, mahogany, dull gold velvet – were much as they had been in the time of Godfrey Barratt's father and grandfather.

Godfrey sat at his desk, staring out at the blue and gold morning. Utterly impossible that Osmond's could fail. A firm of builders known and respected across half the counties of England, providing employment for a host of satellite concerns, sub-contractors, suppliers, manufacturers of everything from a paintbrush to a window-frame. And somewhere pretty far down on that list was Barratt's, woodworkers and turners, a tiny firm – looked at from the standpoint of the giants – but reasonably efficient and prosperous. Or so it had seemed until four days ago.

Godfrey stood up and pushed back his chair. He thrust his hands into his pockets and paced about the room, still a little dazed by the shock that had struck him on Tuesday morning as he ran a casual eye over the businss pages of his newspaper. Just a whisper of rumour at first, the merest shadow of a hint

9

that things might not be everything they should be at Osmond's, but he had felt the muscles of his throat tighten with apprehension.

By Wednesday morning company spokesmen were blandly asserting in radio interviews that nothing was seriously amiss; when the Stock Exchange closed for business on Thursday, Osmond's shares stood at a third of Monday's price; on Friday morning Godfrey assembled his men.

They were very quiet as they waited for him to speak. Their eyes looked back at him with disciplined blankness as if they couldn't as yet abandon themselves to either fear or hope. Unemployment was at a high level; in a seaside town like Chilford there was scarcely any alternative work for a skilled man. But a miracle might yet happen. Currents might move unseen in the City, fresh capital might flow in from a dozen different sources, political pressures might compel the Government to shore up Osmond's.

He'd explained the situation as he saw it, he'd answered their questions honestly, refusing to indulge in meaningless optimism.

All that remained to them now was to wait. Every action that controlled their immediate future would be taken by men they would never even see. Only another week to go and the firm would close for its three weeks' annual holiday. That week would be spent in completing an order for a Chilford builder, the kind of order Godfrey had been accustomed to look on merely as an act of goodwill towards the local community. It occurred to him now with wry force that if his entire order-book had been filled with such benevolent commitments, he would be in a much healthier position.

He flung himself down into an armchair, leaned back and closed his eyes. No point in spending a single further minute in work for Osmond's – unless the miracle happened No point in going into the works this morning; there would be no Saturday opening, no overtime of any kind, till the whole complicated muddle was sorted out.

The whirligig of thought began again . . . This is the end of Barratt's, there won't be any rescue operation for Osmond's, you won't be the only small woodworking firm abruptly stripped of its chief contract, competition will be cut-throat for every other piece of business in sight, you won't be able to hold out, there'll be the men's wages, the relentless overheads, Osmond's won't be paying another penny to suppliers, not even for deliveries already made . . . A light sweat broke out on his forehead at the remembrance of the large consignment Barratt's had despatched to Osmond's only ten days ago, a consignment for which they would normally have expected payment at the end of the month.

He jerked his eyes open and stared up at the ornate ceiling. They'll have a receiver in by the end of the month, he thought, still hardly able to believe it, I can whistle for my money.

On the table beside him the phone shrilled suddenly and he snatched up the receiver, glad to be forced out of his obsessive thoughts.

'Mr Barratt?' The deep soft voice of Theresa Onil, edged now with anxiety. 'I think perhaps you ought to come up to see Miss Tillard, she's not very well this morning. She asked me to see if you would call in.'

'Of course I'll come' Godfrey said at once. Elinor Tillard was his wife's aunt. Headmistress years ago of a girls' school in Africa, she was now seventy. She lived a short distance away, looked after by Theresa, the half-African girl she had brought to England seventeen years ago. 'I take it you've asked the doctor to call?' Godfrey added. Miss Tillard inclined to the view that sending for a doctor during a bout of illness was a desperate remedy to be adopted only when all others had failed.

'Yes.' A touch of hesitation in Theresa's tone. 'It's the new young man, Doctor Nightingale, I'm not sure he's –'

'He struck me as perfectly competent,' Godfrey said reassuringly. The local doctor – ageing, old-fashioned – had taken himself off a week ago for a holiday in Minorca, he wouldn't be back for another three weeks. Godfrey had called in a couple of days ago during the evening surgery to get a renewal of Pauline's prescription, the stuff she took for her headaches. He'd had a word or two with Nightingale, sized the fellow up. 'He may be young, but at least that means his methods are up to date,' he pointed out.

'Mm, perhaps so,' Theresa said without conviction, preferring the man she had known for years. 'Anyway, he said he'd call in shortly after half past eleven. If you could come up about then you could have a talk with him after he's seen Miss Tillard.'

'Yes, I'll do that.' Godfrey glanced at his watch. 'Would Miss Tillard like my wife to come along too?' In the course of the last year or two Godfrey had grown a good deal closer than Pauline to the old lady. He had helped her with one or two business matters, had fallen into the habit of calling in on her on his way home in the evening. She looked on him now as a kind of unpaid confidential adviser. And one of the things she most valued in him was the strict way in which he interpreted the word *confidential*. He might not be related to her by blood but he certainly shared the same close-mouthed attitude to financial affairs.

'Miss Tillard didn't mention Miss Pauline' A hint of coolness now in Theresa's tone. 'I think it would be better if there weren't too many visitors at the moment. And I know Saturday morning is very busy for your wife at this time of the year.'

'Very well then, I'll see you in about an hour.' When he had replaced the receiver, he sat for several seconds frowning down at the carpet, then he stood up abruptly and went over to his desk, pulled open a drawer and searched rapidly through its contents. 'Ah!' he said aloud a few moments later as he found what he was looking for. He sat down, picked up a pen and began to write.

'Mr Godfrey not going into the works then this morning, madam?' Bessie Meacham asked with casual interest when Pauline went into the kitchen at a quarter to eleven in search of coffee.

'No, I don't think he is. I believe he said something earlier.' Pauline dragged her mind back from its preoccupations. She had never set foot inside the works, it had never occurred to either her or Godfrey that she might do so. She made regular conventional inquiries about the state of affairs at Barratt's and received brief reassuring reports of progress.

'I noticed his car still in the garage just now.' Bessie opened the oven door and gazed critically inside. 'That's why I asked.' An appetizing smell of roast lamb drifted out into the kitchen.

Pauline took down a tray from one of the crowded shelves. 'I expect he's in the study. I'll take him a cup of coffee.' She glanced at Bessie who was carefully basting the meat. 'How's the cooking going? Everything under control?'

'Yes, thank you, madam.' Bessie continued to ladle hot fat over the lamb. I do wish she wouldn't address me as madam, Pauline thought with the flick of irritation that still sometimes stung her.

She poured out the coffee and took it along to the study. Godfrey was sitting at his desk, sorting through a bundle of papers. He wore a look of intense concentration, and it appeared to take him a moment or two to realize that his wife was in the room and that she was putting a cup of coffee down on the table beside him.

'Better not let it get cold,' Pauline said gently. He glanced up with an abstracted look and then his gaze focused on her. He pushed back his chair and got to his feet.

'I'm sorry, my dear, I didn't hear you come in, I was deep in documents and figures' He had said not a word to her about his fears over Osmond's, would continue to say nothing until the very last moment – there was still a chance that the moment might never arrive. He picked up the topmost papers, scrutinized them, slipped a couple into his breast pocket and returned the others to the desk. 'By the way, Theresa Onil phoned just now.' He closed the desk and locked it. 'It seems Aunt Elinor is not very well this morning. Theresa's sent for the doctor.'

Pauline set down her cup with a little clatter. 'How bad is she?'

Godfrey began to drink his coffee. 'Don't be alarmed, I dare say it won't prove to be anything very serious, probably just another gastric upset. I know it can't be very pleasant for her, but I should think in a week or two –'

'She's seventy.' Pauline walked over to the window and looked out at the nodding roses. 'Do you think we ought to phone Marion?' she asked in an unemotional voice. 'It's quite a long time since she's seen Aunt Elinor. I feel perhaps she should be told she's ill.' She turned round suddenly. 'Does Aunt Elinor want to see me? Did Theresa say?'

'I did ask but Theresa thought it would be better if you waited till tomorrow or Monday. Aunt Elinor wants me to go up there this morning, and then there'll be the doctor, Theresa thought that would be enough visitors for one day.'

'Theresa Onil takes it on herself to think rather too many things that are not strictly her business She's scarcely one of the family.' And that ridiculous name, Pauline thought with unreasoning prejudice, she can't even have a sensible name like everyone else. Forty years ago Theresa's mother, walking gracefully along a rutted track on the edge of the Ashanti forests, had stopped and given directions to a young Irishman, a mining engineer newly arrived in the Gold Coast. The engine of his car was overheated, he was tired and thirsty, he could see no sign whatever of the cluster of buildings he had been assured he couldn't miss. The girl was young and slender, shyly smiling. Yes, she knew the mine buildings – he had taken the wrong road some miles back; yes, she would come with him in the car and point out the way.

Three months later young O'Neill died swiftly and terribly of blackwater fever and the girl went back to her village. When her daughter was born she called her Theresa after a nun at the mission hospital; there had never been any need for a surname until years later when the baby had grown into a tall, rather silent girl anxious for education. Onil, her mother had said, standing by the desk in the school office, casting her mind back with difficulty to the young Irishman with his black hair and blue eyes, an improbable figure from a brief, incredible time.

'Come now,' Godfrey said with mild reproof. 'Theresa looks after your aunt as devotedly as if she actually were a member of the family.' He finished his coffee, patted the papers in his breast pocket and glanced at the clock. 'I won't take the car, I'll walk up to the bungalow. Young Nightingale's looking in at about half past eleven, I'll have a chat with him after he's seen your aunt.'

'You haven't said yet whether we ought to phone Marion and Stephen.' Pauline gave him a steady look. Marion was her sister, three years older than Pauline, married to Stephen Lockwood, a business executive. They lived some way off, in Barbridge, an industrial town markedly lacking in charm; it was a considerable time since visits had been exchanged between the two families.

'You can phone if you think it necessary,' Godfrey said after a short pause. He was silent again for several seconds. 'Yes, I suppose you'd better.'

Pauline's manner grew suddenly brisk. 'I'll suggest they stay for a week or two. Stephen might be able to take a little holiday, I'm sure Marion would like to see all the old haunts again.' Something rather forced about the brightness of her tone. She picked up the coffee cups and placed them neatly on the tray; her eyes didn't meet Godfrey's.

'Will you be able to fit them in all right?' he asked, a little surprised at the determination in her manner.

'The boys will be going off to camp in another week.' She glanced at the photographs on top of the desk. Her sons looked out of the frames with self-conscious smiles, two sturdy boys, tall and fair like Godfrey. They were due home on Tuesday from the school which had been their father's and their grandfather's. 'Their rooms will be free,' she said. And she always tried to keep one or two bedrooms unbooked for casual holidaymakers looking for overnight accommodation.

'I very much doubt that Stephen will be able to get away for more than a day or two,' Godfrey said. 'And in any case, don't they always go abroad for their holidays?'

Does he really not want them to come? Pauline asked herself with such a fierce stab of the old jealousy that she raised a hand and pressed it to her side as if the pain had a physical cause. Godfrey had been wildly, passionately in love with Marion; they were never actually engaged but everyone had been certain they would marry. And then Stephen Lockwood had taken it into his head on a sunny, idle Saturday morning to go back to Chilford, to his old school, where they were giving a garden party to launch an appeal fund for the building of a new science block. The Tillard girls had gone to the garden party with their father, an old boy of the school. Marion was then twenty years old, at the height of her beauty; Pauline was seventeen, only just liberated from the classroom, still afflicted by adolescent spots and plumpness. Stephen had been coming out of the refreshment marquee where he had been making himself useful handing round glasses of iced lemonade, he had looked across the emerald lawns and seen the two girls coming towards him. Easy enough to find someone to introduce them; six weeks later he and

Marion were engaged, in another couple of months they were married.

'They went to Malta at Easter,' Pauline said. She kept up a regular correspondence with Marion, ruled in this as in many other things by the strongly conventional side of her nature which dictated that if you had a sister you wrote to that sister, whatever thoughts and feelings were sternly denied expression on the smooth-surfaced writing-paper. 'I shouldn't think they'd want to go abroad again for a holiday so soon.' For the first ten or eleven years of her marriage Godfrey had held a commission in the Army and at least half of those years had been spent out of England. Pauline had never really taken to the life; she had longed for the English countryside, had wanted to bring her children up in their own land. She had felt no regrets when Godfrey had resigned his commission four years ago on the death of his father. She had returned to England with pleasure and had ever since retained a certain mild prejudice against foreign shores.

'I'll phone them this evening.' She was now absolutely determined to bring Marion face to face with Godfrey. Some compulsion had gathered force inside her during the last year or two; it had reached a stage now where it could no longer be repressed. She would stand in the same room with the two of them, she would look from one face to the other. She must know. 'And in any case,' she added with a touch of censoriousness, 'Marion really ought to pay more attention to Aunt Elinor. I dare say she'll be left everything – or the best part of it anyway, she's the eldest.' Marion had always been Aunt Elinor's favourite, she had been everyone's favourite. 'Not that there'll be all that much to leave, but still, it doesn't look good.' She suddenly caught the tail-end of her own utterance and was taken aback for a moment at the hypocrisy and petty-mindedness showing through.

'I must go,' Godfrey said. 'I don't want to miss the doctor.' He walked over to Pauline, slipped an arm briefly round her shoulders and brushed her cheek with his lips. 'I'll give Aunt Elinor your love.'

When the door had closed behind him, she crossed the room and stood in front of the screened fireplace, gazing with frowning concentration at her reflection in the oval mirror above the mantelshelf. A faintly-tanned, fine-boned face, blue-grey eyes, delicate brows; but what she saw was the haunting image of her adolescent self, blemished skin, difficult hair. Of course he didn't love me, she thought with savage certainty. How could he have loved anyone after Marion? And least of all that pathetic, plain schoolgirl. She saw all at once with total clarity why he had married her. He had wanted a son to carry on the name, he couldn't have Marion so he had made do with Marion's sister. She felt a searing wave of self-disgust. She'd been so eager to say yes; such an ignorant, blind, foolish creature.

She turned abruptly from the glass and went to the window. Godfrey was walking with an easy pace across the flagged terrace. I'd say yes again, she realized with astonishment; knowing all I know now, with innocence and the first flush of youth behind me for ever, if that starburst instant were to spring into being a second time, if he were to take my hand out there in the garden as he took it before, if he were to ask me again to marry him, I would still say yes.

As he neared the edge of the terrace Godfrey halted and looked back at the house. Pauline instantly moved to the side of the window and continued to watch her husband without fear of being seen herself. She levelled a look of fierce concentration at his calm features. If only she could tell what went on in his mind – but his upbringing hadn't taught him to express his thoughts openly, and his years in the Army had done nothing to counteract that early and decisive training.

His gaze travelled without haste over the whole frontage of the house, the elegant proportions, long windows, slender columns, mellow stone, glossy-leaved creepers. This place means more to him than anything else on earth, she thought suddenly, there is nothing he wouldn't do to keep it . . . The notion sprang into her mind with startling force.

The creek and rattle of a wheelbarrow approached from the shrubbery. Godfrey abandoned his survey of the house and permitted his stance to take on a relaxed air.

'Good morning, sir.' Edgar Meacham appeared with his barrow through a gap in the lilacs. 'It looks as if the fine weather's going to hold.'

Godfrey glanced vaguely up at the soft blue sky delicately

ribboned with white. 'Yes, it would seem so.' He walked across to where Meacham was stooping over a scatter of lopped boughs. The severed ends were reasonably neat, the depth of cutting back not too severe. He nodded in brisk encouragement. 'You're making a pretty fair job of it.' His gaze rested on the pale green leaves. He scarcely ever looked anyone directly in the eyes; on the chance occasions when he did his glance had a lightly veiled quality.

'Thank you, sir.' Meacham gave Godfrey his habitual frank and open look; his voice held both pleasure and relief. His employer's head turned suddenly and with a distinct suggestion of dismay at the sound of the front door opening, footsteps, voices issuing forth.

'Ah! Mr Barratt! I was hoping to catch you – ' A large, imposing lady bore down on Godfrey. She was followed by her daughter, a nervous-looking young woman who seemed perpetually to be trying to obliterate herself from the landscape.

Meacham gathered up the wood, flicking a covert glance of amusement at Godfrey's back as Barratt compelled himself to walk with an air of affability towards the pair of females. Shouldn't have stopped to talk to me, Meacham said to himself, then he'd have been off down the drive, out of harm's way, before they'd had a chance to catch sight of him. His sharp eyes had more than once observed Barratt's little manoeuvres to avoid confrontation with his guests, particularly with the bed-and-breakfasters who were the most mixed bag of all.

'A charming house,' the large lady said with massive patronage. 'Such a stroke of luck to come upon it – ' The trouble is, Meacham thought, taking a pair of secateurs from his pocket and snapping a shoot, there isn't really any type of guest he does genuinely welcome. The pretentious made Barratt squirm, the ill-bred made him shudder, and with civilized folk he was perhaps even less at ease, imagining how they might be pitying – or even despising – him for having to throw open his house in this manner.

He stood now listening to the oration of the majestic lady; his face wore a slight, interested smile. 'I'm so glad we managed to make you comfortable,' he said when she paused for breath. If he didn't protect himself with those good manners, Meacham thought as he looked round for his garden broom, I dare say he'd run the risk of breaking out, letting fly perhaps with a really nasty show of temper, could even go berserk, that type. Meacham had seen a thing or two in his time. Watch out for the disciplined man when the discipline wears thin; he'd learned that lesson the hard way.

'I do hope you enjoy the rest of your holiday,' Godfrey said pleasantly, at the same time removing himself by another couple of paces from the two women in order not to have to shake hands at the moment of farewell. He looked down at his watch. 'I must ask you to excuse me, I have an appointment.'

Meacham swept the debris into a heap, listening with keen interest to the final exchanges, observing with an appreciative movement of his head the skilful way in which Barratt avoided touching either lady by the hand. Not that any man in his senses would want to, Meacham thought as he transferred the heap to the barrow. He sent a shrewdly assessing glance after the two women who were now walking back to the house. Not much joy to be had there, not from either of them. The daughter he might perhaps, at a pinch, have gone as far in the old days as, well, running his eye over her, sizing her up, not likely to have gone any further than that. But the old girl – he shook his head and allowed a soundless whistle to escape his lips – he'd have known better than to tangle with the likes of her, even for a single moment. Not even in his palmy days. He sent a smiling sigh towards the past. Not even in his prime.

Chapter 2

Godfrey walked rapidly away down the drive. Only three or four weeks ago he had told himself that he might not have to endure for very much longer the presence in his house of a succession of total strangers. And now – he drew a long appalled breath at the notion – it might be years before he could finally close the door on that motley horde.

He halted for a moment, brought all at once face to face with a thought that had been bobbing about somewhere in the recesses of his brain and now sprang out to confront him with chill reality . . . It is no longer a question of tolerating or not tolerating holidaymakers at Oakfield. If the Official Receiver walks in through the gates of Osmond's, the unimportant little firm of Barratt's will slide into bankruptcy a week or two later without the attentions of whirring television cameras or crackling microphones. A couple of paragraphs in the *Chilford Gazette*, a few lines in the trade section advertising the machinery to be disposed of for what it would fetch. And the forthcoming auctions page displaying a photograph of Oakfield, details and measurements relentlessly listed below.

He came out on to the road and turned right, in the direction of Miss Tillard's bungalow, away from the centre of the village. The soft air strayed against his cheek, bringing with it the scent of the sea.

It had been Elinor Tillard's idea in the first place, he remembered suddenly, that they should take paying guests at Oakfield. She had thrown the words half-jokingly into a tea-time conversation not very long after the lawyers had finished winding up old Mr Barratt's estate. There had been the death duties of course – Godfrey had expected that – but what he hadn't expected was the leanness of his father's bank balance and share holdings.

Looking back on it now, he could see that his father simply hadn't been much of a businessman. In his youth he had followed the family tradition of spending some years in the Army, then he had lived a pleasant enough life in the village where he had been born, withdrawing to some extent from local society after the death of his wife, becoming increasingly absorbed as the years went by in purely private interests and hobbies. He hadn't been a shrewd investor and time had eroded much of the fair-sized fortune he had inherited.

Not that I seem to be turning out a financial wizard myself, Godfrey thought ruefully. But he couldn't see, even now, that he had behaved foolishly four years ago when he had decided to sink what remained of his father's capital in a run-down firm that could with diligence and shrewdness be restored to prosperity.

He'd gone to Tillard and King's, the Chilford estate agents –

his father-in-law, now dead, had been a partner in the firm; he'd listened to their advice, furrowed his brow over the lists of properties and settled at last on this little woodworking business. The owner had been in poor health and had recently suffered a heart attack which had left him with no alternative to retirement. The price was very reasonable and Godfrey had always had a liking for the sounds and smells of workshops littered with curling woodshavings, ever since his first attempts at carpentry in his schooldays.

The concern had appeared fundamentally sound. House-building looked a very healthy growth industry. He had been confident of success – too confident, he could see that now clearly enough – and he had moved little by little, like many another inexperienced man, into the vulnerable position in which the greater part of his production depended on a single outlet. He let out a groan as he contemplated the extent of his folly.

'It will take a little time before we're really on our feet,' he had said cheerfully over the teacups four years ago.

'Meanwhile – ' Pauline had said, with a questioning glance that spoke of school fees, domestic help, repairs and rates.

'Meanwhile,' Aunt Elinor had echoed smilingly, 'you could take in summer visitors. You're only half a mile from a good beach, you've plenty of room, it would give Pauline something to think about while the boys are away at school, it would help to pay the expenses of Oakfield.' Neither of the women had suggested that he should sell Oakfield, perhaps because they were well aware his ears would be closed to the idea. The family solicitor had raised the matter once, without conviction, knowing his man. 'I am bound to say,' he had observed, looking blandly into Godfrey's eyes, 'that the best advice I can offer you is to put Oakfield on the market and move into a smaller house.' Godfrey hadn't troubled to reply. He had merely shaken his head once, decisively, and that was the end of that.

But Aunt Elinor's joking remark had lingered in his mind, had imperceptibly turned at length into decision. 'Only for a year or two,' he'd said to Pauline, 'just until we're on a firmer footing.' Characteristically he had informed her of his decision without even making a show of consulting her. It wasn't that he had a bulldozing temperament or harboured outdated theories about women's place in the scheme of things. he was simply following instinctively the pattern his father had laid down. Godfrey's mother had died when he was a child, so long ago that he had no memory of her; he had been an only child, more or less brought up by Bessie Forrest – Bessie Meacham as she was now, of course. There had been no one to question his father's edicts and Godfrey had grown up under the impression, which it had never seriously occurred to him to question, that a household arbitrarily ruled by one man represented a perfectly normal and in no way undesirable state of affairs.

Pauline was seven years younger than her husband. At the time of her marriage she had been overwhelmed by a sense of her outstanding good luck, and she had been brought up in a home where the mother was gentle and compliant, the father ruled the roost and there were no sons to challenge this arrangement. The early part of Pauline's married life had been spent in a military environment in which it seemed quite normal for men to issue orders. If she had ever felt resentment after their return to civilian life, if she had come to wish to be treated as a partner rather than as an uncritical subordinate, she never actually got as far as opening her mouth and saying so.

Godfrey turned a bend in the road and glanced up at the top of the next rise, to where Miss Tillard's bungalow stood over on the left with a narrow belt of trees to the rear but unscreened in front, looking out over the wide countryside, down towards the village of Westerhill a mile or so away.

A small green car was parked beside the house. Nightingale's car. The doctor was standing on the verandah with his bag in his hand, talking to Theresa Onil. It was clear from his stance and the way he was facing that he was just about to go inside. Godfrey slackened his pace. A good ten minutes or more before Nightingale would be ready to leave. A few moments later Theresa turned and led the way indoors.

The bungalow would have looked a good deal more at home under the burning skies of Africa than in its orderly setting in the gentle English landscape In the early nineteen-fifties the old colonial life on the Gold Coast had ended for ever in a series of changes and upheavals that Miss Tillard had viewed with dislike and apprehension. She was no longer young enough to adapt herself and her professional attitudes to new ways; when she learned of the proposal by which Europeans in her position were to be allowed to opt for an early pension – together with a handsome lump sum – it didn't take her long to make up her mind to leave the country where she had worked for thirty years.

She had come back to the neighbourhood of Chilford where she had been born and brought up. Her father, a partner in a local firm of estate agents, was now dead, but her brother, of whom she had always been fond, had taken over the half-share in the firm and lived on the outskirts of the town with his wife and two daughters. He had found Elinor a small furnished house in which she and Theresa Onil had lived for the year during which the bungalow had been designed and built to Miss Tillard's very precise specifications.

She had reconstructed as nearly as possible the dwelling she had occupied for the last fifteen years as headmistress of the African school. The bungalow was raised up on a kind of plinth in a way that made sense in the tropics where any whisper of breeze was welcome. A wide verandah supported by slender pillars ran along the front of the house; even the wicker chairs and tables arranged in casual groups carried a note of that other way of life, remote now, part of the past, already beginning to be fossilized.

Godfrey's easy pace brought him to the top of the rise and the gate that led into Miss Tillard's garden. Flowerbeds filled with brilliant cannas were cut into the smoothly sloping lawn. He paused and looked down towards the village, at the church, the central green, the satellite cluster of buildings, and beyond, near the summit of the gentle incline that rose up at the far side of the village, the clubhouse on the golf-course.

He let himself in through the gate. The bungalow stood at a physical remove from the village, and its occupants were isolated also by the way in which they kept themselves aloof from local contacts. This was partly because Miss Tillard found it very difficult to get about; she kept an unwelcome souvenir of her final days in Africa in the shape of an exceedingly troublesome hip joint. The farewell ceremony had taken place at the school; the leather trunks stood locked in the hall. On the day before she was due to wave good-bye, Miss Tillard took it into her head to enjoy a nostalgic ride in a local bus. She hadn't done such a thing for a quarter of a century, since the days when she was newly out from England, a young and humble member of staff, without a dignified position to keep up.

The buses were strange, not to say fearsome vehicles, ramshackle to the point where it was astounding that every jolt over the roads didn't cause them to fly apart. Decorated in garish colours, crammed with passengers, and invariably ornamented with painted signs of a religious nature, at once stoutly optimistic and realistically aware of peril implicit in the next lurch.

Miss Tillard had been accompanied on her fateful excursion by Theresa Onil, then a young woman in her early twenties. She had been enrolled as a pupil at the school not very long after Elinor became headmistress; a couple of years later her mother had died and Theresa had been kept on as a boarder, her fees being paid by Elinor who liked the girl and felt sorry for her. Besides, there was really nowhere else for her to go. She seemed to have no knowledge of any relatives back in her native village, and Miss Tillard knew that a light-skinned child was unlikely to be welcomed by any connections who might be discovered. Inquiries were made through the District Commissioner but no one came forward to claim Theresa.

She had formed an ambition to become a teacher, probably in imitation of her admired Miss Tillard, but she hadn't managed to pass the examinations. When she was eighteen she had begun to take on a number of unofficial duties which she allotted to herself and discharged with care. By the end of another year or two she was supervising the welfare of the youngest children, occasionally acting as a classroom assistant, helping Miss Tillard with a number of irritating minor tasks and in general making herself useful and agreeable all round.

Elinor had felt a blend of sentimental nostalgia and holiday gaiety as she boarded the bus. Theresa had worn an unsmiling look, considering the expedition both undignified and unwise. On the front of the vehicle a short length of wood hammered into place above the driver's seat bore the flowing inscription : 'The Lord Will Lead Me. Beneath it a second piece of wood said simply but alarmingly: To The Cemetery.

Half a mile outside the town Theresa had suddenly seized Elinor's arm and pointed with horror at the road ribboning out behind them. Elinor had just time to catch sight of a wheel from the bus bouncing along on its own before the vehicle fell over.

When Elinor came out of hospital some weeks later it seemed a very good idea for Theresa to accompany her on the voyage home and see her settled into temporary accommodation. Two or three months had lengthened into six, into a year. And then there was the move to the new bungalow, Theresa would be so useful at such a time. Miss Tillard had always intended to lead an active life during her retirement, but the England in which she perched her exotic bungalow was a good deal changed from the country in which she had grown up; in fact she frequently felt herself in the first year or two after her return as much of an alien as she had felt during the recent upheavals in the Gold Coast.

And physically she had never been the same woman since her disastrous trip in the bus. Time drifted by and she made a cosy little nest for the two of them on the outskirts of this quiet English village. She saw a certain amount of her brother and his family, but nothing like as much as she had expected.

She had barely moved into her bungalow when her brother's elder daughter got married and took herself off with her new husband to the other side of England. A year later the second girl also married; Miss Tillard had scarcely had time to congratulate herself on the fact that Pauline would be living at Oakfield, more or less on her own doorstep, when she learned that Godfrey Barratt intended to make his career in the Army.

Eighteen months later Elinor's brother died and his widow sold her house, disposed of the half-share in the estate agency to a Tillard cousin – neither of the girls having the slightest inclination to concern themselves with the firm – and took herself off to Spain to live.

The next eight or nine years floated past Elinor like a none too pleasant dream. She no longer even raised the question of sending Theresa back to Africa; without her she would have felt herself totally isolated, a prey to melancholy. It scarcely ever occurred to Godfrey Barratt's father, perfectly content with his life at Oakfield, his long-settled hobbies and interests, to invite Miss Tillard in for a meal or to share in an outing, nor did it ever cross the mind of Bessie Forrest – who ran Oakfield after the death of Mrs Barratt – that she might make overtures of friendship to the young African woman at the bungalow.

Miss Tillard was able to feel little regret when old Mr Barratt died and it was with deep relief that she learned soon afterwards that his son was leaving the Army and coming home to settle.

Godfrey stood now just inside Miss Tillard's gate. Must be about time for Nightingale to be leaving; he walked briskly up the path and pressed the bell. The door was opened a minute or two later by Theresa who gave him her usual calm glance.

'Do come in.' She stood aside to let him enter the bright airy hall decorated with mementoes of Africa. 'I don't think Dr Nightingale will be much longer.' She opened the door into the sitting-room. 'If you wouldn't mind waiting in here.' A little heavier than when she had first come to England but still trimly built, rather tall, with a graceful, erect way of walking. Not a particularly handsome woman but pleasant enough to look at. Large brown eyes, a smooth skin the colour of milky coffee, shining black hair with a strong wave, taken neatly back and arranged in heavy coils.

A few minutes later Godfrey heard the murmur of voices and after a brief interval the sitting-room door opened and Theresa ushered in the young doctor.

'I gather you're worried about your aunt,' Nightingale said cheerfully when Theresa had discreetly removed herself.

'Actually, Miss Tillard is my wife's aunt,' Godfrey said in precise tones.

Nightingale smiled affably. 'I've written her a prescription, we'll see how she gets along with that. I'll look in again on Monday.'

'She's had a number of these upsets over the last few years.'

Nightingale raised his shoulders. 'Colonial types,' he said lightly. 'Like their curries and their groundnut stews. A bit hard on the digestion. I've had a word with Miss Onil she seems a sensible woman.' He glanced round the walls, at the wooden masks, crossed spears, curious shaped objects of incised brass. 'Quite a little outpost of Empire.' He picked up his bag. 'No reason why you shouldn't go in and see your aunt.'

Chapter 3

Miss Tillard had raised herself against the pillows when Theresa ushered Godfrey into the bedroom. 'I feel a little better already,' Elinor said with an air of thankfulness. 'I don't know if it's just the effect of Dr Nightingale's manner.' She smiled faintly. 'He's rather bracing.'

Theresa went along to the kitchen to make the coffee. 'I'm worried about her,' Miss Tillard said with an anxious look.

'I'm sure you've no need to be.' Godfrey patted her hand. 'She always appears very content.'

Miss Tillard put up a thin hand and touched her hair, once so long, so thick and dark, now sparse, almost totally white. She sighed and shook her head. 'It isn't the present I'm thinking about, it's the future. Theresa's future.' She shot a direct look at Godfrey. 'My own future may not extend all that far.'

'You mustn't talk like that. You'll be up and about in no time at all.'

'I haven't been fair to Theresa,' Miss Tillard said as if he hadn't spoken. 'I've always been a very selfish woman. Whether I die this year or in ten years' time, what is to become of her when I'm gone?'

Godfrey frowned. 'Surely I understood from you that you've made provision for Theresa?'

Elinor made an impatient movement of her head. 'I added a codicil to my will ten or twelve years ago,' she said with contempt. 'I've left her some money.'

Godfrey had never actually seen a copy of the will but he believed that he had a pretty good idea of its contents. Miss Tillard was fond of asking his advice, there were a number of matters in which she allowed him to handle affairs directly but certain nooks and crannies of her financial concerns she kept to herself.

'A thousand pounds,' Elinor said now, mentioning the figure to him for the first time, uttering the words with scorn. 'It seemed a substantial sum at the time. It isn't worth much today.'

'It strikes me as very fair,' Godfrey said mildly. It occurred to him with bitter amusement that in a month or two a thousand pounds might strike him as a princely sum. For a moment he entertained a wild notion of opening his mouth and saying, 'I am very probably on the verge of bankruptcy,' and allowing events to move on from there. But he merely passed a hand across his mouth as if obliterating all traces of the unspoken words. 'I'm sure Theresa wouldn't expect more,' he added.

'She has no friends in England,' Elinor said fiercely.

'Oh, come now!' Godfrey's tone held reproof. 'There's myself, Pauline – '

'And none in Africa.' Elinor's expressive look appeared to attach little importance to the warmth of the Barratt family's feeling for Theresa. 'Where would she go? What would she do?'

'I really think we can forget the question of Theresa's future for the present,' Godfrey said soothingly. 'We'll discuss it thoroughly when you're quite better.' He put a hand into his breast pocket and drew out some papers. 'By the way, I need your signature – ' Elinor listened with an abstracted air as he explained, she gave a brusque nod when he had finished.

'I could simply increase the legacy.' She frowned down at the bedspread. Godfrey picked up a magazine from the top of a rose-wood chest and laid it in front of Miss Tillard. 'Or I could cancel the legacy,' she added. 'Leave her the bungalow and a small income for life.' She took the pen Godfrey held out, glanced at the papers he placed on the firm surface of the magazine. 'Or I could make it a decent income and cut down on the bequests to the girls.' She wrote her signature to each paper in turn in the place where Godfrey's finger indicated. 'Both the girls are well enough provided for,' she said in a musing tone as if she were simply speaking her thoughts aloud and had forgotten that there was anyone else in the room.

Godfrey gathered up the papers and returned them to his

pocket. There was a faint rattle of a tray outside the door, a light knock and Theresa came in with the coffee.

'If I might ask you something,' she said quietly to Godfrey a few minutes later. 'You mentioned over the phone that Mrs Barratt might be calling in later on. I wonder – if she thought of coming this afternoon – if she would mind if I went off to Chilford while she was here to sit with Miss Tillard. I'd like to go in on the bus to have the doctor's prescription made up. I wouldn't really care to leave Miss Tillard on her own just yet.'

'Nonsense!' Elinor said loudly. 'I'll be perfectly all right on my own. Pauline wouldn't find it in the least convenient to come over on a Saturday afternoon at this time of the year.'

'Of course she'll come over,' Godfrey said. 'She would have come with me this morning except that Theresa felt that two visitors at once might be too tiring for you.'

'I won't hear of her coming,' Elinor said resolutely. 'I don't in the least mind being left by myself.'

'I shall settle the matter,' Godfrey said, 'by going into Chilford myself and getting the prescription made up. It won't take me any time at all in the car.'

'That's a much better idea,' Elinor said. 'And then Pauline can come to see me just when it suits her.'

Godfrey held out his hand. 'I'll take the prescription now. Before I forget it.'

Elinor looked on as the paper was handed over. A trace of reluctance surely in Theresa's movements. Elinor felt a pang of remorse. Theresa had in all probability been looking forward to the little outing to Chilford, a brief escape from the tedium of her duties. She must be given a whole day off the very moment Elinor was recovered.

Anxiety about Theresa's future began to thrust at her again. I can't let it slide, she thought, it must be settled.

'The boys will be home from school on Tuesday.' Godfrey had not yet finished his coffee. 'If you're feeling strong enough by then they'll come over to see you.'

'I shall look forward to that,' Elinor murmured. She continued to nod and smile as Godfrey talked about the boys and their summer camp. It isn't really right and proper to discuss the question of Theresa's legacy with Godfrey, she thought suddenly.

He is almost an interested party, in fact he definitely is an interested party – married to Pauline, father of the two boys, all beneficiaries under the present arrangement. It was putting him in an impossible position to ask for his advice. Even supposing he was willing to discuss it again at present.

No, the thing was – she saw it quite clearly now – to say nothing more about it to Godfrey but to talk it over with Henry Whittall; Henry would give her impersonal professional advice.

'You might give Henry a ring,' she said with a casual air as Godfrey set down his cup and stood up to go. 'Ask him to call in and have a word with me. It's all right,' she added reassuringly, seeing the look on Godfrey's face, 'I'm not going to wear myself out talking to him for hours about my affairs, or anything foolish like that. But there are one or two little things – if he would just look in for a moment some time during the next few days, no desperate hurry, then we could fix a time for later on, when I'm well again, to go into things properly. In the meantime, he could be looking up one or two details for me.'

'Very well then,' Godfrey said without enthusiasm. 'I'll phone him.' Henry Whittall was a clerk in the firm of Chilford solicitors who handled Miss Tillard's affairs. He was a local man, a bachelor, a couple of years younger than Godfrey; he had known the Tillard girls since they were all youngsters growing up in Chilford; he lived now on his own in a cottage a mile or so from Oakfield. His firm also counted the Barratt family among its clients, so Godfrey had known Whittall for a number of years on a business level; in his more privileged boyhood his path had crossed Henry's only on those occasions when young Whittall had been up to Oakfield with a legal paper to be signed by Godfrey's father.

Godfrey stooped now and kissed Elinor lightly on the cheek. 'Look after yourself,' he said. 'I'll call in about four o'clock with the medicine.'

He was half-way down the slope leading from the bungalow when he glanced over to his left, at the road coming from the village and saw, a couple of hundred yards away, a toiling figure weighed down on each side by a shopping bag. Henry Whittall, he recognized the figure at once; no other adult male in this region plodded along on Saturday mornings with his week's fodder slung about him. I'll catch him at the crossroads, Godfrey thought, save me a phone call. The sight of Henry aroused in him no emotion of any kind. Either you wanted to speak to Whittall on business or you did not want to speak to Whittall on business and apart from those two concepts Henry really had no existence in Godfrey's mind, or for that matter, in the minds of very many other people.

Godfrey reached the intersection and stood waiting by the grassy bank. When Henry was within earshot he called out pleasantly, 'Good morning, Whittall, I'd like a word with you.' Henry gave a single nod in reply. 'I've just been to see Miss Tillard,' Godfrey said when Henry had reached him and set his burdens down.

I wouldn't mind in the least if Barratt called me Whittall in the friendly way that men do when they're on an equal footing, Henry thought with suppressed anger, but he always speaks to me as if I were a servant. He listened with an air of scholarly concentration to Godfrey's account of Miss Tillard's latest illness, her wish to see him. He didn't look Godfrey in the eye but kept his head inclined at a polite, impersonal angle, his gaze fixed on the creamy florets of a luxuriant weed in the hedgerow. A very tidy sum to leave, Miss Tillard.

'Certainly I'll call at the bungalow,' he said as soon as Godfrey had finished. 'I can look in during the next day or two.'

'That should suit very well.'

'I trust Mrs Barratt is in good health? And the boys?' Henry said as Godfrey showed signs of setting off again for Oakfield. He made up his mind sometimes to refer to Godfrey's wife by her Christian name when he was talking to her husband. He had after all called her Pauline when they knew each other as children. But when it came to the point his nerve always failed. In conversation with the lady herself he had since her marriage grown quite skilful in avoiding calling her anything at all.

'Very well, thank you.' Godfrey added a few remarks about the busy season and end of term and then suddenly said, 'Oh yes, you knew the Lockwoods, didn't you? My wife's arranging with them to come and stay with us very soon. I dare say you'll see them about the village.' It would never cross his mind, Henry thought with savagery, to ask me up to Oakfield for a meal while they're here.

He stooped and grasped the handles of his shopping bags, he spoke in an expressionless voice. 'I was at school with Stephen Lockwood.' A fact he was likely to remember when most of the other facts of his existence had dwindled into hazy recollection. He found it difficult to realize that he would shortly see Marion again. It was some years since he had caught a glimpse of her going by in a car on one of her brief visits to the area. It was more than sixteen years since he had spoken to her. He wouldn't mention her name now, wouldn't by any word of his own evoke her image to hover like an airy ghost in the brilliant sunlight, he hugged the memory of her to him, away from casual tongues.

'By the way.' Godfrey held up a warning finger. 'Don't say anything to Miss Tillard about the Lockwoods, not about their visit, that is. It isn't definitely settled, in fact my wife is ringing them up about it this evening. I wouldn't like Miss Tillard to be disappointed in case they can't come. Or if they don't come for some time.'

'No, I won't mention it.'

'I'm pretty certain they will come, though,' Godfrey said in a flat tone. The last thing he wanted just now was for Stephen Lockwood – reasonably successful, securely placed – to go poking and prying into his business, asking shrewd questions about the future of the firm; he would probably want to go into Chilford with him and prowl round the workshop. Oh – that'll be all right, he remembered suddenly, the men will be on holiday from the end of next week. He closed his eyes briefly against the notion that as far as Barratt's was concerned the holiday might be a permanent one. 'July the twenty-fourth,' he said aloud, forgetting for a moment that he was standing a yard or two away from Whittall. 'I was just thinking,' he added, recollecting himself, 'that Barratt's will be closed for three weeks from the twenty-fourth. It would be pleasant if my wife could arrange for the Lockwoods to come at that time.'

The twenty-fourth, Henry repeated in his mind a few minutes later as he trudged round yet another curve in the road. He had three weeks' holiday still owing. Might take a week or two soon, he pondered; things were fairly slack at the office. By the time he set the shopping bags down on the doorstep he had reached a decision.

Chapter 4

'I'm just slipping down to the post, dear.' Marion Lockwood was patting her hair in front of the hall mirror when her husband came slowly down the stairs. She gave him a mechanical half-smile and let herself out into the warm sunlight of early evening.

Stephen went into the sitting-room and crossed to the window. He stood looking out at Marion walking down the path to the gate, casting his eye – without the faintest trace of affection – over the back view of her rather short, slightly plump figure. He yawned and glanced at his watch. Half past six. Not a minute before seven, Fiona had said. He thrust his hands into his trouser pockets and began to pace moodily about the room. How did Fiona occupy herself away from the office during the long stretches of hours when she wasn't seeing him? She never offered any information, certainly didn't encourage direct questions, answered teasingly or evasively if he so far forgot himself as to ask one. 'Not really any of your business,' her smile would imply, 'I'm not married to you . . . yet.'

A few minutes later he was roused from his thoughts by the sound of his wife returning. He flung himself down into an arm-chair and stared critically at the walls, the furniture, the proportions of the room. They should have moved out of this part of Barbridge ages ago when he got his first really good promotion at Alpha Fabrics, but Marion had always been ready with an apparently sound reason why they shouldn't make a change just yet. During the last couple of years he had at last ceased to bother taking Marion out for those evening and weekend runs in the car which had always ended up in front of desirable residences sporting *For Sale* boards. His attention had finally

3

wandered from Marion, strayed about for a while and eventually settled firmly on Fiona Brooke.

'I thought we could have the last of the lamb for supper,' Marion said as soon as she came into the room. 'I saw a very nice recipe in a magazine at the hairdresser's. I copied it out while I was under the drier.'

'I won't be in to supper,' Stephen said brusquely. Marion's standards of domestic economy, suitable enough in their early married life but no longer relevant, now merely the result of a temperamental inability to adapt to changing circumstances, grated on him with increasing force.

'Oh, you have a business appointment.' Marion didn't appear in the least put out. She would quite enjoy fiddling with the bits and pieces of her recipe, would eat the resulting dish in contented solitude, would settle down happily enough afterwards in front of the television set or pick up one of the romantic novels she was so fond of.

Stephen didn't bother to reply, merely flicked over her an expressionless glance. I do believe, he thought, that it is mostly thrift which keeps her tied to this arid marriage, she simply cannot countenance the idea of throwing away something that is legally hers. She would mind scarcely at all if I were dead, she would see widowhood as a common and natural sequel to marriage, she would bed herself cosily down into it – but divorce . . . He shook his head. She would have nothing to do with divorce. However the case was conducted she would feel herself besmirched, marked with failure, inadequacy, she would be unable to relax pleasurably into cushioned singleness as she could if she had first of all watched his coffin descend towards the consuming flames.

'She hasn't rubbed that dirty mark off the window sill,' Marion said suddenly. She fought a genteelly vicious campaign of attrition against whatever cleaning woman she currently employed. She got to her feet and went out to the kitchen in search of a damp cloth. 'I told her twice yesterday before I went to the hairdresser's,' she said when she returned. 'You really have to watch them all the time,' she added in that tone of satisfaction and self-congratulation that caused a tremor of irritation to run along Stephen's nerves. She attacked the mark with vigour.

All that endless concern with microscopic detail, never a large sweeping notion of transforming the entire interior of the house by some new and imaginative scheme of decoration . . . Stephen closed his eyes in distaste. He sometimes felt that the word *housewife* was the most terrifying in the English language.

'There, that's better.' She turned and gave him the same automatic low-voltage smile that she gave the butcher, the baker and the man who came to read the meter. 'What time is your appointment?'

'I'll leave just after seven.' She must know perfectly well that I haven't got a business appointment on a Saturday evening, he thought with cold distaste; deep down inside that knitting-wool brain she must know with total certainty that I have a mistress. But nothing in the world would tempt her to dig down and take an honest look at that knowledge. He experienced a moment's wild desire to say, 'My mistress asked me not to arrive before seven,' just to see if anything would force her to tear the sealing strips from her eyes.

'We really ought to settle something about your other two weeks' holiday,' she said when she had disposed of the cloth and settled herself into an easy chair. Stephen went abroad two or three times a year to trade fairs and exhibitions and would have felt little deprived if his official four weeks' holiday was abolished. In recent years he found an undiluted dose of his wife's society so grey and dull that it was really only because of the look of the thing that he troubled to take his holidays at all. Last year he had been able to nerve himself to enjoy only three out of his four weeks and this year he was hoping to be able to get away with a bare fortnight.

'Perhaps in October. Or November,' Stephen said without enthusiasm. He had a sudden startling flash of memory, Marion coming towards him over the velvet lawns sixteen years ago, so fragilely beautiful in her pale floating dress.

'Chilford,' he said aloud into that treacherous vision from the past, astounded yet again by the way the glorious romance he had grasped at had turned into this sterile union stapled now chiefly by custom and notions of respectability.

'Funny you should mention Chilford,' Marion said amicably.

'I was only thinking the other day I wouldn't mind running down there again.'

She was just a small-souled, small-minded, small-town girl, he said dismissingly in his mind. But she had been so lovely, so breathtakingly beautiful. He closed his eyes. How much our lives are ruled by chance, he thought with recurrent wonder. But was that after all the case? Didn't every action spring from character seizing and moulding chance to its own purposes?

'I don't suppose Pauline will be all that keen to see us,' Marion said ruminatively. 'I dare say she's very well in with Aunt Elinor by this time. I wouldn't be surprised if Aunt Elinor didn't leave her most of her money. Not that she has much to leave.' I bet you'd have trotted down to Chilford fast enough and often enough if the old girl had a fortune to leave, Stephen thought sourly. But a moment later honesty compelled him to admit, No, that isn't altogether true, she isn't passionately interested in money. What she likes is for one day to follow another in cosy, reassuring succession, with just enough excitement to dimple the surface of living. Money was useful to pad the sharp corners of existence, she wasn't really concerned with it for its own sake.

'Elinor might take it into her head to leave the lot to Theresa,' he said with idle malice.

'Oh, Theresa.' Marion's lower lip pouted, a habit left over from her radiant girlhood when there had always been a dozen admirers to find the expression delightful but now somewhat less than entrancing. 'I wouldn't trust Theresa any farther than I could see her.'

Stephen glanced at the clock and saw with relief that it was ten minutes to seven. If he drove very slowly he could leave now. He got to his feet.

'What about it?' Marion said. 'We could use some of your two weeks now, we could have a few days in Chilford. Then we could go to Italy or Spain in October.'

'Please yourself,' Stephen said shortly, conscious now only of Fiona a few minutes' drive away.

'It would be all right then as far as your work is concerned?' Marion persisted.

Stephen raised his shoulders. Not the busiest of times at Alpha, the middle of the summer. 'If you like to fix it,' he said with one hand on the door, 'I dare say it will be all right.' If he was going to be compelled to spend a few days with Marion he didn't much care where it was, and at least Chilford would require less effort from him than a trip to the Continent. He opened the door and paused suddenly as a fresh vista of thought opened up. 'Actually,' he said on a warmer note, 'Chilford isn't at all a bad idea.' He turned and looked at his wife, his eyes had a bright, friendly look. 'Yes, you arrange it. Make it a week if you like.' He paused again. 'Or even ten days.'

Marion was still wrinkling her brows over the pages of her diary when the phone rang a few minutes later.

'Why, Pauline!' she cried as soon as she recognized her sister's voice. 'If this isn't a coincidence! Stephen and I were just talking about you – '

Stephen parked his car in the shade of a clump of trees that screened it from the road, and walked swiftly towards Fiona's cottage. It really was the sheerest piece of luck that she was currently renting this conveniently isolated little place on the outskirts of Barbridge. If she'd still been in the modern flat she occupied during her first six months at Alpha Fabrics, it was highly doubtful that he would have risked embarking on the affair at all. The Chairman at Alpha was a formidable Scot of sixty, bristling with rectitude; he most emphatically would not look with favour on an employee he even suspected of harbouring dubious moral principles. And these days Stephen considered himself in line for a seat on the Board.

He reached the garden gate and walked up the narrow path. The situation was getting a bit tricky, to put it mildly. Fiona was twenty-eight. She very definitely intended to get married and she wasn't going to wait for ever. Stephen didn't in the least resent the core of steel running through the centre of Fiona's backbone. Sixteen years of living with a wife who saw life as a succession of trivia and expressed her views in a stream of banalities had left him more than ready to admire a woman who took a purposeful view of her own existence.

He raised a hand and pressed the bell. Fiona threw open the door almost at once. 'You certainly don't believe in losing time,' she said as the grandfather clock in the hall began to chime the hour.

She didn't look overjoyed to see him, but then she never did. Her habitual manner was cool and composed. One of the things that fascinated him about her was the way in which the surface coolness would gradually fade, disclosing a temperament of a very different kind. Lately though, the coolness had tended to persist longer and return earlier. He knew the reasons well enough. She wasn't a woman to hold a gun to his head in any brash or vulgar way but she was sounding all the same a warning signal, strong and clear.

He waited till the door was safely closed before he slipped an arm round her waist and kissed her gently on the cheek. She was wearing a trimly tailored summer dress; through the open door of the sitting-room he could see a handbag and parcels lying on the table. She had spent the afternoon shopping then, and – even more important – she would have spent it alone. He felt a strong sense of relief as he registered the fact, he was sharply aware these days of time gathering speed, beginning to press in on him, forcing on him the necessity for decision. Fiona was an elegant, striking-looking woman with intelligence and personality. More than one man at Alpha – to say nothing of the wide world beyond its gates – would be only too delighted to slip a ring on her finger. Whenever he stood back and took a cold, level look at the whole situation he experienced a powerful feeling of danger and exhilaration.

'You must be tired,' he said lightly. 'Shall we bother to go out?' He tried this one fairly regularly; it hardly ever succeeded.

She smiled, put up a finger and ran it across his lips. 'I want a very good dinner and I most certainly don't intend to cook it myself.' She was an excellent cook. He saw himself living with style and elegance in a house presided over by Fiona, his entire existence lifted on to another, altogether more harmonious plane. She put her arm through his. 'I was in the kitchen, putting things away. I'd better finish it.'

He followed her into the tiny well-ordered room and helped her to unpack the groceries. He watched her movements with pleasure. She was tall, handsome rather than pretty, with a smooth white skin, very finely moulded cheekbones and straight black hair, very long and thick, taken up in a casual knot on top of her head. He wasn't a man to be ceaselessly infatuated with the same type of beauty; he had in fact fallen in love this time with a woman about as different in appearance from Marion as it was possible to discover within the confines of Barbridge.

It won't last, he thought with sudden piercing sorrow as she smiled at something he had said. I'll marry her – I'll manage it one way or another – and in fifteen, twenty, twenty-five years we will look at each other with indifference or hatred. But I won't mind by then, he told himself with force, by then I will no longer be young enough to care. If he could bargain with the Fates for a limited span of happiness he'd be satisfied, he wouldn't complain.

'Did you have anywhere special in mind for this evening?' he asked as he put the butter, the cream, the cottage cheese in the fridge. They always drove a good thirty or forty miles out of Barbridge; he usually took a discreet look round the bar and the dining-room first. Just in case. So far they'd been lucky.

When they'd settled on a place she went upstairs to change, leaving him to mix himself a drink in the sitting-room. He sat down on the sofa and switched on the radio. A powerful sweep of music, some classical symphony he couldn't identify. He settled back and let the tide wash over him, strong, insistent, filled with yearning. He saw for an instant the dark face of depression that had looked out at him with increasing frequency in recent years. An only child, born to the astonishment of his parents in their middle age, doted on from the day of his birth, he had been the object of all his mother's obsessive love after the death of his father. His mother also had been dead now these five years or more. It was since her passing that he had begun to be afflicted by this terrible sense of aloneness. It would come on him sometimes at strange moments, in a train, walking along a gleaming corridor at work, waiting for a drink in a crowded bar. He had to stiffen himself to resist the compulsion to reach out and touch a hand, any hand. And when the irrational moment passed he would be left with a black surge of depression that might take hours to fade.

He took a long drink from his glass. Above the sound of the music he heard a cupboard door close sharply upstairs. He tilted

39

back his head and glanced up, thinking of Fiona moving about the bedroom. With Fiona he was able to forget depression. In her company he felt himself years younger than the set-faced husband of Marion; gayer, livelier, farther distanced from the arid shores of middle age.

He drained his glass and set it down. Our emotional needs are programmed in the cradle, he thought with resignation, we are stuck with them for the rest of our days. For me it is a deeply loving woman currently wearing the face of Fiona Brooke. And whatever it is for Fiona, he added with a wry smile, I can only hope it continues to be moulded in the image of Stephen Lockwood.

He picked up the heavy table lighter and idly studied it. Silver, good quality, graceful design, set in a base of onyx. Fiona had expensive tastes. He ran a finger over the chilly smoothness of the stone. In a divorce settlement Marion would certainly get the house. And a substantial slice of his salary. He would very probably have to take out a large insurance policy for her benefit. He wouldn't be left with an income of very impressive proportions. Hardly sufficient to create – let alone maintain – the elegant dream world he was to share with Fiona. He let out a long sigh . . . Love might begin with I will give you the moon and stars, but it not infrequently ended in front of a judge with a vicious wrangle about ten pounds a week.

He clicked the lighter switch, he frowned at the yellow flame. What would the fading, suburban Marion do with her share of the spoils, with the house, far too large for a woman on her own? He extinguished the lighter and set it down with a little bang. Why should an able-bodied, childless woman of thirty-six have to be supported in idleness till the end of her life?

A bedroom door opened and Fiona's steps sounded on the landing. He jumped to his feet, smiling, eager; he switched off the radio and went out into the hall.

'By the way,' he said a few minutes later as they came out into the bright evening, 'I may be taking a little leave shortly. A few days or a week perhaps. I'll let you know when it's definite.' Under no circumstances whatever did he allow the name of his wife to pass his lips when he was with Fiona. She knew, and accepted, that there was no question – as yet – of their going off together for a holiday.

He walked beside her to the car. She turned her head and gave him a brief cool glance but she said nothing. Again he had a strong sensation of time pressing relentlessly on behind him, hurrying him forward to an objective that seemed to glitter with the promise of joy but sometimes, disconcertingly, fleetingly, impelled towards him a sense of some obscurely chilling presence waiting for him at the end of the road.

Chapter 5

Twenty-five minutes to nine and no sign of Lockwood yet. Bob Jourdan tilted back his chair and stared out of the window, biting his lip in annoyance. The Alpha staff were supposed to start work by eight-thirty sharp; he had been here himself since ten past, never saw the point of trailing in at the last moment. And on a Monday morning too, with the new week straining at the leash.

He let the legs of his chair slap down on the floor and snatched up a folder of papers from his desk. But it was no good, he couldn't take a decision on his own about the Manchester job – or rather, he wasn't permitted to take a decision on his own, he was perfectly capable of doing so. He had to have old Lockwood's say-so. And he knew exactly what attitude Lockwood would take. The safe, conservative attitude of a man with his eye on a director's seat.

A light rap on his door and Fiona Brooke came in with some files. 'You look pretty grim,' she observed, laying the folders in front of him. 'Let me have these back as soon as you can.'

'Old Lockwood's late again.' But some of Jourdan's grimness began to fade. With his left hand he picked up the top file, running his eye over the cover which was stamped in red with the word *Welfare*; he suddenly shot out his right hand and without looking at her seized Fiona by the wrist. He dropped the file on the desk and idly flicked its pages. 'Have dinner with me this evening,' he said in a challenging voice tinged with amusement. His face seemed about to dissolve into laughter. Still keeping his gaze fixed on the folder he began to draw her towards him with easy strength.

'I'm busy this evening,' she said pleasantly, looking down at him with unruffled calm.

'Tomorrow evening.' He continued to pull her inexorably towards him.

'Even more busy tomorrow.' Her mouth trembled on the edge of a smile.

'Wednesday. Thursday. Friday.' She was right beside him now. In a swift movement he released her wrist and slipped his hand round her waist, holding her in a tight grip.

'Absolutely frantically busy on Wednesday, Thursday *and* Friday.' She couldn't help smiling broadly, it was as much as she could do not to laugh aloud.

He dropped his hand, looked up at her, his eyes suddenly intent and serious. 'I'll keep on asking.'

'No harm in asking,' she said lightly. 'I must get back to Welfare.'

When the door closed behind her he abandoned all show of interest in the files and sat with his elbows on the desk and his chin propped on his clenched fists. Why do I do it? he asked himself yet again. He not only wanted to get on to a more intimate footing with Fiona, he wanted to marry her. Actually marry her! Why? He was thirty years old, had always looked on himself as an astute bachelor, had never wanted to marry anyone before. He'd never even kissed Fiona and yet he had this overpowering desire to put a ring on her finger, to hear her addressed as Mrs Jourdan. Is this what they mean by real love? he wondered with a sense of incredulity. It didn't feel like anything he had previously identified as love. Could it possibly be – he frowned fiercely, trying to pin down the disturbing notion – that I want her simply because she belongs to Lockwood? He'd been transferred to Barbridge on promotion from another branch of Alpha only two or three months before; the liaison between Lockwood and Fiona was supposed to be a deadly secret but it hadn't taken Jourdan half a day to spot how matters stood. It wasn't the way two people looked at each other that was revealing but the way in which they carefully did not look at each other.

He passed a hand across his forehead, pressed his fingers into his scalp. Was it that, wanting Lockwood's job, he was snatching symbolically at his mistress? If he somehow managed to step into Lockwood's shoes at Alpha, would he instantly lose all interest in Fiona? Or was it after all simply that she was herself a tall, composed, elegant, intelligent woman?

Suppose by some chance that she was willing to marry him. And suppose also that by some other chance he took Lockwood's place as Home Sales Manager. Was that a blueprint for happiness? Or would he in a month, six months, a year, find himself a prey to consuming retrospective jealousy? He had observed this ugly phenomenon once or twice in the marriages of contemporaries who had previously fancied themselves tolerant, broad-minded men of the world. The end result had never been anything but disastrous. Could it happen to him? He shook his head slowly. He simply didn't know. He was almost totally ignorant of the depths of jealousy but it seemed to him that very strange fish might swim in those midnight waters.

A few yards away, in the corridor, he suddenly heard the crisp tones of Lockwood's voice. At once he sat up and straightened the papers on his desk. A minute or two later Lockwood came into the room.

'Morning, Bob. If you've got the details of that Manchester job, we can settle it now. Bring all the stuff into my office in – ' he glanced at his watch – 'say ten or fifteen minutes. Must take a look at the post first. A bit late this morning. I've been downstairs, fixing up a spot of leave.' He saw Jourdan's questioning look. 'I'm taking next week off. I fancy a breath of sea air.'

I'll ask Fiona again next week, Bob thought, with a sense that events had somehow taken a decisive turn. He had a strong notion that with Stephen Lockwood out of the way for what? – the best part of ten days? – Fiona might have time to stand back and take a look at his own apparently teasing pursuit of her, might begin to reconsider the situation between herself and Lockwood, might very well, before the week was out, decide that she was not after all perpetually too busy to accept a dinner invitation from the Assistant Home Sales Manager.

In the larger and better-furnished office next door Stephen glanced through his letters. Nothing of world-shaking interest this morning. He raised his head and twirled his pencil between his fingers. That look of surprise and pleasure on Jourdan's face when he told him he'd be away for a week . . . how well he could remember feeling exactly that blend of emotions in his junior days whenever his immediate boss declared an intention to take himself out of the premises for a while. I'll show them, he used to think, I'll make my mark. Into the office every morning at eight o'clock, the last one to leave at night . . . His shoulders moved in wry amusement.

Now he was no longer the young thruster, but the establishment figure the new wave of young thrusters must push aside on their way up the ladder. He caught the way that Jourdan looked at him sometimes, a curious, obsessive look. Did I ever look at my boss that way? he wondered. I don't suppose he cared for it very much either. How rapidly the years slipped by, with what speed the game of musical chairs was played, how swiftly one was forced out of one role and into another. Was there ever any real choice in the matter? Was the whole thing inexorably played out in accordance with a set of rules totally beyond one's control?

He became aware of his secretary standing at the other side of his desk. 'Yes?' He forced his attention back to the concerns of Monday morning. 'By the way,' he added when he had dealt with her query, 'I shall be away next week. Taking a few days by the sea.' He stood up and walked over to a framed map on the wall, jabbed a finger against the glass. 'There, that's the place. Chilford. We're not actually staying in the town. We're going to relatives, a little village a few miles along the coast. A pretty little place. A good golf-course.'

'Westerhill,' Jean Ashton said to her mother. 'I'd better write the address down for you.' She took a pencil from her handbag. 'Oakfield, Westerhill, near Chilford. You can put care of Barratt if you like, but I shouldn't think it's necessary.'

Her mother took the paper and studied it. 'It's not a hotel, then?'

'No, it's some kind of guest-house. I got it from one of the

44

Sunday papers.' One of the better Sunday papers of course, her tone implied, it's certainly not any kind of common seaside boarding-house. What she would really have liked would have been a jet flight to Majorca, she could have sunned herself all winter in the glow of that memory. She smiled suddenly. 'Next year we might be able to afford a holiday abroad.'

Her mother frowned. 'You're not serious about getting Mike to apply for that security job? His heart's obviously in the police, you can't ask him to leave the force.'

The smile vanished from Jean's face. 'He's already applied for the security job.' I saw to that, her look added. 'Far better pay. I'm not just thinking of myself,' she said defensively, 'nor about luxuries like foreign holidays. We can give the kids a better start, we could buy a house of our own.' Instead of living in a police house set in a kind of ghetto.

'He would have a proper career in the police,' her mother said with unusual firmness. 'This Guardcash job would be just that, a job.' She shook her head. 'Mike's the kind of man who needs satisfaction in his work.'

Jean set her mouth in a stubborn line. 'It's an administrative post he's applied for. He wouldn't just be one of the guards riding the vans.' She stood up. 'And anyway, he hasn't got very far in the police. In a couple of years he'll be forty and what is he? Just a sergeant.'

'You're lucky to have a good husband,' her mother said in a low voice. Five years now since she'd been widowed and she still felt the loss almost as keenly as in those first dreadful weeks.

Jean sighed and glanced at the clock. 'I must go, I've got to meet the twins.' Her oldest daughter was fifteen, too late now to rescue her from the clutches of state education, but the twins were only seven and one of the first things Jean intended to do, as soon as Mike's appointment with Guardcash was a definite fact, was to take the twins away from their primary school and send them to a select little private academy in Perrymount. In the best residential area of Perrymount, of course.

'Remember your father's Cousin Arthur,' her mother said suddenly. Jean gave her an exasperated glance and went out into the hall to get her coat. Cousin Arthur was a new one on her but she was only too familiar with her mother's habit of producing

45

outlandish – and, Jean had a shrewd suspicion, mythical – relatives to illustrate a point or drive home a moral. 'He was a plumber.' Her mother's voice winged its way from the sitting-room. 'A very good plumber.' Jean pulled a face of distaste at this fresh plebeian sprouting from the ancestral tree. 'His wife kept on at him to take up some more refined career. In the end he became a sort of glorified clerk in the gas showrooms.'

Jean came back into the room, wearing a light summer coat of pale cream with gilt buttons; after sixteen years of marriage she still looked slim, almost youthful. 'He was as miserable as sin,' her mother said. 'He shrank into himself, he lost weight, he even got shorter.'

'You're making all this up,' Jean said calmly. She picked up her silky gloves. 'There never was such a person as Father's Cousin Arthur.'

Her mother's eyes widened in a look of bland innocence. 'He stuck it for four or five years,' she said, 'and then he ran away with the barmaid from a pub fifty yards away from the gas showrooms. A very vulgar sort of barmaid, I believe, plump and jolly.'

'And the moral of this tale, I take it,' Jean said, repairing her make-up in front of the mirror, 'is that Cousin Arthur went back to plumbing and lived happily ever afterwards.'

'Whether he went back to plumbing or not,' her mother said with an air of subtle cunning, 'I have no idea. Neither he nor the barmaid was ever heard of again. Not in our family, that is. But Cousin Arthur's wife spent the rest of her life wishing she'd left well alone in the first place.'

Jean turned from the mirror. 'You ought to take up writing improving pamphlets.' She stooped and kissed her mother's cheek. 'We're setting off on Saturday morning,' she added amiably. 'I'll try to pop in to see you on Wednesday or Thursday.'

'And you ought to take up something yourself,' her mother said on a sharper, more direct note. 'You've plenty of intelligence, you had a good job before you were married. No reason why you shouldn't earn a decent salary. You've got too much spare energy, that's your trouble. You're young enough, you're only thirty-five, you could make a career for yourself, it would take your attention off your husband, you might let him alone to live his own life.'

Jean flicked her mother an unsmiling glance. 'Don't bother to come to the door,' she said. 'I can see myself out.'

At four o'clock on Friday afternoon Detective-Sergeant Mike Ashton came down the steps of the central police station in Perrymount. The rain had cleared, the sun was shining brilliantly, the air in the streets was heavy with the moist jungly warmth of late July.

'Hope you have a good holiday,' they'd said in the canteen. 'You need it.' Meaning his irritability and moodiness hadn't gone unremarked in the last week or two.

He got into his car and slammed the door shut. Might as well stop by Brigid's school and pick her up. Jean would want her home early today, there'd be plenty of last-minute jobs for all hands if they were going to make a reasonably early start tomorrow. He wasn't in the least looking forward to the drive down to the coast. Or to the holiday itself.

He drove slowly out of the car park, turning his head once and looking back at the clean modern lines of the police station. When he walked up those steps again in a couple of weeks it would very probably be to hand in his notice. He felt again the slow smouldering of suppressed anger. His own fault too, which made it no better. He could have kept his mouth shut about the approach from Guardcash, he didn't have to mention it in casual chat over Sunday lunch. If Jean had never heard about Guardcash, she would no doubt have nagged him from time to time to change his job, but it would have been in a vague, general sort of way, she wouldn't have been armed with a specific point, the offer of an attractive alternative. He'd have got further promotion in the police during the next year or two, there'd have been a little more money, she'd have got used to the whole thing, she'd have stopped grumbling in the end. She'd have had to.

Now he had left the town centre behind, he was driving down the quiet road that led to Perrymount Comprehensive School. His anger began to fade. I suppose it isn't much fun for Jean, he thought with a sigh, it's a restricted kind of life for her. You couldn't blame a young woman, smart and pretty, for wanting more of the material rewards. He sighed again. It ought to be possible to work up an interest in this Guardcash job, make something of it. But he saw with horror a vision of himself trapped all day behind a desk, imprisoned between four walls. He dismissed the bleak image and pulled the car into the side of the road, lit a cigarette and leaned back against the upholstery. Another three or four minutes before the noisy torrent would burst out through the school gates.

'Some frightful dump called Westerhill,' Brigid Ashton said with venom. She swung her bulging satchel on to her shoulder.

'Nothing wrong with the seaside,' one of her cronies said tolerantly, 'as long as you don't go with your family.' She pulled a face. 'My idea of hell, a family holiday. I've denied myself the pleasure for the last couple of years. I can't think why you don't do the same.'

'Because I've got a Victorian father who thinks I'm still in the cradle.' Brigid followed the knot of girls out of the cloakroom. 'Though how he manages to square that with the notion that I'd be up to every kind of mischief if he took his eye off me for a couple of weeks, beats me.'

'You ought to put your foot down,' another girl said helpfully.

'Try putting your foot down with my father,' Brigid said with a fierce scowl. 'You'd be lucky not to have it torn off.'

The other girl laughed. 'He can't be as bad as all that.'

'Can't he? He's a savage brute, that's how bad he is.' They came out of the gates and she suddenly caught sight of the car and her father looking out through the windscreen. 'Oh – there he is!' she cried in a totally altered tone. 'He's giving me a lift. Good-oh!' She broke into a run, at the same time calling back to her friends, 'I'll send you all postcards. Have a good holiday.'

Her father opened the passenger door as she reached the car. She gave him a brilliant smile. 'Thanks, Dad. A nice surprise.'

He jerked his head in the direction of a group of boys pushing and shoving each other some yards away. 'Any of those in your form? They look a right bunch to me.'

She threw a brief glance at the group. 'They're all right.' She

48

dropped into the seat and closed the door. 'They're only kids. Thirteen or fourteen.'

Her father let in the clutch. 'Bit of discipline wouldn't harm them. Or a haircut.'

'It's boiling hot,' Brigid said, ignoring routine irrelevancies. 'And I'm dying of thirst. Do you think you could stop at that café round the corner? I wouldn't be a minute. A Coke and some ice-cream might possibly save my life.' She turned her head and grinned at him. 'If you're feeling in a generous mood, that is. I am, as usual, skint.'

Mike laughed, dug a hand into his pocket and pulled out some coins. 'Here you are.' He dropped them into her lap, slid the car into motion. 'Only a minute, mind. I haven't the faintest intention of getting pinched for parking.'

Chapter 6

Pauline stood for a moment outside the dining-room, listening for sounds of movement. There were none. Good, only twenty minutes to ten and everyone finished breakfast. She opened the door and went in, cast a rapid glance about her. The table had been cleared, the cloth removed. The daily woman could come in and do her morning run-round.

Tuesday. Steak and kidney pie this evening. Lobster salad as an alternative. She crossed to the window and looked out. Guests had a habit of drifting about the garden at this time of day; before long they would take themselves off to swim or sunbathe, wander round local potteries and art shops, often coming back laden with massive slabs of pottery, gigantic vases, sentimental water-colours and other later-to-be-regretted trophies of the hunt.

Several yards away, at the side of the terrace, Godfrey stood talking to Stephen Lockwood. Stephen caught the movement at the dining-room window and flicked a little sideways glance in that direction. Pauline. How much better-looking than Marion she was these days. He had been quite surprised on Saturday, standing chatting in the hall to Godfrey just after their arrival, looking up at the sound of Pauline's approach, catching sight of her. Quite a time since he'd seen her previously. Three years? Four? She was very slender now. All that running up and down stairs, most probably. The sun had deepened the colour of her skin and lightened the colour of her hair; the bones of her face seemed more delicately moulded.

Why, she's beautiful, he'd thought with astonishment. Or would be, he'd corrected himself a moment later, if it weren't for the little line between her brows, the faintly anxious look she wore. Of course she must be worried about Aunt Elinor's illness, natural enough in the circumstances, that slight air of strain.

Stephen jerked his mind back to the conversation. Not much warmth and friendship pulsing out from Barratt, but then he hadn't really expected it. Never a fellow to look you straight in the eyes, old Godfrey, never a man to deal out the big flashing smiles, more of the cold-fish handshake and the low-temperature gaze focused on a spot two inches above your right ear. Partly a question of temperament and partly – no use denying it – the fact that he'd never been able to forget the way Stephen had sprung up from the ground and snatched Marion Tillard from under his well-bred nose.

I wonder what he feels now, Stephen thought wryly, when he looks at Marion and then at Pauline. Perhaps there was some rough kind of justice operating in the world after all.

'We have to take our own holidays out of season, of course,' Godfrey was saying. Funny, Stephen thought, I've never gone out of my way to make people like me, it must have looked sometimes as if I went to considerable trouble to achieve a precisely opposite effect, but it never used to bother me in the slightest, I always took it in my stride, quite relished it in fact ... until just this last year or two . . . He didn't really like it any more . . . it gave him a nasty feeling sometimes of being lashed up to a tree like old Saint Whatsisname with arrows of hostility poised high on every side. So long as they stay poised, he thought with a tinge of amusement, the time to duck is when they start raining down.

'We'll probably go to London,' Godfrey said. 'Pauline likes the snops. And the theatres.' Three or four months away, he added to himself, the Osmond affair will be settled one way or the other long before then.

'What about a game of golf this morning?' Stephen asked casually. He had scarcely uttered the words before Godfrey was shaking his head.

'Very sorry, but I have quite a bit of paperwork to see to.' He gave a fragmentary smile. 'Even though the works are closed just now.' He didn't say, 'Ask me again later in the week,' Stephen noted. As if being in his company for more than a brief spell was something he would take good care to avoid. I know he doesn't like me, Stephen thought, but all the same . . . and again he had that irrational, disturbing feeling of being deeply and intolerably wounded.

'I'll ask Ashton,' he said lightly. 'I notice he's brought some clubs. Seems a decent kind of fellow.'

'Yes.' Godfrey pondered for a moment, striving to resurrect Ashton's identity from the mental limbo where he endeavoured – as far as possible – to keep all the Oakfield guests during their stay. 'Comes from – ' he frowned. 'Perrymount, that's it. Not all that far from Barbridge, surely?'

'No. Thirty, thirty-five miles.'

'Civil Service, I believe. I dare say he'd be glad to give you a game.'

Stephen nodded. 'Yes, I'll ask him.'

Some little distance away, coming from the direction of the kitchen garden, Marion's shortish, heavyish figure appeared in view. On just such another blue and sparkling day she had floated towards him over the glittering grass If he'd had something better to do on that far-off Saturday . . . if he'd never taken it into his head to drop in at the garden party . . . he gave an infinitesimal sigh. How could he have been such a fool as to prefer Marion to Pauline? He saw with sudden perception that fate had after all been kinder to Pauline than she might in her brooding youth have been inclined to accept. She had been much the plainer of the two girls and so had been compelled to develop a certain amount of character, she had taught herself to be a little more interesting, she hadn't been able to sink back into fatal reliance on a captivating but fleeting prettiness.

Still halted by the dining-room window, Pauline watched Marion making her way past the lily-pond towards the rose-garden. There was no longer any suggestion of elasticity in her walk. She's only three years older than me, Pauline thought, but already she moves like a middle-aged woman. At the side of the terrace she saw Godfrey turn his head and look towards the rose-garden; his gaze followed Marion until she disappeared behind the summer-house.

A fierce pang of jealousy – oddly mingled with irritation – shot through Pauline. How was it possible for Godfrey to look at Marion and still see, as she felt certain he did, the graceful girl he had loved? And surely he must be aware of the banality of her words, her opinions, her whole outlook on life. Pauline gave a deep sigh. If only she had been there when the Lockwoods' car halted outside the front door on Saturday afternoon, if only she had been able to catch the look on her husband's face when he first glimpsed Marion. But she had been upstairs, snatching a few minutes to change her dress and do her face. She had heard the car, had raced through the rest of her toilet and hurried from the bedroom, slackening her pace only when she reached the landing and heard the sound of voices, realizing she was too late, Godfrey was already standing in the hall talking to the Lockwoods, all tell-tale facial expressions would have been discreetly rearranged well before she reached the little group.

Stephen made some admiring remark about the splendour of the roses and as Godfrey turned to answer he saw Pauline at the dining-room window, looking out at him Their glances had barely crossed before she stepped back into the room, no longer visible. He had a moment's strong impression that she had been watching him, not to say spying on him.

'Yes, the floribundas have been magnificent this year,' he said pleasantly to Stephen. 'Mostly the fine weather of course, I fear we can't claim much of the credit.' He was certain that Pauline had very little notion of what he really thought about her – or for that matter about a good many other things. He wondered briefly if it was the same in all marriages, if no one ever really discussed the genuinely important things, if there was no true communication, if everyone felt as he did that if totally frank communication ever took place, things might be said which would be intolerable to hear and so it was better all round if contact was kept on an acceptable, superficial level.

Marion reappeared from a small cluster of trees several yards away. At the sound of her steps on the path Stephen glanced over and saw her going round to the rear entrance of the house. He felt a surge of irritation. She hadn't been uprooted more than twenty-four hours from her own kitchen before she'd hollowed out a fresh little nest for herself in the kitchen at Oakfield. If she had chosen she could have been mistress of this house – for the moment he saw the fact that she was not its mistress as a failure on her part, totally forgetting that it was almost entirely due to his own hand in events – but she seemed quite content now to take up the position of Bessie Meacham's crony and unpaid helper. Unutterably and irretrievably commonplace, he thought with vehemence, the soul of an under-housemaid.

'There! That's the last of it!' Bessie slapped the final handful of dripping cutlery on to the draining-board, squeezed out her dish-cloth and began a vigorous attack on every flat surface within her reach.

A couple of feet away Edgar Meacham dried the knives and forks with energy and goodwill. Oh, what a relief to have done with the past! he thought. Heigh ho! for the good life!

'Any news of Miss Tillard this morning?' he asked amiably. As he crossed to the cutlery drawer he caught sight of his head and shoulders in the mirror by the dresser. He flicked at his image a glance of keen appreciation. My word! but he was look-ing rosier and healthier, sleeker and plumper than when he had set off in February for Torquay and the well-heeled widows.

Bessie shook her head. 'I dare say Theresa will be phoning Mr Godfrey some time this morning. A nice chop do you for your lunch? Or do you fancy a bit of liver and bacon?'

Edgar came and stood beside Bessie. 'Oh, the liver and bacon, I think.' He dropped a kiss on her sternly-waved greying brown hair, he ran an approving hand over her ample rump. 'With plenty of fried onions.' The sheer incredible luck of it! 'And perhaps a few sauté potatoes.' A comfortable berth, elegant surroundings, civilized folk . . . and Bessie. He could have gone farther and fared worse.

Bessie suddenly ceased her bright-eyed giggling, smote Edgar's arm from its grip and flung a wary look at the door.

'It's only me!' said Marion's cosy voice from the other side of the panels. When she came into the room Bessie was standing decorously by the kitchen table and Edgar was just about to open a cupboard.

A few minutes later Pauline gave a perfunctory tap on the kitchen door and entered at once without waiting for a reply. She had arrived at this compromise not very long after coming to Oakfield as a bride. It had irked her to have to knock on the door of her own kitchen but if she didn't, Bessie would make it plain from her tone and manner that she considered the privacy of her personal domain had been discourteously breached.

Marion and Bessie were sitting opposite each other at the table, just about to begin preparing the lunch-time sandwiches. Edgar was dealing with the picnic flasks, orange squash, lemonade, tea, coffee; each flask bore its owner's name on an adhesive label. All three of them ceased their activity the moment Pauline entered, looking up at her from their frozen postures as if they were only waiting for her to say her piece and vanish, leaving them to resume their intimate and agreeable little chat. How pleased Bessie would have been, Pauline thought yet again, if Godfrey had brought Marion home as his bride, instead of herself. What absorbing confabs the pair of them would have been able to enjoy over the morning coffee.

'May I have a word with you?' she said a little frostily to Bessie, indicating with a nod that the conference must take place elsewhere. She certainly wasn't going to discuss her household arrangements in front of the other two. Bessie followed her out of the room and along the corridor to a small store room that had once been the butler's pantry.

In the kitchen Marion began to make the sandwiches in accordance with the instructions pencilled in Bessie's notebook which lay open on the table.

'No mustard for the Ashton twins,' she read aloud. Edgar cut delicate slices of cold beef and she laid them on the evenly buttered bread. What nicely shaped hands he had. And so well cared for too, surprisingly so when you remembered that he did so much gardening. She had been astonished but pleased when she heard that Bessie had married. She was invariably pleased to hear of anyone getting married, irrespective of the chances of happiness for the pair involved; it had the effect of reinforcing her own sense of security, of the absolute rightness of her own path in life.

But she felt some shadowy kind of obligation to vet Bessie's choice. Not that there was any real point in doing so now, three or four months after the event, but there it was, she would just like to satisfy herself.

'I think Bessie mentioned you're from somewhere up north,' she said to Edgar in a pleasant conversational tone. 'You worked in a shop, I believe?'

Edgar continued to carve the beef into fine slices. Something of the exuberance he had felt a few minutes ago still welled up inside him. 'Thetstone,' he said on an unusually reckless impulse, mentioning the name that hadn't crossed his lips for more than thirty years. It's all right, said the ceaseless watcher in his brain, Mrs Lockwood would never have heard of Thetstone.

Marion jerked her head up, she was just about to say something when he spoke again. 'I was manager of one of the departments in Hunston's. The finest store in Thetstone,' he said with pride. What an odd, agreeable sensation it gave him, mingling fact with fiction in this tight-rope way. 'Gents' Outfitting, my department.' He rather liked that, at once refined and outside Mrs Lockwood's immediate sphere of knowledgeable interest. He had toyed for a split second with China and Glass but had rejected it, attractive as the notion was, because it was scarcely conceivable that a married lady could know even less about the subject than he did.

He had never needed to be specific with Bessie; a shop up north was as much as he had told her or indeed as she had wanted to know. She had lived in one village since the day she was born; her entire working life had been spent in one house, almost in one kitchen. One place in the heathen north was very much the same as another to her. She had heard of very few and didn't care two hoots for any of them.

'And you retired fairly recently, I suppose?' Marion asked.

'Not quite the usual kind of retirement,' he said with mysterious significance. After all, he was only just turned sixty-two and if he accepted the label of retirement he was as good as declaring himself to be over sixty-five. And a man had his vanities. He prided himself that he could pass anywhere for fifty-seven or eight. 'I took a somewhat reduced pension, some years earlier than the normal age.' He paused in his task, looked up and gave her a confidential smile. His cornflower-blue eyes, which had added a good couple of hundred a year to his income ever since he had come to his senses and fled from the unspeakable barbarities of Thetstone, gazed into Marion's face with an honest and appealing expression. 'I was never the most robust of men.' He allowed the merest hint of a cough to escape his lips. 'The staff doctor advised . . . ' He could almost see the wise old greybeard sagely nodding, placing the tips of his fingers together.

'And this was – what? A year or two ago?' Marion arranged a little stack of sandwiches on a sheet of greaseproof paper. 'That you left Hunston's?'

'Yes, last summer to be precise.'

The door opened and Bessie came bustling back into the kitchen. 'You'd better get off outside,' she said to Edgar with amiable directness. 'Can't have you round underfoot.' She added a brisk reminder about various salad stuffs and vegetables.

Thetstone, Marion said to herself with a very pleasing sensation of mingled suspicion, excitement, alarm and righteous indignation . . . Hunston's . . . During his career with Alpha Fabrics Stephen had been moved to three or four different branches. Ten or twelve years back they had lived for a time in a town quite close to Thetstone. She used to go over there for a morning's shopping now and again; she had often been in Hunston's, had very probably even patronized the Gents' Outfitting section in search of a birthday tie for Stephen. But what drew her brows into faint furrows was the near certainty that Hunston's had been pulled down about eight years ago. Marion had never gone back to Thetstone but she still exchanged Christmas cards with one or two families they had known, very occasionally wrote a letter to a former friend dwindled now into old acquaintance. Surely she remembered hearing – yes, she could almost take her oath on it – that that part of Thetstone had been redeveloped; Hunston's had been losing trade for a long time, had failed to change with the changing times, had been glad to sell out in the end for the very considerable site value.

'Well now, how are the sandwiches coming along?' Bessie asked as soon as the door had closed behind Edgar. Really, Mrs Lockwood could be exasperatingly slow at times.

'I'll finish them for you if you like. Then you can make a start on the cooking.' Marion could scarcely bear to look at Bessie, all unknowingly delivered into the hands of a husband who might be . . . what? A liar? An idler? A potential murderer? A delicious thrill rippled along her spine. 'Have you ever insured your life?' she asked suddenly, seizing a sheet of greaseproof paper.

'What's that?' Bessie could make nothing of this wild interjection. 'I'd better get on with the pastry,' she said brusquely.

Marion was relieved at Bessie's impatient dismissal of her impulsive question. What a stupid thing to have said! Might have caused all kinds of trouble. After all, what did she have to go on? It could very easily have been some quite different part of Thetstone that had been developed. She might even have been thinking of some other town altogether. She bent her attention to her task. Of course . . . all she had to do was drop a line to one of her old contacts in Thetstone, ask about the fate of Hunston's . . . though what would she do if she discovered that the store had indeed been pulled down years ago? She couldn't quite see that far ahead.

Bessie was now busy assembling equipment and ingredients for the major cooking tasks of the day. She wished very dearly that Madam Marion would see fit to go and waste someone else's time. All very well, a nice little gossip, but enough was as good as a feast. Now Mrs Barratt, she had some notion of what work was, she wouldn't dream of hanging about the kitchen, rattling on like a babbling brook, getting in the way. Just as well Mr Godfrey hadn't gone and married the elder sister, Bessie thought, not for the first time; he got a much better bargain the way things turned out, though he might possibly not have been of that opinion at the time. But there again, he might have been, who could tell? She might have more or less brought him up from the time he was a year old and herself a scraggy little girl of fourteen in a gingham frock, but that didn't mean she could read his mind when he was a grown man.

To her irritation she saw that Marion was settling herself down again for a leisurely chat.

'I suppose we shouldn't have taken Aunt Elinor out on Sunday,' Marion said reflectively. 'But she didn't seem unwell. She was so anxious for a little run in the car. And she said she hadn't had one of her turns for a whole week. We really weren't to know –'

'A great mistake. I said so at the time,' Bessie said forcefully. In fact she had not only not said so at the time, she had had no opportunity of saying so, having been neither consulted nor informed about the outing in advance. She snatched a mixing-bowl from a cupboard and banged it down on the table.

'I believe Dr Nightingale is trying to get Aunt Elinor to go into hospital,' Marion said placidly. She didn't in the least mind being criticized, openly or indirectly, by Bessie. All she asked from a conversation was that the other person should play an interested part. 'Dr Nightingale would like to make some tests. He seems to think Aunt Elinor might have an ulcer. And he says they could do something about her hip. But Aunt Elinor won't hear of it. She can be very stubborn.'

'It's that Theresa at the bottom of it, you mark my words.' Bessie shook a bag of flour vigorously into the bowl. 'She'll have talked Miss Tillard into not going into hospital.' Against her will she felt herself being seduced by the intriguing byways of the topic. 'Or bullied her, more likely.' She shook her head, pursed her lips and levelled at Marion a deeply meaningful look. 'Gastric trouble. H'm, that's as may be.' She seized a packet of butter and slashed it in half with a knife. 'All that heathen food. Ask yourself who does the cooking.' She began to rub the butter into the flour with passionate movements. 'And ask yourself what they stand to gain.'

'Oh, surely not!' Marion said with an air of protest underlaid with deep conspiratorial pleasure. 'Of course, Aunt Elinor is sure to leave Theresa something in her will –'

'Something!' Bessie leaned forward and stabbed a floury finger at Marion's bosom. 'You may well call it *something* . . .'

Due at Miss Tillard's at eleven to discuss the matter of the codicil, Henry looked at his wristwatch. That gave him a good hour. Just ahead of him the open gates of Oakfield beckoned. He had every intention of walking through them and marching up to the house. He was – if humanly possible – going to see and talk to Marion. He had provided himself with a paper of no importance whatsoever which would nevertheless enable him to frame a piffling query about a legal matter if he should chance to run into Godfrey, or otherwise feel himself obliged to justify his visit to the house. But he felt in a rather defiant mood, half intended to brazen it out and present himself solely as a social caller. After all, why shouldn't he have a few friendly words with Marion? He'd known her well enough in the old days, had danced half the night with her often enough, had loved her loyally and passionately, would surely have married her had it not been for Stephen Lockwood. He halted for a moment halfway up the drive, immobilized by the fierce strength of the emotion that swept through him.

Several yards away, popping out to have a word with Meacham about the flowers, Pauline glimpsed Henry standing motionless in the middle of the drive. Oh Lord, she thought, better nip back in again, the flowers can wait. Above all else she didn't want just now to have to exchange routine nothings with that old woman. All during her childhood and youth she seemed to remember that nondescript face appearing from behind a pillar or round a bend in a corridor. And here he was again, ever since their return to Oakfield four years ago, inexorably turning up from time to time, but now of course no longer a skinny child starched up for a birthday party or a gangling lad on the fringes of a dance floor, but an adult, a professional man of sorts, and so to be treated civilly if still not to be taken very seriously.

A moment or two after Henry resumed his approach to the house he saw Meacham kneeling in front of a flowerbed a little distance away to his left. He changed direction and plunged across a wide strip of grass, coming up behind Meacham who was examining with an air of bafflement some very miserable-looking begonias.

'Pardon me,' Henry said in his prim way. 'I wonder if you happen to know where I could find Mrs Lockwood?'

Edgar got to his feet. 'Certainly, sir. Mrs Lockwood is in the kitchen.' He watched Henry pick his way between the flowerbeds, making for the back of the house. Rum look he had on his face, Edgar thought, suppressed excitement it looked like. He dropped back on to his knees and fingered a begonia leaf hopelessly, allowing his mind to circle round the central notion of Henry Whittall and the subsidiary ideas radiating from that centre.

Miss Tillard's illness, the situation in which her coloured companion might shortly find herself, the purpose of Henry's visit to Oakfield – Edgar had glanced at all these topics and arrived at a conjecture or two about the state of that mighty fish Osmond's and the possible effect of its possible collapse on small fry like Barratt's, when he decided that it would be much more comfortable to pursue his train of thought in the potting-shed.

He abandoned the begonias to their fate and slipped off unobtrusively by a circuitous route to his peaceful little hideaway. He closed the door and stood looking out of the tiny window, surveying the house, the lawns and borders. The whole lot might have to go if Osmond's fell. Bessie's position, his own cosy berth, could disappear in the dust-clouds of ruin. Which brought him inescapably round again to the image of Miss Tillard in her curious bungalow and the extent and disposition of her assets.

He wouldn't be at all surprised if the old girl wasn't worth a good deal. He'd been up to the bungalow several times on errands from Oakfield, he had listened with unfeigned interest to Bessie's accounts of the history of the Barratt and Tillard families, he prided himself on being able to size things up pretty shrewdly.

Might not be at all a bad idea to keep an eye open and waylay Master Whittall on his way back down the drive, have a little chat with him. Easy enough for a skilful man to pick the lock of professional discretion, he'd done it often enough in his time. He looked down at his watch. Whittall was due at the bungalow at eleven; Edgar knew that fact as he knew a great many other seemingly trivial little facts, it was his business to know them. Individually they might not amount to much but add them all up . . .

In a few minutes he could wander back towards the gates, station himself at a suitable spot with some purposeful secateurs.

And in the meantime . . . He turned from the window and took a couple of paces back, glanced at the shelves with their load of tins and packets, cartons and bottles, and began to whistle a few bars of a dance tune from the innocent days of his youth.

Chapter 7

We shall have the whole ruddy neighbourhood parking themselves in my kitchen at this rate, Bessie said to herself in the early-warning stages of a nasty bout of bad temper. 'If you don't mind,' she said with vehement politeness, indicating to Henry by means of a powerful glance that he should shift his chair a few inches out of the way and allow her enough room to roll out her pastry on her own table, and thank you very much. An old woman dressed up in trousers, that's what he was, sitting there gawping at Mrs Lockwood as if she was a ghost.

'This is very good beef,' Marion said, pushing a plateful of slices a little nearer to Henry so that he might appreciate its quality. 'And not at all overdone. I don't in the least care for overdone beef myself.' Goodness, it was years and years since she'd come across Henry Whittall, she hadn't been able to think who he was till he'd reminded her of his identity. He'd looked so reproachful, standing there in the doorway. But then he could hardly have expected her to remember him all that well. She'd never really known him. He was just a lad from the old days, and a far from attractive lad at that. Wait a moment – now she came to think of it, hadn't there been some joke among her crowd about Henry being a bit sweet on her? She slid him a speculative glance. No, surely not, not this dried-up creature, even as a boy he couldn't have had much notion of romance. It must have been some other youth they teased her about.

'You never married then?' she asked, partly for the sake of something to say and partly to confirm her own impression of his nature.

'No.' He gave her the oddest sort of look.

The back-door bell rang suddenly and sharply. 'Butcher,'

Bessie said flatly. She picked up a cloth from the back of a chair and rubbed her hands more or less free of the pastry mixture. Without haste she took down a meat dish and went out of the room.

Marion glanced at the clock. 'Ten past ten,' she said with a note of vicarious pride. 'Bessie's right, you could almost set your watch by him.' She smiled comfortably. 'I do like tradesmen to be punctual, don't you?'

It is utterly incredible, Henry thought, that Marion Tillard, light, ethereal, bewitching, laughing, could be one and the same person as this clock-watching, beef-conscious, almost podgy creature. He searched her face with near-desperation, sent his eyes boldly over her figure, striving to find some fragmentary remains of her great beauty, something he could recognize with thankfulness, that would allow him to cry out in his mind, It wasn't all a fantastic mirage, I was right, she did exist, I did love her . . . But there was nothing, nothing at all.

I do wish he wouldn't stare so, Marion thought with slight vexation, it really isn't very polite. She gave him quite a sharp glance, just to make him mind his manners and was pleased to see that he at once turned his head and began to scan the walls.

'You're not thinking of going away for your holidays, then?' she asked, a little more friendly again, now he'd taken the hint. 'I never think you get a real rest if you stay at home. Always so many little jobs waiting to be done. Don't you find that?' She was beginning to remember him more distinctly now, it was that trick of staring that had sharpened recollection. Yes, it was coming back to her, she'd been right the first time, he *was* the boy who had that ridiculous crush on her, he had that same irritating habit of staring at her, popping up everywhere.

'I have my hobbies,' Henry said with dignity. He raised a hand and gestured at the camera slung round his neck. 'I take wild life pictures. Among a great many other activities.' He was unpleasantly aware of a turmoil in his brain, as of some massive and difficult process of adjustment taking place.

'I keep asking Stephen why he doesn't get a colour camera, so we could take some nice holiday snaps when we're abroad,' Marion said with mild habitual complaint, 'but he never seems to bother.'

62

The disagreeable turmoil suddenly ceased and Henry was able to look at Marion from a stable plane of sorrowful compassion. How could she help being as she was now, with that ruthless egotist for a husband? He had without doubt treated her abominably. How much happier and gayer, how much prettier and more youthful-looking she would be now if Lockwood had never crossed her path, if it had been he himself who –

The kitchen door jerked open as Bessie returned, much refreshed by a jolly sparring-match with her old pal the butcher. She plonked the laden meat dish on the table an inch or two away from Henry in a manner that spoke loudly of farewell. He got to his feet and mumbled something about Miss Tillard and hoping to see Marion again.

'At last!' Bessie cried loudly as soon as he was at the other side of the door. 'Perhaps now it might be possible to get on with some work.'

'I've finished the sandwiches.' Marion inked the name carefully on to the last packet. 'Now what else can I do for you? Just say, it's no trouble, I always like to help people if I can.'

Bessie closed her eyes briefly. 'Very good of you, I'm sure, but you ought to be out enjoying yourself, not hard at work in here. Won't Mr Lockwood be taking you out somewhere for a trip?'

Marion shook her head. 'I expect he'll be playing golf again. I thought of going into Chilford on the bus.' She looked at the clock. 'It goes in forty minutes, according to Pauline.' Thank the Lord for that, Besssie thought. 'I'm going to have a look round some of my old haunts,' Marion added in a sentimental tone. 'I may call on one or two folk. There's a bus back about six.'

'If you wouldn't mind taking the sandwiches along with you,' Bessie said in a tone suddenly grown much mellower. 'You know where I usually put them in the hall.'

Marion gathered up the packets. She had an abstracted look in her eyes. 'There was that business about the school,' she said thoughtfully. Bessie spoke not a word for fear of luring Marion back into her chair. 'Can't quite remember what it was, exactly.' Marion frowned. 'Was Henry expelled? Or asked to leave?' She walked slowly towards the door. 'Ah well, never mind, it was a long time ago, whatever it was.' She gave Bessie a little parting smile. 'I don't suppose it matters very much now.'

'I'll just make sure Jean has no objection,' Mike said. 'But I'm sure it'll be all right.'

'Good.' Lockwood gave a brisk nod. 'About twenty minutes, say?'

Henry came round the side of the house and saw the two men standing talking a yard or two away. Stephen Lockwood! Looking scarcely any different after all this time! The second man appeared merely as a vague figure on the edge of his vision. Henry didn't say anything, could not in fact have managed to get a syllable past his lips, so unnerving was the feeling that surged through him.

'Well, well, well,' Stephen said with idle amusement. 'If it isn't old Henry.' He introduced Ashton, made a few routine inquiries about Henry's state of health, life situation, career progress, then touched with a due show of gravity on Miss Tillard's condition.

'If you're on holiday,' he said, feeling for some reason quite amiably disposed towards Whittall, 'why don't you come along and have a game of golf?'

'Very kind of you.' Henry's tongue was pretty well under control by now. 'But I don't play all that much nowadays.' In fact he hadn't played at all in the last seven or eight years and not all that often before that. 'And in any case I'm just off to see Miss Tillard.'

'Oh yes.' Aunt Elinor had mentioned on Sunday that he was coming to see her. 'We'll make it another day then.'

Henry put up a hand and scratched his nose. 'Yes, thank you,' he said after a moment. 'I'd like that.'

'You could call in here, we could all go along together. Any particular day suit you?' As Henry was moving away a few minutes later Stephen said, 'I see you still play about with a camera.' He shook his head. 'Ah me, the hobbies of our youth.' He turned to Ashton. 'I remember old Henry at school – we were at school together in Chilford – he thought he was a genius with the camera.' He laughed. 'Do you remember that exhibition of your work? In the Art Room.' He laughed again, more loudly.

'Studies of dustbins in the early morning and other artistic subjects, if I remember rightly.'

'Surely you and he weren't in the same form at school?' Mike asked Stephen after Henry had gone stiffly off, acknowledging Stephen's banter with no more than a cool nod.

'We were, you know,' Stephen said. 'We're exactly the same age. Give or take a month or two. Henry was a day-boy, I boarded of course, my home was sixty miles away.'

'He looks ten years older than you,' Mike said with perfect honesty.

Stephen began to laugh again and Ashton looked at him inquiringly. 'I was just remembering,' Stephen said, still amused, 'that ludicrous business with the French master. I'd forgotten all about it. Funny how things come back to you.' They began to walk towards the house. 'Couldn't keep order, the French teacher, he actually was a Frenchman, didn't speak English all that well, young fellow, don't suppose – looking back – he was all that many years older than us. We led him one hell of a dance. He got so he began to twitch the moment he came into the classroom.'

'I can't imagine Whittall leading anyone a dance,' Mike said without much interest.

'Well, Henry wasn't in it all that much, he really only joined in to keep in with the rest of us, trying to make himself a bit more popular. Never exactly the hero of the Lower Fourth or anything like that, as you can imagine.'

They reached the front door. 'And what happened about the Frenchman?' Mike asked with a civil show of interest.

'My idea,' Stephen said, still with some remnants of pride in his tone. 'Odd arrangement of staircases at Chilford School. It's a very old building, been chopped and changed over the years. Our classroom and two other classrooms were all on this floor and there were three separate staircases running down, each of the three classrooms had its own staircase, if you follow, they converged from different directions on a sort of little hall, not much more than a large landing, really. It came into my head one day, out of the blue. Took a bit of organizing, though. When the bell went for morning break – on this particular day we had French last lesson before break – I'd fixed it so that the very second the French teacher set his foot on the top step of our staircase to go down, the other two classroom doors would open at exactly the same moment, that was of course a few seconds after our door had opened, and all the boys – getting on for a hundred big hefty lads – would run pushing and shoving down to the landing.'

'Did it work?' Mike asked with a strong feeling of distaste.

Stephen nodded, he looked quite pleased at the memory. 'Yes, it worked beautifully. I always had a talent for organization, even as a lad. The first wave knocked the Frenchman off his feet just as he got to the landing and then the other two classes piled in on top, you never saw such a scrum. Or heard such an uproar. Masters came flying from all over the school. And of course all the other classes pelted along to see what was up. And old Froggie down at the very bottom of the pile.' His shoulders shook with glee.

'You could have killed him.' Ashton's face wore a savage look. 'And half a dozen boys as well.'

'To tell you the truth, I never thought of that,' Stephen said lightly. 'Anyway, as it turned out, no one was killed. A few strains and sprains, a hell of a lot of bruises. I seem to remember someone dislocated a shoulder. But it was a glorious sight. Took half an hour or more to restore order. Old Froggie had a nervous breakdown, of course he was heading for a breakdown for weeks before, the staircase business was just the last straw. He also got the sack. I don't know which came first, the sack or the breakdown. He simply disappeared. Packed his bags and left the school immediately. Never came back. Common knowledge he had a breakdown but I can't remember how we found out.'

'You realize,' Mike said without much hope of penetrating Lockwood's hide, 'that you very probably ruined that man's career for him?'

'No!' Stephen said with an emphatic shake of his head. 'People are a good deal tougher than that. He'd have got over it. Bet if I met him now we'd have a good laugh together about it.'

'I rather doubt it.' Ashton glanced at the stack of sandwiches on the table in the hall, picked up those intended for his own family. 'How did Whittall come into it?'

'He was expelled,' Stephen said carelessly. 'Well, not exactly expelled, summoned to the Head's study and asked to leave, you know the kind of thing.'

'But why Whittall? Why not you?'

'Me?' Stephen raised his brows. 'No one could pin a thing on me. Not born yesterday. I may have loaded the gun but it was old Henry who fired the bullet. He gave the signal for the other two classroom doors to open. He did as I'd instructed him, asked permission to leave the classroom just before the bell was due to ring, posted himself in a spot half-way between the other two doors, then as soon as Froggie reached the head of the stairs Henry put a whistle to his lips and blew it.'

A little way inside the gates of Oakfield, to the right of the drive, Edgar stood beside an escallonia in its full rosy flush. He made a few snipping passes at the leaves with his secateurs; through the tracery of branches he could see Henry walking away up the road with a rapid, agitated gait, bound for Miss Tillard's. Been with that firm of solicitors a long time, Edgar thought, pursing his lips and nodding shrewdly over the glossy green leaves. The old lady trusts him, that's for sure, quite possible he's had his hand in the till . . . Or not the type? . . . Though when it came down to it, it was difficult to the point of impossibility to say who might or might not be the type.

Henry reached the spot where the road bore round in a curve. He hesitated, shook his head sharply as if to clear it, and glanced around, not entirely certain of where he was or what he was doing there. Some distance ahead he sighted the roof of Miss Tillard's bungalow – ah yes! He squared his shoulders and set himself in motion again.

The disagreeable churning sensation persisted in his brain, he had a horrid feeling as of an actual kaleidoscope of thoughts physically revolving inside his head Images from the past flashed up at him, brilliantly sharp, filled with pain. I might have been an eminent man . . . I might have been a judge . . . his thoughts began to tumble along well-worn channels . . . there is nowhere I might not have gone, nothing I might not have done if the bell hadn't sounded for break on that particular morning . . . if the Frenchman hadn't placed his foot on the topmost step

. . . if I hadn't stationed myself between the doors . . . if Stephen Lockwood had never existed . . .

He had a shadowy recollection of standing a little while back – this morning? Two days ago? – looking into the centre of a cluster of pink flowers and a voice talking to him with delicate insinuation, searching, probing . . . The recollection fell away and he was back again at Chilford School at one minute before eleven, with the whistle raised to his lips.

Chapter 8

'No, of course I don't mind you going off to the golf-course.' As long as Jean could have her way in the really important matters she was more than ready to be generous over trifles, she liked the sense it gave her of conducting her marriage on an expansive, large-souled plane.

'That's fine, then.' Mike gave her arm a brief pat. She was pleased to see that he was beginning to lose that tense, moody look. He would almost certainly have a definite word about the new job in the next week or two; she had made sure he had given Guardcash a note of their holiday address.

Brigid came slouching into the bedroom. 'Do you know where the twins are?' Jean asked her.

'Yes, they're in the attics.'

'I suppose it's all right for them to play up there?' Mike said with a frown.

'I'm sure the Barratts don't mind,' Jean answered lightly. 'Mrs Barratt saw them running down from the attics yesterday and she just looked across at me and smiled.' She glanced at Brigid. 'You might run up and fetch them down, they'll have to get ready to go to the beach.'

The attics were two dusty rooms set on top of the central wing; they were stacked with the intriguing accumulations of the years. On her way down again with the chattering twins Brigid saw Godfrey Barratt crossing the hall. He paused to exchange a word with a bed-and-breakfaster, an elderly spinster with decided opinions. Brigid leaned over the banisters and looked down at him standing there; tall, broad-shouldered, that stiffly upright carriage, that pale blond hair.

'Mr Barratt has such an odd way of holding himself,' she said to her mother as she closed the bedroom door firmly behind the skittish twins. 'As if he daren't relax. And when someone's talking to him he keeps his whole head and face rigid, he just moves his eyes, I think he's sort of weird-looking.'

'Take the twins next door and clean them up.' Jean couldn't summon up much interest in Mr Barratt's facial expressions.

'I should think,' Brigid said with frowning seriousness, 'that he's a man of strong passions.'

'And don't forget their ears,' Jean said briskly.

'Very strong passions.' Brigid savoured the words.

'We'll go up in the attics again tomorrow morning,' Kate said to Vicky in a low, decisive voice. 'We'll look in the trunks at the far end of the other room.' They were not identical twins, not even very much alike. Vicky was small and chubby; she had long straight flaxen hair and a dreamy expression. Kate was taller, thinner, with a quick bright look and short dark curls.

'Just mind that you don't go running in and out of any other parts of the house,' Jean said with casual firmness. 'And see that you don't make too much noise either.'

'I take it you're going to the beach as well?' Mike said as Brigid shepherded the twins through the doorway.

'Oh yes.' She gave him a guileless smile. She certainly intended to pass half an hour or so lolling about in the sun, idly watching the twins – who needed no company but their own – busying themselves with sand and shells. Then when her mother's eyes grew somnolent and her voice languid, Brigid would casually mention a Coke or ice-cream, some girls met in the beach café, a trip with them into Chilford; her mother would murmur something that would be interpreted immediately and indisputably as permission and Brigid would vanish at once, reappearing at Oakfield in due course after as long an absence as she thought she could get away with.

There had in fact been an encounter with some girls at a beach café – Brigid had rather liked one of them, Eileen, who was on holiday with a bunch of friends. But Brigid was most certainly

69

not going on any trip into Chilford with a beach crowd. An hour or two after springing out of the family car before the front door of Oakfield, Brigid's eyes had locked glances with those of a very likely-looking lad tinkering with a motor-bike beside the path that ran down to the shore. He was as thin as a reed but tall and supple. He was wearing a pair of unbelievably old jeans and a blindingly new flowered shirt, a combination which had taken him a solid quarter of an hour of brow-furrowing to arrive at.

Within five minutes they knew enough about each other to provide a good working basis. His name was Ian Ripley, he was seventeen years old, a sixth-former at a grammar school seventy miles from Brigid's home town of Perrymount. He was spending the summer holidays with three of his mates, sharing two rooms above a greengrocer's shop in the centre of Chilford. The four lads made up a group called Blueberry Pie; they had formed it a couple of years ago in a top-of-the-world moment during a party, had begun after a time to take it seriously, worked at it, achieved a few bookings, astonished their friends before long by securing some good regular engagements and finally confounded their foes with the news that they were going to play for six weeks in a seaside nightspot.

On Saturday Brigid and Ian had regaled themselves with sandwiches and coffee at the beach kiosk – this was by way of being his breakfast, he had as usual been up till all hours. On Sunday he had ridden out to Westerhill again, they had walked all round the village, the golf-course, the seashore. She had tried to work out how she could manage to get to the Sweet Potato Club to hear him play. Today he would be waiting for her by a bus shelter a quarter of a mile along the road out of Westerhill; he would wait until half past twelve. If she managed to join him he would take her back with him to Chilford, riding pillion on his bike.

'Don't go getting up to any mischief,' Mike said to her now in a tone that spoke of a world filled with pitfalls for young girls. She flicked him a single resigned glance and closed the bedroom door. She took the twins along the corridor to their own room and set about making them look presentable for the beach. If only she had had an older brother or two, her father might not have been so ridiculously watchful over her, he might have been able to comprehend that the average lad of her own age wasn't a potential delinquent. The trouble is, she thought, rubbing a flannel over Vicky's face with an energetic scouring action, the only young men Dad comes much into contact with are either suspected criminals or well-scrubbed policemen, he can't seem to get it into his head that there are millions of decent lads in between.

'You're rubbing Vicky's face too hard,' Kate said with stern rebuke. She had to keep an eye open for her twin's welfare; Vicky would stand there and allow herself to be pummelled clean by a strong and absent-minded grown-up.

'Oh, I'm sorry.' Brigid dropped to her knees and kissed Vicky's fiery cheek. 'I wasn't thinking. I didn't mean to hurt you.'

From his position beneath the flower-laden branches of a philadelphus Edgar watched Ashton and Lockwood walking towards the car. Civil Service my foot, he thought with massive cynicism, Ashton's no more a civil servant than I am. Those shoulders, that look in the eyes, spelled out one word and the word was copper. Couldn't blame him, of course, passing himself off as a harmless member of society; would any man in his senses march into a guesthouse hoping for a couple of weeks of relaxed and friendly living and announce himself as a policeman on holiday?

He'd make pretty certain he kept on the right side of Ashton, however he chose to describe himself. And he'd have a little word with the twins, just to be absolutely sure. No trouble at all in winkling the truth out of them. The older girl, no use trying there, she'd have been too well drilled into the Civil Service spiel before too many past holidays.

Mike's keen eye caught a flicker of movement beneath the snowy blossoms. He paused for a moment and tilted his head to one side. Meacham. Handyman gardener . . . His brain automatically flung up the scanty details. Not all that long at Oakfield. A late-flowering romance on the part of the housekeeper . . . and for Meacham? . . . What was it for him? Something he didn't altogether care for about the way the fellow was standing there under the branches, he looked a good deal less like a gardener than someone casing a joint.

Edgar took a couple of brisk paces forward and seized the end of a philadelphus bough with a firmly authoritative gesture.

'Lovely morning, Mr Ashton,' he called in a strong, courteous tone. 'And Mr Lockwood.' He frowned knowledgeably at the waxy flowers, patted the branch and released it; it swung vigorously up in the air and descended an instant later to deal him a smart blow on the head that caused him to stumble sideways.

'It certainly is a glorious morning,' Mike said. The fellow had no earthly reason to be skulking among the shrubs, no horticultural reason, that is. He suddenly became aware that Lockwood was holding open the passenger door, was waiting for him to get into the car, was giving him a curious glance. At once he wiped from his face the look of concentrated thought and replaced it with a friendly half-smile.

'I was just thinking,' he said with an apologetic air, 'that Meacham seems rather a citified type to find working in a place like this.' Almost gave myself away there, he told himself with irritation. Ordinary men didn't go round training two-hundred-watt stares on casual citizens . . . but then, he added to himself a fraction of a second later, neither did ordinary casual citizens peer out of shrubberies with that alert and watchful eye. He felt the faintest tingle move along his spine. That particular quality of the gaze, wary, disciplined, and yet comradely, innocently trusting . . . characteristic, unmistakable. He slid into the passenger seat and settled himself back.

'Where did Mrs Meacham meet her husband?' he asked idly as Lockwood got in behind the wheel. 'On holiday somewhere, wasn't it?'

Bob Jourdan glanced at his watch. Twenty minutes to five. He frowned. Perhaps Fiona wouldn't be going down to the typing pool at all now, she might leave it over till the morning. In which case he would either have to walk into her office and make no bones about it, ask her to come out with him this evening, or he would have to forget about it for today and engineer the whole thing a little more intelligently tomorrow. He wasn't particularly keen on either course.

Ah! The sound of a door opening Fiona's voice, speaking back into the room she was leaving. A few brisk paces took him round the end of the corridor, then he slowed down, began to stroll in her direction, looking with an absorbed gaze at the sheaf of papers in his hand.

When her crisp footsteps were only a few yards away he allowed himself to look up.

'Oh, hello there! Fiona!' he said in a tone of lively surprise. She didn't appear in the best of humours, she had the air of someone who, given any opportunity at all, would have great pleasure in snapping out a brusque retort. She's just about in the right mood, he thought with pleasure. She can't have seen Lockwood since Friday, she must be getting a bit tired of her own company in the evenings, she'll be beginning to ask herself what on earth she's doing sitting round waiting for Lockwood to snap his fingers.

'I've been meaning to ask you,' he said, giving her a full, open, uncomplicated smile, 'if you'd like to have a drink with me one evening this week.' He knew damn well she'd been certain he would make a play for her the moment Lockwood took himself off; after four days without any approach from himself she had probably come to the conclusion that he'd lost interest. He'd avoided her office, kept out of her way in corridors, picked a distant seat in the canteen. 'Any evening to suit you,' he added now. He had the curious feeling that he could actually read the thoughts passing through her mind . . . If I play hard to get now, she was probably thinking, he might never ask me again. Some other girl, eighteen or nineteen perhaps, might have edged her way into his consciousness, might begin to take up his free evenings. In two years' time I'll be thirty. And Jourdan is firmly set on the ladder to promotion. He's younger, fitter, better-looking than Stephen Lockwood. And . . . I rather fancy him . . .

She gave him an appraising look. 'I might like that,' she said with a detached air.

A girl came stepping along the corridor, light and graceful. He let his eyes linger on her for several seconds, saw that Fiona followed his look. He turned his gaze back to Fiona, he invested it with a certain abstracted quality. 'Dinner too if you want. If you're by any lucky chance free this evening.'

'Well now.' She smiled, her voice took on a decisive tone. 'As it happens, I am.'

At the Sweet Potato in Chilford things didn't really begin to warm up before eleven. Until half past nine Brigid had been able to tell herself that she was going to catch the last bus out to Westerhill; until twenty minutes before midnight she reminded herself frequently and fairly firmly that she must on no account forget to watch the time, she must be quite certain to leave when the girl with the frizzy hair decided to push off as the frizzy girl was the daughter of the steward of the Westerhill golf-club and – so Brigid had learned in the course of sundry jigging and screeching interchanges in the last couple of hours – had arranged to meet her father outside the Sweet Potato and get a lift home; she had no objection if Brigid came with them.

At midnight the lights dimmed even further, an unearthly purple spot was directed on to the stage, Ian Ripley and the other members of Blueberry Pie emerged from the wings in a series of kangaroo leaps, a great shriek rose up from the auditorium and Brigid's mind was suddenly riven by the realization that the frizzy-haired girl had vanished into thin air.

She let out a dreadful groan, imperceptible in the general uproar, she held her wrist an inch away from her face and screwed up her eyes at her watch. Twelve o'clock! Nothing for it, utterly, absolutely, totally and inescapably no help for it, she would have to wait till it was all over, get Ian to take her back to Westerhill on his motor-bike. The lad sitting next to her – or to be more accurate, jumping up and down and howling next to her, a lad she had never knowingly clapped eyes on till this moment, seized her in a powerful grip and pulled her to her feet.

'My dad's going to murder me!' she screamed in his ear. 'He's going to tear me into a million pieces!'

The lad sank his face on to her neck, gave her a swift break-the-ice biting kiss and sprang upright again.

'You gotta go some time,' he yelled unarguably. The music took hold of her, snatched her up, whirled her along, Ian was up there in front of the mike, singing in that gorgeous harsh nerve-endy voice for her alone, singing of how abysmally foul and hopeless everything was but how in spite of all the mind-blowing horrors he would continue to be her ever-loving fella, her dreamy-eyed baby boy. She threw back her head, let the whole lot wash over her, she began to laugh and sing and cry.

Something had woken Marion up. Some noise down there in the garden perhaps? Slight, subdued, but disturbing all the same to a sleeper with a digestion somewhat disordered by an unwise – and overlarge – second helping of Bessie's apple pudding richly laced with thick country cream.

She sighed in the darkness. Might as well go down to the kitchen and root about for bicarbonate of soda, otherwise she'd be tossing and turning till morning. From the other bed she could hear Stephen's deep rhythmic breathing; she drew back the bedclothes and reached for her slippers.

The whole house was still. The luminous hands of the bedside clock showed twenty-five minutes past two. She eased open the bedroom door and made her way slowly along the corridor. Better not switch on a light till she was well away from the sleeping quarters. But as she rounded the end of the passage she saw a dim glow coming up from the hall. Someone had been careless, had gone last to bed without turning off the lights – or perhaps it was now the custom at Oakfield to leave on a lamp or two all night to discourage burglars?

She went noiselessly down the stairs. At the far end of the hall a standard lamp shed a pool of yellow light over the carpet. As she walked towards it her ear caught the sound of a little bubbling snore, her eyes made out the shape of an arm hanging slackly over the side of a wing chair. She took a few more silent paces and peered in at the sprawling figure. Mr Ashton, fast asleep, fully clothed. She stood looking down at him in a moment's indecision and then shrugged her shoulders and went cautiously off to the kitchen.

The bicarbonate had dynamited her heartburn and she was standing by the stove waiting for a pan of milk to warm up when she heard quite distinctly the sound of powerful giggles partly repressed. She turned her head sharply and at the same instant there was the crash of a heavy object falling over, a stifled cry and a few seconds filled with agitated shushing. Marion seized the handle of the milk pan, torn between a desire to investigate and an instinct to flee.

Footsteps – Ashton's surely? – coming rapidly from the hall, an outside door opening and closing, someone running lightly round the back of the house, an engine kicked into pulsing life.

Brigid Ashton, Marion registered with an agreeable feeling of censoriousness, staying out till this time, keeping her father up out of his bed waiting and worrying. She poured the milk into a beaker, extinguished the light, and tiptoed from the kitchen, listening expectantly for tones of recrimination and defiance. The standard lamp was still on but the hall was empty. Mike had seized his daughter by the arm and marched her into a small sitting-room opening off the hall so as not to disturb the rest of the house; he had closed the door and let loose his shafts of anger. Marion saw the line of light under the door, she walked silently over and stood for two or three minutes with her ear close up against the panels, a look of lively interest on her face. Then discretion stirred itself, she gave a tiny sigh, glanced down at the beaker to make sure she wasn't spilling the milk, and went softly off towards the stairs.

Chapter 9

'Oh dear, I do beg your pardon!' Marion clapped a genteelly curled hand over her mouth and extended the fingers of the other hand over her well-upholstered chest in an attempt at one and the same time to apologize for the resounding burp that had just escaped her lips and to prevent its successor from following suit; in this latter effort she was signally unsuccessful. 'Do forgive me, it's Bessie's cooking, so very tempting.' She turned her head and smiled in a refined way at Godfrey sitting beside her in the driver's seat. 'Do you suppose it would be possible for us to call in at that shop in the village? They're sure to have some magnesia tablets. Thursday afternoon – it isn't their half-closing day or anything?'

Godfrey shook his head. 'They don't bother with any half-closing day. Certainly we can call in there.' At the next intersection he turned the car in the direction of the village.

'I can get some cigarettes while we're at it,' Stephen said from the rear seat. They were on their way back from a visit to Miss Tillard who was now a good deal recovered from her nasty turn of a few days ago, although Dr Nightingale hadn't ceased to press her to go into hospital for observation.

'What time does the store shut?' Stephen asked. 'It's getting on for half past five.'

'Plenty of time,' Godfrey said calmly. 'They're open till well after six, they never close as long as there's a customer on the horizon.'

Fifty yards farther along the road a pale green saloon car slackened its pace and the driver stuck his head out to read the road sign.

'We can go on to Chilford. Or take a look at Westerhill. Just a village of course. Chilford's quite a sizeable place. What do you think?'

'I want some aspirins,' Wyn Paget said. 'We can decide where to stay later. But if I don't get the aspirins soon the shops'll be shut. And I've got one hell of a headache. It's all this driving round,' she added crossly. 'About time we stopped somewhere for a few days.'

'You wanted a touring holiday,' Jack Paget said without animosity. 'And a touring holiday you're getting.'

'Enough is as good as a ruddy feast,' Wyn said with a scowl. 'Come on, let's try Westerhill, there must be some place there where you can get an aspirin.'

In the village shop Wyn found not only aspirins but a good selection of postcards, a brand of crystallized figs to which she was very partial and a table stacked with huge floppy-brimmed straw hats in brilliant colours. She spent several cheerful minutes in front of a small mirror nailed to the wall, balancing on her head one monstrous creation after another.

'They're all gorgeous,' she said happily. 'What do you think?'

'Have them all if you want,' Jack said without looking at her. He was watching a little group through a gap in the shelves, two men and a woman, talking to the proprietor who was treating them with deferential courtesy.

'We've now got the chestnut purée Mrs Barratt was inquiring for,' the shopkeeper said. 'And a new delivery of Swiss black cherry jam. Would you like me to send some up to Oakfield? No trouble at all, I assure you. Say, a dozen of each?'

'Thank you, there's no need to put yourself out. I'll mention it to my wife,' Godfrey said without enthusiasm.

'Business good?' the man asked in a way that managed to combine obsequiousness with the comradely notion of all being in trade together. 'Pretty well full up at Oakfield?' Godfrey said nothing, he closed his eyes for an instant, then opened them and studied with an air of intense concentration a placard concerned with a startling reduction in the price of frozen faggots.

'Not completely full,' Marion said chattily, seeing that Godfrey didn't appear to think the question had been addressed to him. 'Still a few of the small bedrooms vacant. They were part of the servants' quarters in the old days of course.'

'Enjoying your visit to the old haunts, then, Mrs Lockwood?' Like everyone else in the neighbourhood, the shopkeeper knew Mrs Lockwood was a local girl, had as near as dammit married Mr Barratt. He was agreeably intrigued to see her staying at Oakfield, wondered exactly how much each member of the foursome was enjoying the situation.

'Oh, very much,' Marion said at once. 'I went into Chilford the other – '

'Marion dear.' Stephen slid fingers of steel under her arm. She glanced at him and received again the odd impression she had registered with increasing frequency during the last few years, that he was just managing not to grit his teeth. 'I think we ought to be getting back to Oakfield,' he said. 'I'm sure Godfrey has a great deal – '

As they came up to the exit with the shopkeeper still assiduously attending them, they found their passage blocked by a customer standing almost facing them, looking with an appraising frown at a tempting shelf display. 'Excuse me,' Stephen said. The abstracted look vanished from Jack Paget's face; he took a couple of steps to one side.

'I'm so sorry.' He looked in apology at the trio who gave him back the courteous, impersonal glances of strangers. Then Godfrey paused for an instant, looking back at Paget who had now moved on; he put up a hand and passed a finger slowly across his upper lip. The shopkeeper's voice pursued them with farewells out into the soft caressing air.

'I'm very fond of black cherry jam,' Marion said. 'I always say you can't beat the Swiss.'

'Indeed,' Godfrey murmured. He opened the car door and stood back to let her get in. I know that face, he thought. I remember that tone of voice. Where had he met the fellow before? Had he in fact ever met the fellow before? Was it perhaps that he was just reminded of someone else? But it seemed to him that it had been that face and that voice and for some reason he had a powerful and totally irrational sensation of being pierced to the marrow by an icy wind.

For the best part of a quarter of an hour after he had read through Friday morning's post Bob Jourdan sat at his desk with his head cradled in his hands, the tips of his fingers pressing hard against his skull. Just before half past nine he jerked himself upright, flexed his shoulders, riffled through the letters and carefully selected half a dozen from the pile. He stood up, hesitated, and then sat down again, looking consideringly at the phone.

No, he wouldn't go down to Welfare, Fiona must come up here. She had gone out with him not only on Tuesday evening but on Wednesday and Thursday evenings also; the greater part of their Thursday date had been spent in his comfortable flat. If there was ever a time to establish who was going to be the dominant one, that time was now. He settled himself comfortably into his seat, stretched out a hand and picked up the receiver.

'Several birds with one stone,' he said across the table to Fiona a few minutes later in a cheerful positive tone. He experienced a moment of exquisite pleasure at the sight of her sitting opposite him, silent, attentive. 'I can call in to see these people – ' he stabbed a finger at the topmost letter – 'on Monday morning, they're only fifteen miles or so from Chilford, couldn't be more convenient.' He picked up two other papers. 'I can fit both of these calls very comfortably into Monday afternoon.' He flicked a finger at the remaining letters. 'I must talk to Lockwood about these. Can't take the responsibility on my own.' He grinned at her. 'Not that I'm not capable of it, or that I wouldn't like to.' He gave her a glance edged with significance. 'But as of this moment Lockwood is Home Sales Manager. And these matters should not be decided without his say-so.'

Fiona continued to listen. She didn't say, 'But what has all this to do with me?' She simply sat waiting for him to tell her what it had to do with her. He rather liked that, in fact he liked it so much that he had great difficulty in refraining from springing over the top of the desk and seizing her in his arms.

'So I propose to go down to Westerhill for the weekend,' he said, 'and have a little chat with Lockwood. I can leave, say, at three or four this afternoon, I can see to the other things on Monday, come back to Barbridge on Monday night, I'll be here in the office again on Tuesday morning.' He tilted his chair and linked his hands behind his head. 'It occurred to me that you might like to come too. I rather thought a whiff of sea air might do you good.'

She gave him a long slow smile. She had a deep conviction that she knew what was going on in his mind. He was forcing her out into the open, proposing to set her down between himself and Lockwood for an entire weekend, make her choose. 'I take it you're intending that we should stay in the same house as the Lockwoods?' she asked. She had reasons of her own – reasons which she very definitely proposed keeping to herself – for finding the suggestion intriguing.

'Yes, that was my intention.' A line appeared between Jourdan's brows. It occurred to him suddenly for the first time that it was quite possible, in fact at this season of the year more than likely, that the Westerhill house might be full. In which case was there any point in going off on the expedition at all?

'I'd have to go upstairs and ask permission of course,' he said lightly, jerking his head towards the ceiling in acknowledgement of higher powers in loftier regions, providing himself with a let-out in case a phone call revealed that the house was in fact full. 'They might have other notions.' He shrugged his shoulders. 'But I take it that if I get the okay, you'll come with me?'

She nodded. 'Yes, I'll come with you. But what reason am I to give for going? Just why should it be so necessary for Welfare to contact the Home Sales Manager?'

'It isn't. You don't have to tell anyone you're coming with me or ask anyone's permission to come. You can simply take a day of your annual leave on Monday. As far as the tail end of this afternoon is concerned, you can have a hairdressing appointment or a date with the dentist. No need actually to pin it up on the notice board that we're going off together.' He stood up. 'I'll let you know definitely one way or the other in about three-quarters of an hour. Will that suit you?'

As soon as the door had closed behind her he picked up the sheet of paper on which Lockwood had written his Westerhill address. He glanced at the phone number, perched himself on the edge of the desk and lifted the receiver.

'Enjoying it ever so much,' Wyn Paget said. 'As I remarked to Jack only this morning over breakfast, if Mrs Barratt could possibly see her way to letting us stay on over the weekend, it really would be just the job. We wouldn't mind at all if we had to move to another room or if we had to squash in somewhere smaller – '

'That's perfectly all right,' Pauline said into the flow, suppressing with difficulty a powerful desire to yawn. 'It won't make any difficulty if you stay over the weekend – '

'Till Tuesday, that would be,' Wyn said swiftly. 'Or possibly Wednesday.'

'We'll take it as Tuesday for the moment. You can make up your minds about Wednesday later.' Pauline gave the woman a determined smile, chiding herself for finding it so wearing to be friendly to the wife of a man who had served with her husband in Germany. Several years ago, it appeared, and then only for a few weeks, Paget being just about at the end of his term of engagement and Godfrey newly arrived at his posting. 'That very severe winter,' Paget had reminded them when he disclosed his identity. 'You must remember, sir.' Godfrey had smiled and murmured suitable sentiments. 'But I have only the haziest recollection of the fellow,' he'd said to Pauline afterwards. And she had been no more successful recalling Mrs Paget, although

Wyn had assured her that they had worked together at organizing one or two social events for the troops.

Paget came strolling towards them, keeping an eye open for Mr Barratt who was even more efficiently keeping an eye open for Paget and so contriving to remain invisible.

'All settled, Jack,' Wyn called out on a high gay note.

'Good-oh!' He put up a hand and fingered his little moustache, flashed Pauline a smile at once ingratiating and comradely. 'Delightful place you have here, my dear lady . . . ' The house really will be full now, Pauline thought, with that couple coming down this evening from Stephen's firm. She could put Mr Jourdan in the tiny room with the flowered wallpaper and Miss Brooke in the slightly larger room next door. Stephen had been out when Mr Jourdan had phoned, she'd passed on the message as soon as he came in. He'd said nothing for a moment, she'd thought him gripped by – surprise? Or some other stronger emotion? But then he nodded and said quite casually, 'Yes, these matters do crop up in business, I'm not altogether surprised.' As if he found the prospect of their arrival boring or at worst irritating.

She realized suddenly to her astonishment that Paget in the course of making a point had laid a hand forcefully on her bare arm. He would never have dreamed of doing that in the Army, she thought, wondering briefly whether to disengage herself discreetly. Ah well, she decided an instant later, allowing her arm to remain where it was but in a disembodied, lump-of-wood fashion, we are none of us in the Army now. And asked herself almost in the same breath if perhaps that had been the point Paget was intent on making.

'It's our wedding anniversary on Sunday,' Wyn said suddenly. She turned to her husband. 'I bet you'd forgotten it. You always do.'

'Never!' he said firmly. He gave Pauline a massive wink. 'No reason why we shouldn't celebrate it here. A few bottles of champers. Plenty of jolly chums to help us celebrate. My word, we can have quite a party.' His small regular teeth gleamed whitely at Pauline in dazzling good humour 'I take it you would have no objection, dear lady? It'd be quite like the old days.'

They'll be gone by Wednesday morning at the very latest, Pauline told herself bracingly, you can put up with anything in the world until next Wednesday. 'No objection at all,' she said in a pleasant tone. 'Now, if you'll excuse me, I do have one or two things – '

Paget raised a hand. 'Of course, of course, by all means, quite understand, say no more.' As Pauline took herself off to a place of safety she heard him say to his wife, 'What about some of those squeaker things? They're sure to keep them in one of the Chilford shops. Do you think they'd go down well? And those jolly little hats with elastic?' His voice took on an animated note. 'I feel we should seriously consider balloons. I always say you can't really go wrong with good big balloons.' Oh dear, Pauline thought, pressing the palms of her hands together, Godfrey isn't going to be one little tiny bit happy about this.

'Lockwood.' Wyn sat on the edge of her bed and stared reflectively at the opposite wall. 'That man, you know, the one who did you down that time you worked for that big firm, what was it called, when we lived in, you remember, that little house, that pretty little house with the delphiniums, you know, wasn't he called Lockwood?'

'No-o . . . ' Jack said on a long-drawn-out note of dismissal. He twisted round to look at his back view in the long mirror on the front of the wardrobe, flicked a speck from a shoulder. 'Isn't it about time we were going down for dinner?'

Wyn leaned forward so that she could see herself in the glass of the dressing-table. 'Well, what was his name, then? I was pretty certain it was Lockwood. Every evening when you came home at that time, it must have been weeks altogether, you never stopped talking about him, about the dirty trick he'd played on you, I ought to remember that name, I heard it often enough.'

'Well, whatever it was, it wasn't Lockwood,' Jack said briskly. 'Come on, love, look lively, time's getting on.'

She got to her feet. 'What was it then if it wasn't Lockwood?'

He shrugged his shoulders. 'I don't know, forgot the fellow's name years ago. Doesn't do to go round harbouring grudges. Anyway, what does it all matter now? He may have done me out of a bit of promotion once, but what of it? Did me a good turn, really. If I hadn't got so damn mad about it and cleared out of the firm, it might have taken me years to get up the nerve to start out on my own.' He went over and gave her an unsubtle kiss. 'We'd never have been where we are today, nice little business, no one to answer to.' He gave her an affectionate thump on the back that propelled her half-way across the room. 'We're doing all right, kiddo, and don't you forget it.'

As Wyn flicked a powder puff across her face he said on a sudden inspiration, 'We could go into Chilford tomorrow and find one of those joke shops, you know, rubber poached eggs, exploding cigars.' He threw back his head in a loud laugh. 'We could have a bit of fun at the party. Wouldn't mind seeing old Barratt bite on a squirting bun. Toffee-nosed blighter. Just the same now as when he was out in Germany, hasn't changed one iota. Thought he was doing you a favour if he wished you good morning.' He threw open the bedroom door.

As they walked along the corridor Wyn turned her head and gave him an unsmiling, level look. 'I'm right, aren't I? It was Lockwood.'

'Ready when you are, dear.' Marion picked up her handbag, smiled comfortably at Stephen who was lying stretched out on his bed with his hands linked behind his head, frowning up at the ceiling.

He didn't seem to have heard her. She leaned over and took hold of his foot in its conservative dark grey sock, she shook it in an amiable fashion. 'Dinner-time, dear. Put your shoes on.' He jerked his head in her direction, glanced at her as if she were a total stranger who had wandered into the bedroom and started taking liberties with him.

'That codicil,' he said abruptly. 'Your aunt's will. Did Whittall happen to mention to you how much she's thinking of leaving Theresa?'

Marion looked surprised. 'No. Why should he? I don't think it can be all that much, Aunt Elinor isn't a wealthy woman.' She found his shoes, held them out to him, watched as he put them on. 'I was remembering that old business about Henry. You know, when he had to leave school.'

Stephen stood up and walked over to the dressing-table. 'What of it?' he asked brusquely.

'I was just wondering. He's only a solicitor's clerk, I know he's supposed to be a good one, Aunt Elinor seems to think very well of him, but still, he isn't a real solicitor. I suppose being asked to leave school – that meant he couldn't go to a university or get himself properly articled.'

'He'd never have got any farther than he is now,' Stephen said with force. 'He was never over-gifted with ability.' He made a sound of contempt. 'He's a weak character, always was, always will be. Probably likes to kid himself that little caper at school ruined his chances, but don't you believe it. A little thing like that wouldn't have held back a man of real talent.' He stooped and peered at his face in the mirror. 'It wouldn't have hindered an able and confident man.' He picked up a comb and ran it fiercely through his hair. 'Dare say it suits him to have a good excuse for being what he is.' He flung the comb down on to the china tray. 'Keeps him happy.'

He turned from the mirror. 'Did Godfrey say anything to you about your aunt's affairs?' he asked in a mild, casual tone. 'I wouldn't like to think you weren't going to get your fair share of what's going when the old girl snuffs it.' He smiled at her fondly, really quite a long time since he'd smiled at her like that.

'Well, he did talk about Aunt Elinor in a general sort of way, about her health and so on, not exactly about her business affairs.'

Stephen came over and put an arm round her. 'If he does have another little chat with you, you might just see if you can get him to – oh, I don't have to spell it out for you, I'm sure.' He laughed. 'An intelligent girl like you.' He squeezed her shoulders. 'I just want to make sure your aunt doesn't forget you.' He looked down into her face with a teasing smile. 'I'm quite sure you can get old Godfrey to tell you anything you want. He was very sweet on you at one time.' He gave her another squeeze, bent his head and dropped a fleeting kiss on her cheek. 'But he wasn't as lucky as I was. He didn't actually get you.'

He released his grip and walked beside her to the door. He held it open for her, stood glancing out of the window at the beautiful evening sky of high summer, a clear bright blue with fluffy white puffs and streamers. A wild surge of melancholy rose inside him. He turned his eyes from the window and followed Marion out into the corridor.

'I meant to ask you,' Stephen said suddenly to Godfrey as they took a turn along the terrace after dinner. 'That Osmond affair – any effect on you? Do any business with them?'

Godfrey felt as if a huge and brutal hand had seized the central muscles of his body in a crushing grip. 'A little,' he said casually. 'Nothing to speak of. And some time ago at that.'

'That's good,' Stephen said with energy. 'Must be a terrific relief to you. Great temptation to a small firm starting out, put all your eggs in one basket, land a good contract with one of the big lads, think you're made for the next ten years.' He shook his head. 'Never does. Seen it happen more than once. Not a mistake anyone makes twice.' He laughed without mirth. 'Takes a bit of doing to survive a first mistake like that, I can tell you.' They reached the end of the terrace, turned, started back again. 'Still,' Stephen added in a more cheerful voice, 'doesn't apply to you, I'm glad to hear. Order book nicely full, is it?'

'Pretty full,' Godfrey said. He had a cramp in his side now that made it quite painful to walk. 'Let's go in and have a drink,' he suggested. 'We might get hold of a couple of the others, see if we can drum up a game of bridge.'

In the distance he saw Meacham walking towards the house, coming from the rose-garden. He'll have to go, he thought in an oddly detached fashion. And Bessie too. After the best part of forty years at Oakfield she'll be sent packing when the crash comes. He would do what he could for her of course, there had been a time when he had almost looked on her as a mother. But he might not be in a position to do anything at all for her. He glanced back at Meacham walking confidently round to the back of the house. Could he be relied on to look after Bessie? Seemed a decent enough fellow. Godfrey had been pleased for her when she'd got married, had hoped sincerely that she was making a happy old age for herself, had been glad to make a niche for her husband.

When he was busying himself with the drinks a few minutes later a restless impulse took hold of him, he felt the need to take a look at Bessie, for no reason that he could formulate, he simply wanted to see her. He murmured something about ice to Stephen and went off to the kitchen. He rapped lightly on the door and entered almost at once. Meacham was standing very close to Bessie, they both turned as he came in, looking at him with lively, slightly startled eyes. Bessie's cheeks were very pink.

'We need a little more ice,' Godfrey said lightly. He opened the fridge door. 'No need for you to bother, Bessie, I'll see to it.' Oh, it's all right, he thought with pleasure, with unutterable relief, she's happy, they're fond of each other, he'll be good to her. He lifted out the ice tray. Next week the fateful meeting was due to take place, the Minister and the top brass from Osmond's. He took a dish down from the shelf.

'That was a very good cheese *soufflé*,' he said to Bessie, smiling at her across the table.

She smiled back at him with that old look of love. 'Thank you. It's always a pleasure to me when they come out well.'

In another week at the most he would know one way or the other. He tipped the cubes carefully into the dish, went over to the sink and filled the ice tray with water.

'I had a word with Godfrey earlier.' Stephen looked out at the advancing twilight, the dark mass of trees against the deep blue sky. 'I was glad to hear he hadn't been doing business with Osmond's.' He laughed, without humour. 'A weight off your mind too, I should imagine.'

'Oh – yes,' Pauline said vaguely. Osmond's? The name had a familiar sound. She stared down at her hands, trying to remember.

'Osmond's,' Stephen said with reproving emphasis. 'You must know – the big firm there's all this fuss about, going bust . . .' His voice ran on, explaining, simplifying for her lay mind. 'Just as well Godfrey hadn't any of their orders on his books.'

But he had, she thought, looking back at Stephen with a relaxed air, surely he had . . . she was almost certain she could remember Godfrey coming in one day in the spring, pleased, triumphant, telling her about another big order . . . hadn't that been Osmond's? Or merely some name like it?

Stephen turned his head and looked over at the bridge table where Godfrey was reckoning up points, carefully watched by a pair of one-nighters. 'I'd better get back.' He stood up, smiled at Pauline. 'Must go and find out what the damage is.'

Pauline watched him walking over to the table, bending down to see the score. Are we really in bad straits? she wondered, trying to come to grips with the notion. Is it possible? Surely Godfrey would have said something? Or would he? She put up a hand to her face. He seemed to say very little to her of any real significance these days.

All at once she had a clear vision of Aunt Elinor lying back against the pillows, pale, exhausted. Her heart began to beat with uncontrollable rapidity. And there had been Marion, no more than half an hour ago, engaging her in casual-seeming chat, coming back more than once to the topic of Aunt Elinor's will . . . the possible amounts of any legacies . . . wondering if after all they might have been mistaken in supposing there wouldn't be very much to leave . . .

At the bridge table Godfrey looked up, met Pauline's gaze, gave her a faint smile, raised a hand in idle greeting and turned his attention again to his cards. She felt the breath catch in her throat. Was it possible, was it remotely conceivable, that all she represented to him now was a convenient source of cash?

She got to her feet, went out on to the shadowy terrace and stood leaning against a pillar, trembling slightly in the breeze.

Chapter 10

'I'm not going to the Pagets' stupid party,' Brigid said with deliberate insolence. 'You're determined to see I don't have any of the kind of fun *I* want on this so-called holiday. I don't see why I should join in when a load of old deadbeats are trying to live it up.'

'Look here, my girl,' Mike said belligerently, but Jean put a restraining hand on his arm.

'Ssh, dear, we can't have a scene, everyone will hear.' She glanced calmly at her daughter. 'Do try not to be so difficult,' she said in a pleasant, even tone. 'You could ask that girl to come round. You know the one I mean – Eileen. You might enjoy the party if she was with you. Why don't you phone her?' Quite a nice girl, Jean had thought, when Brigid struck up a beach friendship with her a couple of days ago.

'I'm going to bed,' Brigid said loftily. 'I'm going to read. I bet it'll be a weird party.' She pulled a face. 'Honestly, those Pagets. So frantically cheerful all the time.'

'Wouldn't do you any harm to be a bit more cheerful,' Mike said in a low incisive voice.

'Oh, do stop it, you two,' Jean said with irritation. 'Neither of you has a grain of consideration for anyone else.' Mike threw her a dark look, she gave a deep sigh. It was going to be a gay evening with the lot of them. For a moment she wished herself back in Perrymount, watching television in comparative peace, with the twins in bed, Brigid doing her homework in the other room and Mike out on duty. Then she remembered that this was supposed to be one of the happy times, one of the carefree golden interludes you pasted into memory's scrapbook to illuminate the grey twilight of old age. And furthermore, it was costing them good money.

'Oh, all right, Brigid,' she said with an attempt at affability. 'You go on up to your book. Keep an ear open for the twins, make sure they don't get up to any tricks.' She gave Mike a placatory smile. 'Come on, let's go and join the festive throng, I gather there's going to be champagne.'

Marion was quite enjoying herself. The Pagets seemed to be very good at organizing nice romping games that took her right back to the days of her youth, made her feel gay, pretty, desirable, a charming butterfly, licensed to emit little shrieks, clap her hands, bump laughingly into people, all without anyone – even Stephen – being able to look at her with lofty disapproval.

It was just this twinge of indigestion that was spoiling her evening. The cake had been very rich, and champagne, delicious as it was, always had a way of making its presence felt after a brief interval. She glanced round the room. The Pagets were in the throes of getting another game going, some kind of guessing competition. No one would notice if she slipped out through the other door and went upstairs for a few antacid tablets. And she could take the opportunity to repair her make-up, she felt her face to be flushed, which meant without doubt that her nose was brightly shining.

As she went up the first flight of stairs she heard a door close a little way along the corridor. A light scurry of feet came towards her. A moment later Vicky Ashton raced into view with her long pale hair flying out behind her. She was wearing pyjamas, her feet were bare. Marion put out a hand and brought her to an abrupt halt. The child stood looking up at her, panting, with an expression half of amusement, half of entreaty.

'You're supposed to be in bed, aren't you?' Marion said firmly. 'What would your father say if he knew you were running about like this?'

'Oh, don't tell him, please!' Vicky said in a small intense voice. 'I'll go back to bed right away, I won't get out again, I promise!'

'I'll take you back myself,' Marion said. 'Let me see, which is your room?' As she led the child up to her door she saw a small bright face peep for an instant round the end of the corridor. There was an interval of a few seconds and then Kate came walking towards them with an air of breezy nonchalance.

'It wasn't Vicky's fault,' she said as soon as she reached them. 'It was all my idea.'

'It doesn't matter whose idea it was,' Marion said. 'You're both going back to bed now.' She opened the door and urged them inside. 'By the way,' she said suddenly, 'where's Brigid? I should have thought she'd have kept an eye on you.'

Vicky shot a speaking glance at Kate who said nothing but kept her gaze fixed on the coverlet of her bed. 'Jump in then, both of you!' Marion said. 'I'll have a word with Miss Brigid before I go downstairs.'

'There's no need to.' Kate wriggled herself into a comfortable position under the bedclothes. 'I expect she's fallen asleep. She was reading a big thick book.'

Marion paid no heed but marched along the passage and rapped on Brigid's door. No reply, no sound of movement. She rapped again. Still no answer. Had the girl gone to sleep then? Should she just let her be? But some prick of malice, some impulse to needle at this young headstrong girl with her sulky, striking looks, rose inside her – presenting itself to her simply

90

as a wholly admirable desire to behave in a neighbourly and responsible fashion towards the Ashton family. She put her hand on the knob and tried it. The door swung silently open.

The room was dark, the heavy curtains drawn. By the light coming in from the passage she could see Brigid hunched up in bed, her dark hair spread out on the pillow. She hesitated, then went over to the bed and brought a hand purposefully down on the girl's shoulder with a brisk shaking movement. 'Brigid!' And in the same instant she realized that her fingers were sinking into a soft mass of skilfully arranged pillows and blankets, that the dark hair sprouted from the head of a large doll that tumbled sideways and looked up at her with an innocent trusting smile.

'Well!' she said aloud in a swift thrust of righteous anger. 'That's a nice trick to play!' She would most certainly go straight downstairs and have a word with Mr Ashton, party or no party.

She went out of the room and closed the door, she walked slowly to the head of the stairs. From the sitting-room in which the Pagets were manhandling the evening along came muffled sounds of good cheer.

She glanced down, her mind still occupied with thoughts of Brigid. Outside the sitting-room door two figures stood locked in each other's arms, the man with his mouth pressed down on the lips of . . . she clutched the banister rail and peered down . . . of that girl from Alpha – Miss Brooke! The man straightened himself and she saw with a terrifying stab of shock that it was Stephen. She remained clinging to the rail, one foot poised towards the next step. Down by the door a little rapid smoothing of hair and general rearranging was taking place, lighthearted whispering drifted upwards. The sitting-room door opened suddenly and they were both standing in the broad shaft of light, at ease, apart. Voices called gaily to them to come in and have a shot at guessing. Stephen put out a hand and placed it gently under Miss Brooke's elbow. They went into the room, the door closed.

When Marion slipped unobserved into the room by the other door a few minutes later the guessing game was over and a fresh piece of nonsense was about to get under way; it involved pairing everyone off into couples and setting them to perform tasks which would bring them into very close proximity. The champagne, the unswerving and unsnubbable efforts of the Pagets had combined by now to produce a sort of defiant merriment which was affecting even Godfrey. For the first ten minutes of the proceedings he had longed to be in a position to put Paget on some kind of charge, for the next half hour he had viewed the evening with barely-masked distaste, and then the ludicrousness of the whole performance, the sharp contrast between the carefree atmosphere and the dark tides surging in his brain, had somehow released him – from one moment to the next, it seemed – into a reckless mood of irresponsible gaiety.

He sprang to his feet, he would join in the game, he would seize hold of a partner. He glanced round, his gaze fell on Marion, looking at this moment rather different from the staid matron of the last few days. She had a certain wildness in her eyes, she seemed suddenly much younger as if she had torn herself free from the strait-jacket of suburban respectability. Their eyes met, she gave him an unrestrained smile, she took a step towards him. And he remembered all at once how desperately in love he had been with that other Marion, that beautiful, bewitching girl. He stretched out his hand and took hold of her, he slipped his arm round her waist and without waiting for the complicated gyrations of the Pagets' comical chores to begin he bent his head and gave her a powerful lingering kiss that seemed to them both like a smooth sweet picking up again of something that had been dropped a long and foolish time ago.

Bob Jourdan saw the kiss. He shot a glance at Stephen who briefly permitted his eyes to rest on his wife and Barratt, and then directed a look of steady goodwill at no one in particular.

'That's the spirit!' Paget cried loudly at the sight of an ex-officer unbending in public. Pauline turned her head at his shout and followed his approving gaze. She turned casually away again and regarded herself in a near-by mirror with an air of good-natured detachment, patting idly at her hair. A frail, elderly bed-and-breakfaster appeared beside her and said cheerfully, 'Mrs Barratt. If you would be so kind. Most honoured.' He swept her an exaggerated bow, held out a hand and indicated the other couples ranging themselves into position. She smiled, put her hand in his and took her place beside him in the circle.

Stephen moved a few paces to the right and leaned forward

to attract Fiona's attention; she was helping herself from a dish of *petits-fours*. But just as his fingers were about to rest on her arm Jourdan spoke her name from somewhere behind Stephen, over to the left. She looked round at Jourdan, half smiling.

'All right,' she said gaily. 'I'm coming.' Stephen let his arm drop back to his side. Jourdan took a firm grasp of Fiona's hand and pulled her to him.

'Partners, everyone!' Paget commanded. Which left Stephen with the stout female half of the elderly bed-and-breakfast couple. He resigned himself instantly to his destiny and took her gallantly into the ring.

Opposite them Marion stood looking about with restless animation; Godfrey's arm was still clasped round her waist. A few feet away Mike Ashton kept a proprietorial hand on his wife's arm. It had totally escaped Marion's mind that there had been something she had intended saying to the Ashtons.

Chapter 11

'Pity Ashton can't join us today,' Stephen said. 'He's taking his family off on some expedition. I'd have liked a last round with him.'

'You're off back to the treadmill tomorrow then?' Paget said. Stephen nodded. 'Nothing like a break to freshen you up,' Paget went on. 'I'm my own boss, of course, I take a holiday when I please these days.'

Not at all a bad chap, Stephen thought. A type you often came across in business, took a bit of swallowing at first, bit of a rough diamond, but good-hearted. And shrewd enough. He glanced at his watch. 'Whittall should be along shortly. Mark you, I don't know what kind of a game he plays, he tells me he hasn't handled a club for a year or two.'

Marion crossed the terrace, she passed within a few yards of the two men as she went in through the front door but she gave no sign of recognition, she had an absorbed, inward look. Her hands were thrust into the pockets of her blue waterproof jacket;

her fingers toyed with the folds of a letter that had come in the morning post in answer to one she had written to a woman she had known in the old days up north.

It was as she had suspected. 'You're quite right,' her friend had written. 'Hunston's disappeared eight years ago. There's a large supermarket on the site now, the whole of that part of Thetstone has been redeveloped, you wouldn't recognize it.' So whatever Edgar Meacham had been doing last summer, he hadn't been getting himself put on the early retirement list at Hunston's.

She took off the anorak and laid it across the back of a chair in the hall, only partly aware of her actions. I suppose I ought to tell Bessie about Meacham, she thought, without any real sense of mission. If he is a liar and God knows what else as well, I suppose she must be told. But she couldn't feel the sense of prickling pleasure that the notion had roused in her a few days ago, it no longer seemed of such overwhelming importance. Her mind kept slipping off to other preoccupations.

Wherever she looked she saw before her a shadowy mental image obscuring the face of the real world . . . the Brooke creature standing with her head tilted back, gathered into Stephen's fierce embrace. And a detached calculating section of her brain was all the time engaged in an exhaustive review of Stephen's conduct and attitudes during the last year or two, the things he had said and the things he had ceased to say, his absences and the reasons for those absences, little discrepancies she had half noticed at the time, larger discrepancies she had closed her mind to.

She didn't in the least want this manic activity of her mind to continue; it was wearing her out, consuming her, she had slept scarcely at all last night. But she seemed to have no control over it, it went remorselessly on and on as if an irreversible switch had been pressed in her brain.

She set herself in motion towards the kitchen, her mind all at once made up. No, she definitely would not say anything to Bessie. The woman was by no means as friendly as she used to be. And Heaven knew, she was old enough to take care of herself.

She went down a narrow passage and suddenly, there he was,

Meacham, coming round the end of the corridor, walking briskly towards her, smiling cheerfully. When he was a couple of yards away he opened his mouth and said, 'Beautiful morning, Mrs Lockwood,' and everything seemed to focus on his treacherous smile. A wave of bitter resentment, sharp animosity, sour vengefulness, swept over her, picked her up and carried her forward. She heard her own voice say on a high, light note, 'I had a letter from an old friend this morning, Mr Meacham.' He halted instantly, every line of his body froze into rigidity, the cheerful look vanished from his face and was succeeded by a disciplined, wary blankness.

'I knew you'd be interested,' she said with that same odd feeling of listening to the words being spoken by some other woman. 'This friend lives quite near Thetstone, she knows the place well.' His eyes continued to rest on hers as if to remove them would involve a fatal admission. 'She tells me the town has been redeveloped, that Hunston's was pulled down years ago. Eight years ago, to be exact.' Kate Ashton came running along the passage, she had to brush past Edgar as she ran, she actually put out a hand and pushed it against his side as she passed, in order to keep her balance, and neither of them could have said a moment later who had gone skimming by, though each had a dimly-registered impression of something happening on the fringe of awareness.

'Quite so,' Meacham said with an air of mild interest. 'The Thetstone branch most certainly ceased to exist some years ago. I was transferred to the Larchend branch at that time, I worked there until last summer. Larchend – I don't know if you've ever been there? It's what – oh, about seventy miles to the east of Thetstone.' His face broke into a disarmingly apologetic smile. 'I think I must have confused you a little the other day.' He placed a hand on his chest, slightly left of centre, gave a hint of a bow. 'Do forgive me, dear lady.' A couple of seconds later she realized that he was gone. She swung round and glanced along the passage. He had reached the end of the corridor, he had turned and was looking back at her. They remained like that for a long moment and then he disappeared from view.

Bessie had already made a start on the sandwiches when Marion came into the kitchen. Hello, Bessie said to herself at the sight of the lack-lustre face, had a bit too much champagne at the party last night, did we? She said a word or two by way of greeting and got scarcely a syllable in reply. She felt very little inclined herself on a Monday morning to exert much effort at making conversation, so she set Marion to buttering bread and got on with carving the remaining half of a very fine leg of cold roast pork. She jerked her head in the direction of some small glass dishes. 'Apple sauce in that one. Sage and onion stuffing there.' She nodded towards her open notebook. 'Don't forget, keep an eye on that. Mrs Paget can't touch anything with onion. But she'll have plenty of apple sauce.' She wasn't at all sure she could rely on Marion's careful attention to detail this morning; something absent-minded, even upset, about her today. Gave her a look once or twice as if she intended to say something and then just couldn't be bothered, or forgot what it was she'd been going to say.

'You haven't had bad news?' Bessie asked suddenly. Marion leaned back in her chair and contemplated her as if from a considerable distance. And at that moment the back-door bell rang loud and clear.

'Ah!' Bessie laid down her knife and fork, snatched at a towel and rubbed her hands. 'You carry on in here,' she said, briskly affable. 'Won't be long.' She whisked a straw basket down from a hook and took herself off for an enlivening pow-wow with her cousin on her mother's side, a red-faced jovial man who drove his mobile shop around the countryside six days a week.

The sound of Bessie's laughter floated back to one of the daily women as she knocked at the kitchen door. 'Always likes a joke with her cousin, does Mrs Meacham,' the woman said, entering the kitchen on Marion's answering call. 'That Miss Onil's here, she asked if Mrs Barratt or you happened to be about. I can't seem to catch hold of Mrs Barratt.' Not that she'd spent a lot of time looking for her, she wanted to get off early today. She smiled at Mrs Lockwood. 'Do you suppose you could come and have a word with Miss Onil?'

'We're going over to see some caves.' In spite of herself Brigid couldn't manage to sound as contemptuous as she could have wished, she had a sneaking feeling that the caves might turn

out to be rather interesting. 'We're setting off about eleven
o'clock. I can't possibly get out of it.' There was a short silence
as she listened to Eileen's voice at the other end of the line.
'No, I didn't mean that at all,' she said. 'I'm pretty certain I'll be
able to get out this evening. We'll be back – oh, somewhere
about teatime, I should think. We can't be terribly late because
of the twins' bedtime and anyway they have dinner in this place
at about half past seven and my mother likes to dress herself
up for that. Let's say nine o'clock. If I'm not there by half past,
don't bother waiting any longer, I won't be coming . . . Yes, I
think the drummer fancied you too.' She broke into a long
giggle. 'You might get a chance to sing with them if you play
your cards right . . . No, I can't sing for toffee, never could.' She
giggled again. 'Yes, sure it'll be all right, it was all right last night,
it worked like a dream.'

'It didn't work like a dream,' said a voice a couple of yards
away. Brigid let out a little scream and leapt back, still clutching
the receiver. 'Oh, it's you, Mrs Lockwood! You gave me a fright.'

'The twins were running about all over the place.' Marion
felt the dark surge rise up again inside her. 'I had to take them
back to their beds. I looked in your room, I saw the pillows
and the doll you'd set up. Very clever of you, I'm sure. I had
every intention of going straight downstairs and telling – ' She
stopped suddenly and put a hand up to her face.

'Then why didn't you tell him?' Brigid said defiantly. 'I should
think that's exactly the sort of thing you'd enjoy.' She became
aware of tiny squeaking noises coming from the receiver in her
hand. She flashed a look at Mrs Lockwood who was standing
with her eyes closed, her fingers pressed into her cheek. Brigid
bent her head and hissed fiercely into the receiver, 'Scrub round
tonight. Can't explain. See you some time,' and put the receiver
back on its rest. She threw another look at Mrs Lockwood and,
seeing again that baffling expression, raised her shoulders, pulled
a face and with all possible speed removed herself from the
scene.

Stephen's brows were drawn together in a frown as he came
down the front steps. Nothing he could actually put his finger
on in Jourdan's manner. They had stood together on the terrace

after breakfast, Jourdan had talked at some length about one of his business appointments later in the day, he hadn't uttered a word that anyone could take exception to and yet every syllable he spoke came to Stephen's ears with an edge of challenge, even of contempt.

He walked rapidly towards the large garage. He must snatch a last word with Fiona, must make quite sure she understood how things were, he mustn't leave any element of doubt – any loophole for Jourdan to take advantage of in the next forty-eight hours.

The garage door stood wide open and he saw at a glance that Jourdan's car was no longer there. So they'd left already. He remained motionless for a couple of minutes, looking into the interior of the garage, then he sighed, shook his head and made his way back to the house, kicking a stone along in front of him, his hands thrust into his pockets. Marion was standing by the front door, staring out at the shimmering day. He ran up the steps and took hold of her hand.

'You're coming with us today, aren't you?' He smiled and pressed her fingers. She looked at him with intense scrutiny, she saw the pleading in his eyes, her lips turned up in a slow smile.

'Yes, I'll come,' she said. 'I really quite enjoy a picnic.'

'Certainly I'll call in at the bungalow. I can suit Miss Tillard's convenience.' Henry nodded at Theresa Onil, looked over at Lockwood and the pair of casuals he was chatting to, raised a hand to indicate that he wouldn't keep them waiting long, then turned his attention back to Theresa. 'Some time this afternoon? Yes, of course.' He didn't in the least mind seeing to a trifle of business during his holiday, it gave a point to his day. 'Would half past four be convenient?' There was the question of witnesses for the codicil, might ask that fellow Ashton and his wife. Or the cottagers from the lane below the bungalow. 'That's settled then, half past four. I'm very glad to hear Miss Tillard's feeling a little better.'

'Quite a bit better,' Theresa said. 'I wouldn't have been able to come out and leave her otherwise.'

Ashton walked towards the house at a furious rate. It was

scarcely credible that in a few days he might find himself having to say yes to Guardcash . . . and yet, if he didn't, if he did what every nerve in his body commanded and told them to go to hell, he was going to have to live with the domestic consequences of his act of mutiny for months, years even.

He went up the front steps at a run, almost knocking into Barratt who was standing in the doorway talking to the African woman from the bungalow.

'Oh – I'm sorry.' Mike's pace slackened abruptly. They both gave him abstracted glances and resumed their interchange; they had a serious, rather intimate air, as of people who understood each other well.

Mike took a few hesitant paces, frowning, striving to recall just why it was that he had come rushing indoors. Oh yes, the twins. He nodded to himself. Jean had asked him to ferret them out, immobilize them in their bedroom until she came along in a few minutes to get them ready for the outing. He glanced along the corridor leading out of the hall, looked into a ground-floor sitting-room. One of the daily women was running a duster over a table. 'You haven't by any chance seen my little girls?' he asked, but she shook her head.

'No, sir, I'm afraid I haven't.' From upstairs he suddenly caught the sound of lightly scampering footsteps. He went rapidly across the hall, seized the banister rail and ran up the stairs two and three at a time. On the first-floor landing Stephen Lockwood was washing his hands at the sink in a little recess that dated back to the days of housemaids and under-housemaids.

Lockwood turned his head, smiled jovially at Ashton; he looked cheerful and vigorous, pleased with life. 'Sorry you couldn't come along with us today.' He rinsed his hands under the tap with forceful movements. 'But duty calls you, I can see that.' He gave a short friendly laugh, sympathetic to the family man. 'I've roped in the Pagets for a game, it seems she plays golf too.' He snatched up a towel, rubbed energetically at his fingers. 'Don't know how well, of course. But I gather he's pretty good.' He laughed again. 'Or so he keeps telling me.'

'You haven't seen the twins by any chance?' Mike asked. 'It's worse than rounding up sheep, trying to get them both into one spot for any length of time.'

Stephen shook his head. 'No, haven't seen hide or hair of them. I suppose you've looked in the garden?'

Mike sighed. 'I've just come in from the garden. Ah – ' Over to the left, the bubble of Vicky's laughter. 'Have a good game,' he said as he went swiftly in the direction of the sound.

'Thanks. We've got a fine day for it, anyway.' Stephen strode briskly off towards the stairs.

'Hi – Vicky! Come back here!' Mike called. She was just about to disappear round the end of the corridor. She stopped, looked back at her father. Her whole attitude changed to one of resigned, slack helplessness; her face took on a pouting, sorrowful look. She uttered a long groan.

'I suppose we've got to get washed and changed.' She stuck out her head like a tortoise, pulled an agonized face, and gave several dejected nods. Mike took a firm grasp of her hand. 'Who wants to go down a lot of silly caves?' she said provocatively. 'I'd much rather stay here and play.'

Mike didn't answer, he merely jerked her along by his side. Was there the remotest chance that Guardcash wouldn't come up with an unqualified acceptance? Any faint possibility that he might still be able to wriggle out of it and yet maintain marital harmony? He chewed the inside of his cheek in fierce thought.

'Where's Kate?' Vicky asked, abandoning now the delights of the attics and beginning to view with cheerful interest the prospect of a trip underground. 'Did you find her before you found me?'

They had reached the door of the twins' bedroom. Mike said nothing, he propelled her inside, marched her over to the wash-basin and, without giving his actions more than a superficial flick of thought, inserted the plug, ran the taps and seized a face flannel. Vicky closed her eyes at once in habitual meek accept-ance of the onslaught to come. 'I wonder where Kate is,' she said, more or less addressing herself, knowing from long experi-ence that in one of his shoulder-grabbing, frowning moods, her father was scarcely likely to engage in rational conversation.

The door opened gently and Kate slid into the room with a wide bland smile. 'Oh, there you are,' Vicky tried to say through a faceful of savage lather but the words came out as an incoherent mumble.

Kate crossed instantly to the basin with an air of reprimand and laid a restraining hand on Mike's sleeve. 'You're doing it again!' she said, loudly and clearly, pressing down on his arm.

He came out of his thoughts, turned and saw her look of stern criticism. He half-smiled, glanced at Vicky's face, snowy with suds.

'You must wash that off,' Kate said commandingly. '*You* wouldn't like your face scrubbed like that. It stings.'

He rinsed the flannel and dabbed obediently at Vicky's beet-root cheeks. 'Well now,' he said in a light and friendly tone, 'are you both looking forward to the expedition?'

By one o'clock a slight breeze had sprung up, just sufficient to blunt the fierce edge of the sun's heat. A perfect day for golf. In the small dining-annexe opening off the club-house bar a cold buffet lunch had been set out, as was customary on a Monday in the season. They came drifting into the room, the usual assort-ment of members and visitors, a few locals, a sprinkling from neighbouring villages and further afield, a scatter of holiday-makers.

'The food's not at all bad.' A businessman from Chilford propelled his guest gently towards the array of dishes. 'I can strongly recommend anything to do with fish. Can't go wrong with fish here. Absolutely first class.'

A sensation percolated into the atmosphere of the dining-room as of some kind of disturbance taking place outside.

'I'm not all that fond of fish,' the guest said apologetically. 'Doesn't always agree with me. I think I'll try the veal and ham pie.' He turned his head. Other heads turned. A sound – of distant shouting?

'The beef's pretty good,' the Chilford man said on a hesitant, listening note. A woman screaming? No, surely not, probably just youngsters larking about on the edge of the course, you got that sort of thing a bit in the school holidays, could be very irritating. 'I'm a red beef man myself,' he said affably. 'Can't stand it overcooked.'

Unusual movement, no doubt about it now. Feet, running feet, coming nearer. Voices, louder, confused, calling to each other. In the annexe they stood with arrested forks, rigid heads.

Someone came panting up the steps of the club-house – two, three runners, a little wave of incoherent agitation. They shouted as they burst into the room.

'A doctor! Get a doctor!' A young man, a local lad, from one of the big farms.

'There's a man. Out there. I think he's dying. He might be dead.' A schoolboy, on a morning's hunt for lost golf-balls. He got his breath back, seized someone by the sleeve. 'It's where people go to picnic. By those trees. He picked up the beaker. I was watching. I just happened to be there.'

A man came out from the bar, moving with controlled haste. Solidly built, a serious, disciplined face. 'Excuse me. If I might get past. I'm a doctor.'

The boy fell in by his side. 'I can show you where it is.' The doctor began to nod, continued to punctuate the lad's jerky utterances with briskly professional nods continuing all the while to press forward with a smooth, purposeful and rapid gait, out of the door, down the steps. He thrust his hand into his pocket as he went, pulled out a bunch of keys, isolated one key, glanced round at the throng of faces, called out a name, spoke clearly and forcefully to the man who ran to his side.

'My car.' He jerked his head. 'Over there. Get my bag. Hurry.' He closed the man's fingers over the key. With the same quick stride he went on towards the picnic ground. A good two hundred yards. No sense in breaking into a run. Not at his age, with his build. Get there just as fast walking. And in much better condition to deal with whatever was waiting.

He turned his head and threw a questioning look at the boy – still determinedly keeping up with him – encouraging the lad to resume his flow of information. Didn't waste his breath framing questions, simply nodded every time the boy paused, more or less drained him of facts by the time they got within hailing distance of the tableau under the trees. The Pagets coming to meet them, Jack – still fairly fit – managing a jog-trot, Wyn skittering and panting just behind. Whittall on his knees, staring down, moving his hands in an amateur rhythm of massage. Marion, sitting in an awkward position, white, silent, drawing long trembling breaths.

And Stephen, stretched out on the sun-dappled grass, with his head for the first time in ten years cradled in Marion's lap. His eyes closed, his lips drawn back, no rise and fall in the chest, no flutter of living from the mouth or nostrils. And his face a very nasty colour indeed.

Chapter 12

'Accident.' Detective-Inspector Kenward stared reflectively at a crystal bowl of peach-coloured roses on the window sill. 'The first thing that comes to mind is undoubtedly – accident.' He leaned back in his chair, allowed his gaze to wander round the little ground-floor sitting-room that the Barratts had put at his disposal. 'Enough cyanide in that tin to wipe out half the village.' He passed a hand across his face, let out a massive sigh. 'Always beats me why that kind of criminal carelessness isn't a punishable offence. If you think about something else for half a minute while you're at the wheel of a car, they'll have your hide fast enough if you kill someone. But you can shove a tin of cyanide on the kitchen shelf, the entire household can take it into their heads to sprinkle it on their cornflakes, and as like as not the coroner will express his sympathy for your sad loss. You might even get a pound from the poor-box.'

No one knew how the tin of cyanide had come to be standing on one of the cluttered shelves in the Oakfield kitchen – or at all events, no one was admitting to that knowledge. Bessie Meacham gave it as her opinion that the tin had very probably strayed in from the garden shed. When asked how long ago this might have been she glanced vaguely about and shook her head. 'I really couldn't say, might have been years ago. The last gardener we had, he was a great one for destroying wasps' nests.' She frowned. 'I seem to remember him saying something about cyanide, but he used to get so agitated about wasps, I never really paid all that much attention to what he was going on about.'

Godfrey Barratt on the other hand was inclined to believe the cyanide might have belonged to his father. It seemed old

Mr Barratt had had a passing fancy once for photography. 'But he'd scarcely have been quite so careless with a lethal poison,' Kenward had suggested. An intelligent, educated man like that. Godfrey had looked doubtful. 'He was always rather absent-minded,' he said with an air of apology. 'It got worse as he grew older.'

'We are not actually totally and positively certain that Lockwood's death was caused by cyanide,' Sergeant Trevitt said now to Kenward in a mild detached tone. Been with Kenward on many a little foray, used to his ways, let him ramble on a bit at first, pontificate, get the social observations off his chest. And then the real thinking could start.

Kenward flung him a glance, didn't bother to reply. Cyanide, unless he was a Dutchman. Seen a cyanide death more than once, could recognize the trade marks. He looked at his watch. It would be a bit yet before they'd have the official word, of course.

'It's always seemed to me,' Mike Ashton said, 'that it's a great deal easier to get hold of cyanide than is commonly admitted by the official mind.' As a lad in Perrymount, helping his father on the allotment, he'd never noticed any difficulty when one of the allotment holders wanted to deal with a wasps' nest; there was always someone with a brother or neighbour employed at the local plating works. It had always seemed easy enough to come by a nice little quantity of the deadly stuff and not only with no questions asked but without even an injunction to keep one's mouth shut about the source of supply.

'I wouldn't dispute that,' Kenward said bleakly. 'Beats me sometimes, what with that kind of carelessness about poisons, fiddling and pinching bits of stuff here and there. to say nothing of dumping lorryloads of chemical waste and generally carrying on like a race of lunatics, why there's a single soul in the whole of these islands still drawing breath.'

'Mrs Meacham certainly doesn't strike me as particularly fussy or careful by nature,' Ashton said. 'But I never imagined – ' It would have blunted the edge of his appetite for Bessie's pies and savouries if he'd had any notion of that lethal canister nestling among the domestic bottles and cartons.

'I've known Bessie for years,' Kenward said. A local man – like

Sergeant Trevitt. Not many folk in the area Kenward didn't know in one way or another. 'Bessie Forrest, she used to be,' he said ruminatively. His eyes took on a reminiscent shine. Lively young woman she'd been in her time. Very lively.

'However the cyanide came to be on the kitchen shelf,' Mike said politely, 'I can't quite see how it could have got into Lockwood's flask of coffee by accident.' A tricky position, to say the least, the holidaying copper actually staying in the same house as Lockwood, anxious to offer what help and information he could, even more anxious to avoid treading on sensitive official toes. Could be as temperamental as prima donnas, some of these lads in the force, when it came to a man from the other side of the county sticking his oar in.

Kenward raised his shoulders, let them drop again. 'Could have been stirred in, thinking it was sugar.' A piece of luck, having Sergeant Ashton on the spot, as it were. Nothing like the trained eye when it came down to it. And under the same police authority too, thank heavens, simplified matters where officialdom was concerned.

'We are not utterly and completely positive that any noxious substance which may have been administered was present in the flask of coffee,' Trevitt said automatically, wondering if phase one of Kenward's ritual posturing was likely to be lengthened or shortened by the presence of Ashton, the outsider.

Kenward pressed a hand against his fleshy nose. 'Lockwood took a couple of bites of a sandwich, poured himself a beaker of coffee, drank one good mouthful and began to gasp and choke.' He struck his nose energetically with his index finger. 'They all seem agreed on what happened. I'm willing to gamble on the coffee.'

Outside the window the twins skipped by, laughing and chattering. And a pace or two behind, the lad from the golf-course, the hunter of golf-balls. Ashton's brows came together in a momentary frown. Seemed a sensible enough lad, not likely to disregard the stern warning not to let one single syllable about Lockwood's death reach the ears of the children. Mike had been standing in a seaside queue, waiting to buy ice-cream for his family – still unsatisfied after their lunchtime sandwiches – when he'd heard the first word of what had happened out at

Westerhill. There'd been enough hard fact in the distorted and embroidered version that had filtered out to the gossiping holidaymakers to send Mike hurrying off to a phone-box, to ring Oakfield. Five minutes later he had bundled his family – still protesting the urgent need for tubs and wafers – into the car, and the afternoon's trip to the second series of caves was abruptly written off.

'Bessie's husband,' Trevitt said thoughtfully. 'Edgar Meacham. He helps in the kitchen quite a bit. If it was an accident, it's quite a possibility that it was the husband, coming in from the garden, say . . . ' He tried to visualize the circumstances, Meacham called by his wife, perhaps when he was in the middle of an outdoor task, dealing with a wasps' nest maybe, actually holding the tin of cyanide, caught up in some domestic emergency, setting the tin down on the table. forgetting it, some other person later on, absorbed in chat or laughter, dipping in a casual spoon, dealing hastily with impatiently-awaited flasks of lunch-time drinks . . . I suppose it's possible, he thought. Not very likely, in fact highly unlikely, but just about possible.

'Ye . . . es.' Kenward stretched out his arms flexed his shoulder muscles. 'The husband. M'mm.'

'A thought occurs to me.' Ashton kept his tone light and unemphatic. 'Just an impression, you understand. Nothing specific to go on – but I wouldn't be at all surprised if Meacham had a record.' Kenward jerked his head round, he looked at Mike with a totally altered expression, alert, penetrating. Ashton spread his hands. 'A look, his manner. A way he has of working about the place and yet keeping part of his attention focused on what everyone else is doing.'

'Any particular kind of record?' Kenward said. 'Anything strike you?'

'Con man,' Ashton said at once. 'The eyes, the smile.'

Kenward nodded slowly. 'Yes. Could be.' Poor Bessie, if it turned out to be true. Married a few months, fancying herself warm against old age. 'Should be able to check without much difficulty.'

'If you're right about Meacham,' Trevitt said, 'and if Lockwood's death was not an accident, it occurs to me that Meacham might have had good reason for wanting Lockwood out of the

way. Lockwood might have spotted him. Come across him somewhere before, maybe, under another name.'

'We're scarcely likely to be able to confirm that now,' Kenward said without much interest. 'Lockwood won't be doing much talking.'

'Lockwood might have mentioned something to his wife,' Trevitt persisted.

Kenward shrugged. 'All right.' He threw a look at Constable Yarrow sitting at the end of the table. 'Make a note.' He raised his eyes to the ceiling. 'Not that she's likely to be in a fit state to be questioned yet awhile.' Marion was lying down in her room, the curtains drawn against the gilded afternoon.

'One other thing.' Ashton allowed an apologetic note to colour his tone. 'A ridiculous notion very probably, but I feel perhaps I ought to mention it.'

'Spit it out,' Kenward said brusquely. 'No need to dance on eggshells.'

'I can't help wondering,' Ashton said, a good deal more positively, 'if there could be any question of a practical joke having gone wrong.' Kenward's eyes blinked wide open. 'It's the Pagets,' Mike went on. He leaned forward and stabbed a finger at the list of names. 'Those two. Very extrovert types. They had a party here last night.' He let himself go on the topic of the party, the excruciating jollity, the sledge-hammer merriment.

'Could be,' Kenward said with lively interest when Mike had finished. 'Could very well be.' Practical joking was often the expression of a hostile, aggressive personality, whether manifest or concealed. 'We'll have the Pagets in right away.' He sat up, smiled jovially. 'If it was a joke that went wrong and if they'll admit it, it'll save everyone a lot of trouble.' He smiled again, less jovially. 'With the possible exception, of course, of the Pagets.'

The nurse opened the door leading out into the corridor. 'Miss Tillard really will be quite all right now,' she said in a low tone. 'She'll settle down perfectly well as soon as you've gone.' She opened the door more widely. 'You'll be able to visit as often as you like. Within reason, of course,' she added, suddenly remembering the eccentric manner in which a relative of another patient had recently interpreted that permission. 'We shouldn t care for you to call in with a bottle of whisky at two o'clock in the morning.'

'I shouldn't dream of doing such a foolish thing,' Theresa said with a surprised look. She glanced back at the bed, at Miss Tillard seeming frailer, older, infinitely more vulnerable. She sent her a fleeting smile, raised her hand in farewell. 'I'll be back this evening at seven.'

'I am prepared to enter any witness-box in the United Kingdom,' Jack Paget said in a voice that only just stopped short of a bellow, 'and swear before Almighty God – ' he drew a sustaining breath, momentarily restoring himself after the repeated outrages of the last five minutes – 'that I in no way interfered with – ' he threw an embracing glance at his wife who looked back at him like a mesmerized rabbit – 'or caused any other person to interfere with any food or drink, or indeed any substance whatsoever – ' The insubstantial memory of Army courts martial that had till this moment upheld his rhetoric suddenly deserted him. He frowned, blinked rapidly and then, realizing that there was no help for it, finished his sentence in a mortifyingly civilian fashion. 'Anything that Lockwood had at the picnic. I never put anything into anything. Nor did Wyn. Not for a joke or seriously or for any reason at all.' He flung a defiant look at Kenward, he had the air of a man who expected to be clapped into irons but who intended to give a very good account of himself before he was finally overpowered.

'Well now,' Kenward said mildly, 'that would seem to take care of that.'

'You mean I can go?' Pagent said in an incredulous tone.

'You may go wheresoever you will,' Kenward said, vastly bland, adding however on a more realistic note, 'You will, of course, both of you, hold yourselves available for further questioning, should this be necessary. And there will in due course be statements to be signed. I take it that you have no urgent reason for leaving Oakfield right away?'

Paget shook his head. 'No, but of course we'll be glad to get off as soon as we can. It's supposed to be a holiday.'

Kenward gave a brief nod, tired now of Paget with his irritating air of being perpetually engaged in giving a hammed-up impression of a military man. 'We have no intention of prolonging our enjoyment of your company beyond the bounds of strict necessity,' he said pleasantly, leaving Paget a little uncertain whether the remark was intended as a compliment or an insult.

Sergeant Trevitt studied Paget's face with a moment's sharp curiosity. Was the man all outward activity? No interior life whatsoever? Or was that never true of anyone? I suppose not, he thought, waiting for the Pagets to go. The husband turned to the door with haste, glanced a command at his wife. But she remained where she was, still wearing that apprehensive look. Her eyes seemed to be trying to say something to Kenward. A couple of seconds went by. Paget said 'Wyn!' a trifle sharply. She half rose from her chair, still levelling a glance at Kenward. He became at last aware that she was suspended over the seat of her chair, he looked up from his notes and met her unhappy gaze. At once his lips curved up in a smile of impersonal affability, he said as if something had just occurred to him, 'Oh, by the way, Mrs Paget, a little detail, I wonder, if you could just assist us, a woman's instinct, you know how it is – ' he flicked a good-humoured glance at Paget. 'No need to detain you, Mr Paget, won't keep your good lady many minutes, I'm sure you'll be glad to get along.'

As soon as the door had closed behind Paget's suspicious and questioning back, Kenward spoke to Wyn in a completely different tone. 'Come now, Mrs Paget, what is it you want to say to me?'

She bent her head and burst abruptly into tears. Kenward drew a long breath of weary resignation, leaned across the table and patted her hand. 'You'll feel a lot better if you tell me about it,' he said gently, aware that his words had in all probability no basis whatever in reality. 'Some little thing you've remembered perhaps? I dare say it's of no consequence.' He patted her hand again. 'But I'd like to hear it all the same.'

The phone was answered by Edgar Meacham. 'I'd like to speak to Mrs Barratt,' Theresa said rapidly. 'Would you go and get her right away? I'm speaking from a call-box at the hospital and I can't stay more than a minute or two, there are people waiting to use the phone.'

'Certainly, Miss Onil,' Edgar said. 'I'll go at once.' He hesitated for a moment. 'I suppose you've heard?'

'Heard what?' she asked with a trace of impatience.

'About Mr Lockwood?' The pleasure that is never entirely unknown to those who announce important and dramatic news – however disastrous or unwelcome – touched his voice. 'He's dead. At the golf-club. He died about one o'clock.' He became aware of silence at the other end of the line. 'Are you there?' he asked sharply. 'I said Mr Lockwood's dead.' He heard the sound of her breathing, harsh, irregular. But she made no reply. 'I'll get Mrs Barratt,' he said at last, and laid down the receiver.

'She's mistaken of course,' Paget said loudly and cheerfully. He gave his wife a look that seemed to Kenward, watching closely across the table, to be totally devoid of reproach. Wyn continued to stare down at her folded hands. Paget smiled at the inspector. 'You know what women are. They get a notion into their heads. You can't get it out again. However hard you try.'

Kenward felt no inclination to pronounce idiotic judgements on the opposite sex. 'So you never met Stephen Lockwood before you arrived in Westerhill a few days ago?' he asked in a clear trenchant voice. 'You never had any business dealing with him? You were never a member of the same firm?' At each question Paget shook his head emphatically.

'I never clapped eyes on him in my life before,' he said with force as soon as Kenward ceased to speak. He leaned forward. 'I am prepared to swear –'

Oh, for heaven's sake, Kenward just managed to refrain from saying, spare us another round of the amateur theatricals. Instead he raised a hand and said pleasantly, 'No need to swear just yet, Mr Paget, time enough for that if you should find yourself in a court of law. And this firm you worked for some years ago – ' he jabbed a finger at his notes. 'No connection of any kind with Alpha Fabrics?' He drummed a rhythm on the sheaf of papers. 'Easy enough for us to find out,' he said lightly.

Paget moved slightly in his seat. 'Well,' he said after a long moment. 'I do have some kind of recollection that they might have been taken over by Alpha. After I left, of course. But I'm not at all certain about it.'

'Nevertheless,' Kenward said gently, 'you maintain that Stephen Lockwood was a total stranger to you until last week?'

Paget looked round the room with a swift unseeing glance. His eyes came back to the inspector, darted away again. 'It is of course perfectly possible,' he said, fixing on his lips an imitation smile that instantly fell off again, 'that I may have come across him somewhere or other. Both in business, after all. One doesn't remember everyone one meets.'

Kenward stroked his left cheekbone. 'So you wouldn't, when it comes down to it, be prepared to enter any witness-box at all in the United Kingdom and swear that you never met Stephen Lockwood before?'

Paget gave a kind of a laugh. 'Well, if you put it like that.' He turned his head and looked at Trevitt, inviting a humorous look in return – but without success. His eyes came to rest again briefly on the inspector. 'I suppose I wouldn't.' He laughed again, more loudly. 'It almost makes me out to be a liar, doesn't it?'

No one offered any reply.

When Jean Ashton put her head round the door of the sitting-room Kenward was seated at the table and the two sergeants were standing, one at either side of him, listening, as he stabbed his way through his notes. At the end of the table Constable Yarrow did his best to preserve an attitude of lively interest although no one had addressed a word to him for ten minutes and the air in the room was growing rather warm.

'Tea?' Jean said. Doing what she could to give a hand in the disrupted household. 'Shall I ask Mrs Meacham to send in a tray?'

'We'd be very glad of some tea,' Kenward said with a smile. 'But I don't see any need to trouble Mrs Meacham.' In order to enjoy a cup of tea it was necessary to have unqualified confidence in the hand that brewed it. 'I wonder, Mrs Ashton, would it be a dreadful imposition if I asked you to make the tea yourself?'

She was taken by surprise for an instant. then she caught her husband's eye, and suddenly saw the inspector's meaning.

'Oh – yes, certainly,' she said at once. 'I'll make it myself, no bother at all. And if you want anything to eat, just tell me, I can get that for you too, I'm sure that can be arranged.'

Chapter 13

'Or murder,' Kenward said in a flat, expressionless voice. He wouldn't even glance at suicide. A man didn't commit suicide in that particular fashion. Or at least no man that Kenward had ever heard of. He looked down at the list of names. 'Anyone we can cross off?'

Ashton and Trevitt focused their attention on each name in turn; Constable Yarrow had been despatched – to his own relief – to make a search of Miss Tillard's bungalow, not forgetting outhouses, garden sheds and the like, to see if he could sniff out any little caches of cyanide. He was then to take himself off to Henry Whittall's cottage and set about the same task there. In the meantime the inspector was going to dispense with Yarrow's note-taking services, having had as much of firing questions at folk as he wanted for the present, and being glad to sit down in comparative peace and clear his thoughts.

'Theresa Onil?' Trevitt said. 'Can't see any motive there.'

'Mm, perhaps not.' Kenward blew out his cheeks. 'But I have a notion we might see one before we're done.' His mind sent out a swift encompassing beam that ranged over Miss Tillard and her recurring bouts of illness, shreds of gossip from the past, speculation about the present and the future. 'I am certainly not going to eliminate Miss Onil.'

He looked at the list again, thrust a finger at a name, one of the daily women. 'She's gone off to attend her daughter's confinement, some distance away, won't be back till tomorrow.' According to Mrs Barratt the woman was never employed in the kitchen, never had any hand in the preparation of the packed lunches, probably wouldn't have anything to tell them. 'We'll have a word with her when she gets back. Anyone else we can rule out?'

'These two,' Ashton said with assurance. He indicated a pair of names. 'The bed-and-breakfasters who left this morning.' An elderly couple, booked in for the night only, departed after an early breakfast, well before anyone at Oakfield had made any start on preparing the picnic food.

'Ye-es.' Kenward could see no objection to that. And there was an address beside their names, they'd come to the end of their holiday, had gone back home; simple enough to contact them if the need arose. He ran his eye down the list yet again. 'Is that the lot? Anyone else we can get rid of?' There was a short silence, then Trevitt shook his head slowly and Ashton said, 'Not as far as I can see.'

Kenward stood up, stretched himself and walked over to the window. He stood looking out at the sunny garden where the Ashton twins were playing a skeletal form of rounders with the golf-ball boy.

'Any special reason why we're hanging on to that lad?' he asked. 'Surely he can cut off home?'

'He's been invited to cut off home two or three times already,' Trevitt said, 'but he can't be persuaded.' Couldn't blame the lad, probably storing up self-importance for next term, possibly the only chance he'd ever get.

Across the lawn the lad suddenly turned and caught sight of Kenward standing at the window. At once he abandoned the game and came racing towards the house with a look of joyful optimism on his face. Kenward shook his head at the boy, raised a prohibiting hand, saw the lad halt, his expression change to one of fierce disappointment. 'I see what you mean,' he said, turning back into the room. 'Well now.' He resumed his seat, looked without eager anticipation at the pile of notes.

'Motive, method, opportunity,' he said with heavy ritual. 'I suppose we'd better get cracking.' He passed a disciplinary hand across his face, sat upright, stared challengingly at the screened fireplace. 'Assuming that Lockwood was poisoned, and that he consumed the poison in something he ate or drank on the golf-course, who had the opportunity to administer that poison?'

Ashton visualized the flask of coffee, the packet of sand-

8

wiches, the fashion in which these items were normally prepared in the Oakfield kitchen, he sent his mind back over the entire morning. He made a helpless gesture. 'Almost anyone,' he said with a sigh.

Kenward pursed his lips, nodded slowly. 'Yes.' Hopeless to hunt about in such a limitless field. 'Motive,' he said, a little more cheerfully.

'Jourdan,' Ashton said at once, astonishing himself by the push-button speed of his response.

The inspector raised his eyebrows, inclined his head. 'Jourdan,' he repeated. 'You came to that conclusion with remarkable swiftness.'

'It seems to me,' Ashton said, trying now to rationalize what had been totally instinctive, 'that Jourdan benefits immediately and considerably from Lockwood's death. He was Lockwood's assistant, I imagine he'll be doing Lockwood's job as from tomorrow morning, I dare say there's a very good chance he'll be permanently appointed to it later on. And the girl – ' Not much doubt about Jourdan's intentions in that quarter, nor about Lockwood's feelings either. It was three or four minutes before Ashton stopped talking.

'Could very well be something there,' Kenward said with renewed vitality. He glanced at his watch. 'Where would those two be now? Jourdan and the girl? Back in Barbridge?'

Ashton cast his mind back. 'No,' he said at last. 'Jourdan had some appointments in this area. He wasn't going back to Barbridge till this evening.' He closed his eyes, concentrating. 'I remember the name of the first place he was going to, and the customer he was calling on.' He opened his eyes, smiled. 'Belling. Same name as the electric cooker we've got at home.' He stood up. 'I could phone Belling's, Jourdan might very well mention to them where else he was going, we could catch him at one or other of his calls this afternoon.' He had a sudden inspiration. 'I can have a word with Barratt. And Paget. They were both there when Jourdan was talking about his trip. One of them will probably remember something.'

'Right.' Kenward looked pleased. He jerked his head at Trevitt. 'You can go along with Ashton.' Unheard of to send the outsider off on his own. 'Don't be all day about it. Phone in if you come up with anything. And get their fingerprints while you're at it.'

When they had gone he felt an overpowering urge to get up, stride out of the house and go down to the beach, make his solitary way along the shore, let the wind blow through his brain. For a moment he wrestled with the notion, then let it go. Impossible to disappear out of range of communication. And it was high summer, there would be no solitude on the beach. No wind, either. He yawned, groaned, threw himself down again in his chair and bent a hostile eye at the wretched list . . . Theresa Onil at the bungalow . . . Henry Whittall at the cottage . . . The whole ruddy boiling at Oakfield. He closed his eyes and let thought wander idly through his brain.

The possible closing-down of Barratt's firm in Chilford . . . Kenward had a neighbour whose son worked at Barratt's, he knew pretty well how things stood in that quarter. But how could Barratt possibly benefit from Lockwood's death? No way that Kenward could see. There was that old business of course, years ago now, Barratt had been as good as engaged to marry the girl who was now Mrs Lockwood. What of it? Kenward sucked at a tooth that was beginning to make its presence felt. After all this time Barratt was scarcely likely to take it into his head to murder the man who had carried off his sweetheart. And looking at the two sisters now, surely Barratt had cause to feel gratitude to Lockwood, rather than any uglier emotion.

The inspector folded his arms on the table, leaned forward and cradled his head comfortably with his nose a couple of inches above the polished surface. Pauline Barratt . . . no earthly reason to wish Lockwood gone that he could see . . . Meacham and Bessie and Paget . . . his thoughts began to swim and slip about . . . perhaps just for a couple of minutes he might let it all go, make his mind a blank, give himself a chance to . . . a chance to . . . A little while later Pauline walked softly up to the door, listened, and hearing nothing, gently turned the handle. She peeped in, raised her brows at the inspector serenely oblivious on her good mahogany table, was about to tiptoe off again and then hesitated, glanced out into the passage, and turned back into the room.

*

Ah! Cyanide! Quite a respectable amount too. Neatly labelled, securely stoppered in a small glass jar. Constable Yarrow made a note of the time and place of discovering the item, took possession of it with a feeling of calm satisfaction. Of course Whittall had a perfectly good reason for owning cyanide. Yarrow glanced round at the orderly assemblage of photographic materials. But all the same . . . that didn't mean he might not have used it for some other more deadly purpose. Quite a good cover, really, when he came to think about it. If you were going to finish someone off with a poison, you might just as well choose a poison you were entitled to possess. Difficult to prove anything then, one way or the other. Yarrow halted suddenly. Yes, very difficult to prove. 'We . . . ell,' he said aloud, with a half smile. Just suppose old Whittall had done it . . . and just suppose old Whittall got away with it . . .

Still intrigued by the notion, he finished his search of the cottage, neither finding nor expecting to find anything else of much significance. When he had finished he secured the door behind him. Back to Oakfield now. There had been nothing at Miss Tillard's bungalow, at least nothing in the way of cyanide. There had been some exceedingly strange-smelling spices in the kitchen, African, he supposed, being unable to ask Miss Onil who was out somewhere. He walked down the path, made sure he closed the gate, strode over to his car and slid into the driver's seat, whistling loudly and cheerfully.

Jourdan had been closeted with the head buyer for several minutes when Trevitt and Ashton spoke to the manager of the department store, not all that busy on a sunny Monday afternoon.

Yes, Jourdan was alone; the manager had seen nothing of any woman. Damn, Trevitt thought as they followed the manager up the service stairs; it would have been worth a bucketful of more conventional evidence to have seen Jourdan and Fiona Brooke together when the news of Lockwood's death was broken to them . . . to have watched the expressions on their faces or the controlled lack of expression, the way their eyes met or carefully avoided meeting.

Miss Brooke is most probably at this moment sitting in the

store's tearoom, Ashton guessed. Passing the time till Jourdan had finished his business, reading a newspaper, waiting to order tea till he could join her, thirsty from discussion. Wouldn't make much difference if we had encountered the two of them together, he reflected. Fiona struck him as the kind of woman who could never really be taken by surprise; even in an earthquake her ear would have caught some warning rumble. And Jourdan was in command of himself in the way a panther or tiger is always in command. The gaze might be concentrated or sleepy, the muscles tense or deceptively relaxed, but awake or asleep, in the presence of friend or foe, the alarm signal in the brain never ceased to operate.

Which by no means indicates that the man is guilty of murder, Ashton reminded himself as they came up to the final landing. Only that he lived a life in which innocence and spontaneity were merely words in a dictionary.

'I'll go in first,' the manager said, a good portion of his existence being spent in protecting the store from unpleasantness of one kind or another. Trevitt stepped forward, about to insist with bulldozing courtesy on going in without the benefit of a public relations exercise, but Ashton laid a hand on his sleeve, indicating by a glance that it mattered very little one way or the other. Yes, I suppose he's right, Trevitt thought, signalling acquiescence with an infinitesimal nod; if Jourdan is guilty he'll have been expecting this visit or something very like it for the better part of the afternoon. Precious little chance, after all, of catching him unawares.

His interest in the whole encounter suddenly dropped by several degrees. It was merely going to resolve itself now into a series of questions and answers . . . At what time precisely did you and Miss Brooke leave Oakfield? . . . Did either of you have any reason to enter the kitchen this morning? . . . And so on and so on . . . He followed the manager into the office, running a swiftly assessing eye over Jourdan, who remained seated while the store buyer got to his feet with a surprised look.

Jourdan was young, younger-looking than Trevitt had expected. Well-built, tall, broad shoulders. Not conventionally handsome but with the kind of strongly individual good looks underlaid with more than a suggestion of thuggishness that

Trevitt knew from long sour-grape experience were powerfully attractive to women.

We shall have to rout Miss Fiona Brooke out of wherever she is temporarily nesting, Ashton thought as he watched Jourdan's face. She might be sitting in the car outside on the concrete strip or upstairs in the café among the glass-topped tables and the music piped in from the borders of a dream . . . He saw himself and Trevitt advancing towards her, saw her walking between them down to the buyer's office . . . If you wouldn't mind, Miss Brooke, take that chair if you please . . . did you by any chance observe Mr Robert Jourdan lifting down a tin of cyanide from a shelf – Ashton's meandering notions ceased abruptly as he saw that Jourdan was looking at Trevitt with an air of crippling shock, he seemed scarcely able to take in what the sergeant was saying.

'We do not know precisely as yet the cause of death, but you will appreciate that as a visitor to the house you may very well find yourself in a position to give us some assistance, some piece of information perhaps, some little thing you may not have paid much attention to – '

Jourdan's eyes slid to the window. His face was very pale. Either he's a first-class actor, Ashton thought with deep bafflement, or he's no longer listening to Trevitt running on, he's slipped his brain into another gear, he's giving his entire attention to some other irresistibly compelling matter that has sprung into the forefront of his mind.

Chapter 14

'Fingerprints.' Kenward assumed his disarming, affable look. He marked the way Meacham's shoulders relaxed instantly like a man preparing to ride a blow he cannot hope to dodge. 'Nothing to get alarmed about,' the inspector said reassuringly to Bessie, who had thrown him a startled look. 'We're taking fingerprints from everyone with any kind of connection with the case, however remote. We must have them for elimination purposes, you understand.' She wasn't absolutely certain what that implied but it had a soothing official sound. She smiled and looked with interest at Constable Yarrow setting about the task.

Meacham allowed his prints to be taken in silence. A bit different from five minutes ago, Kenward thought; Meacham had been fluent enough then in his assertions that he knew nothing whatever about the tin of cyanide on the kitchen shelf, that in any case he could never have mistaken cyanide for any other substance, would never have been fool enough to go stirring it into flasks of coffee, that the tin must have been acquired before he ever set foot in Westerhill, might date back ten years for all he knew. And furthermore, there had been no trouble with wasps' nests during the short time he had been at Oakfield, nor had there been any other conceivable reason why he should wish to go ferreting about for tins of cyanide.

And Bessie had rejected every insinuation of her own careless-ness with flashing-eyed vigour. Astounded, wounded, mortified, to think that anyone could imagine for one single moment . . . et cetera . . . et cetera . . . Ah well, Kenward had said to himself, it was just a thought, never did think very highly of the accident theory anyway, dare say neither of them did go sloshing the stuff around out of sheer *joie de vivre*.

It occurred to him all at once that if they were dealing with a case of murder, then it didn't really matter where the tin of cyanide on the kitchen shelf had originally come from. If it was from that tin that the murderer had abstracted the fatal dose, then it was pretty obvious that he was confident the poison couldn't be traced back to him.

Meacham sat looking on as his wife allowed Yarrow to take hold of her hand. Ashton could be quite wrong about Meacham, Kenward thought. Might be exactly what he seemed, a gentle-manly sort of fellow, pleased to have found happiness at this stage of his life. The inspector's fingers, idly rolling a pencil to and fro along the table, suddenly ceased their playing as a notion presented itself to him with arresting force. Of course – Meacham or Bessie – or the two of them together, could have deliberately dosed Lockwood's lunch with cyanide and then put the tin up on the kitchen shelf so that the death might be written off as an accident. Or the tin might in truth have been on the shelf for some considerable time, giving birth to the idea – in one or both of them – of committing murder under the guise of mishap.

In which case, Kenward realized with a sense of shock, the plan might very well work. He looked at Meacham with passionate interest, wondering if he might be in the presence of a cunning and successful murderer; almost he felt something resembling admiration begin to wash against the edges of his mind. He dismissed the feeling with stern resolution and was aware a moment later of a surge of exhilaration, an immense and hugely attractive challenge. He stood up, unable to remain seated under the thrust of energy that rose inside him. His glance shifted from Meacham to Bessie, returned to Meacham, he took a pace or two back so that he was able to look at the pair of them together . . . This one? . . . That one? . . . Or both of them? . . . Two in one flesh?

The tide of energy ebbed a little as the question of motive reared up before him. Only tnat frail suggestion of a shady past for Meacham – would he have murdered for that? And no motive whatever for Bessie, no conceivable reason why she should wish Lockwood dead. He felt confusion begin to addle his brain. He must talk to Mrs Lockwood soon, see if her husband had said anything to her about Meacham . . . and if he hadn't? If Meacham's past turned out to resemble the driven snow? . . . Ah well . . . Kenward sighed In that case he'd do what he'd done a hundred times before, drop that unprofitable line and start again, on another. He tilted back his head and stared at the ceiling. If Mrs Lockwood felt up to it . . . wouldn't do any harm, surely, just to put one or two simple queries, nothing in the way of serious questioning yet of course, nothing at all exhausting . . .

He suddenly lowered his head and met Meacham's eyes, seeing from the briefly unguarded look in them that the man had realized the significance of that upward glance in the direction of Marion Lockwood's bedroom. And that the implication disturbed, not to say frightened him; he saw the faint glisten of sweat on his forehead. Meacham got to his feet, gave a little smile and said, 'If you've finished with us then, Inspector – ' he looked across at his wife – 'we'll be getting along. It really is a trifle warm in here.'

'Still waters,' Trevitt said with a hint of admiration in his voice. 'Miss Fiona Brooke. Very still waters.'

'And a remarkably good-looking young woman,' Ashton said. They came out into the sunlight, headed towards the car park. They'd got nothing of any note from the two interviews. Except that Ashton's impression of Jourdan as a calculating man-on-the-make had been strongly reinforced.

'I feel he has the personality of a man who could commit murder,' he said as they walked past the fire-escape, past the staff entrance. Capable of planning the deed in scrupulous detail, or of taking a suddenly decisive step if events presented him with an unlooked-for opportunity. Capable too of sticking it out to the end, keeping his nerve, resisting the temptation to unburden himself. And, most difficult of all, capable afterwards of enjoying the fruits of his crime through the long slope of years with an easy conscience, an undiminished appetite for life.

'Doesn't mean to say he actually did commit a murder, though.' Trevitt picked his way between the cars. 'And if he did, I doubt if we'll be able to pin it on him. He's the type who'll sit tight and say nothing. Not even to his lady-love.' Fiona had indeed been drinking tea in the café at the top of the store. The manager wouldn't hear of their walking up to her among the little knots of thirsty shoppers but had insisted on despatching a waitress with a discreet message. So by the time the two men laid eyes on her she was already armoured. She had closed her eyes and sat leaning forward with her head bent for a minute or two after they had broken the news, then she had raised her head, drawn herself upright and answered their questions, but still with her eyes closed. An odd experience; Trevitt had felt as if they were interviewing a blind woman. The face so calm, the voice so controlled and even. And yet one knew that she was unable to expose her eyes to their gaze, that behind the calm, beneath the control, there must be a turmoil of emotions; by closing her eyes she had as it were issued a statement to that effect.

They reached the car. Trevitt opened the door. 'Seems to me,' he said over his shoulder, 'Mrs Lockwood had some very good reasons for wishing to bid a long farewell to Hubby.' Now that he'd actually laid eyes on Miss Brooke he could scarcely blame Lockwood for wishing to effect whatever changes in his life were necessary to bring it about that he came home to that young woman every evening instead of to Mrs L. 'You're pretty certain she knew about her husband and Fiona Brooke?'

Ashton inserted himself into the passenger seat. He looked back at the weekend, at Lockwood's eyes following Fiona Brooke, wandering from Jourdan to Fiona, back again to Jourdan, resting on his wife scarcely at all and then with either deliberate blankness or veiled hostility.

'I'd be willing to gamble next month's salary that she knew. If she didn't she was the only adult at Oakfield that was in any doubt about it.'

Trevitt began to ease the car out. 'I don't believe she'd have cared for a divorce, our Mrs L. That suburban type always regards it as a disgrace, do anything to avoid it.'

'Scarcely murder, though,' Ashton said.

'I don't know so much about that.' They were out of the car park now, edging into the traffic. 'She might think: Better murder, widowhood, and all the loot, than divorce and half the loot at best.'

'She was at the picnic.' Ashton began to revolve the notion. 'She helped to prepare the packed lunches.' It began to seem rather more than possible.

'And unless she's made a speedy recovery,' Trevitt said, 'she's lying upstairs in her room at Oakfield at this moment, resting after her exertions, being sympathetically allowed to tranquillize herself, being shielded from any awkward little questions.'

'Miss Tillard has always been a shrewd investor,' Henry Whittall said with detached approval. 'Her father left her a nice little sum which she never touched, it's been in very sound investment trusts for well over thirty years.' He regarded Kenward with a knowing eye. 'I'm sure I don't have to spell out for you just how much the original capital has increased.'

He needn't bother to butter me up with his assumptions that I'm a good judge of an investment portfolio, Kenward thought sourly. By the time he'd shredded his salary over regular clamorous claimants there wasn't enough left to buy a healthy-looking postal order, let alone a fistful of shares.

'She always had a good salary,' Whittall went on. 'And she always saved. She came in for a handsome lump sum when she retired, she has a pretty sizeable pension.' Kenward nodded encouragingly. A little baffled by Whittall's readiness to discuss the affairs of a client. Not that he was specifying actual sums but all the same . . . The inspector had certainly not expected anything like this degree of frankness although he had taken the precaution of speaking to Whittall without the inhibiting presence of Constable Yarrow and his notebook. But after only one or two really quite mild bits of probing Whittall had suddenly said, 'If you insist,' and immediately begun to give tongue. Now why precisely would that be? I'm damn sure he doesn't make a habit of it, Kenward thought, wouldn't keep his job long if he did.

'She's made rather a hobby of studying the financial papers since she retired,' Henry said 'She's played the market with a good deal of flair. Only comparatively modest amounts, you understand, never any question of touching the bulk of the capital, too level-headed for that. She's done very well, very well indeed.' He pursed his lips. 'A good head for business. And the time to give to it. That's important, that's where a lot of people fall down.'

'And how far does Miss Tillard disclose details of her business affairs to members of her family?' Kenward found himself falling into solicitor-like modes of speech.

'I couldn't be very exact about that.' Henry pulled down the corners of his mouth. 'She is by nature inclined to reticence. But . . . Mr Barratt perhaps . . or Mrs Barratt . . . Miss Onil . . .' He spread his hands. 'I really couldn't say.' Leaving the field wide open, the inspector noted. He gave a moment's concentrated thought to the framing of his next question but he couldn't come up with any subtle way of putting it. What he wanted to know was whether Barratt had had the opportunity to dip his fingers into Miss Tillard's savings, a pretty uncompromising sort of notion however it was dressed up.

'Mr Barratt has been acting in the capacity, as it were,' he said at last, 'that is to say, he might be called a confidential adviser –'

'He handles a good deal of her business,' Whittall said at once.

'And you have oversight of his handling?' Kenward felt able to stop fencing now.

Whittall shook his head. 'Only very occasionally. Miss Tillard relies a good deal on Mr Barratt, she trusts him implicitly.' His eyes, bland, unsmiling, looked calmly into the inspector's.

Something began to stir at the back of Kenward's mind, some recollection involving Whittall . . . Lockwood . . . something surely to do with school . . . what was it? . . . He hunted the idea down the twisting byways of memory but each time he fancied he had it, it slipped away from him. To give himself time, he picked up a page of notes and ran a finger over it, asking a confirmatory question here and there about some detail of the fatal picnic; Whittall answered easily, without hesitation.

I know! Kenward suddenly had the snippet from the past triumphantly in his grasp. Expelled, Whittall had been expelled, or as near as made no difference. And Lockwood had been mixed up in the expulsion. Trevitt might know the ins and outs of what had happened, he was more or less the same age as Whittall. Into the little silence that Kenward had unwittingly allowed to arise, Henry said suddenly, 'Lockwood offered me a sandwich, you know. At the picnic.' He pulled a face, shuddered.

'But you didn't take it,' Kenward said soothingly.

'I certainly did not. It was pork. I wouldn't dream of eating dead flesh. Never have done and never will do.'

'Indeed?' Kenward said politely. 'In any case,' he added, 'we have no reason for thinking there was anything wrong with the sandwiches.' He put up a hand and stroked his chin. 'You knew Lockwood at school, I believe?' he said a moment later, easing the question gently forward.

'Yes.' Just that. But Kenward saw that Whittall had ceased to fidget about, was holding himself rigid in his chair. He felt a slight prickling across his scalp. Two common types of murderer – apart from the most common of all, the member of the family, the nearest and dearest; the meek and mild little man, and the man who wants to make a mark in life, any kind of mark, to be remembered for *something*. Was it possible that Henry Whittall combined both types in one personality? How much of his behaviour under questioning was skilful play-acting? Yarrow had found cyanide at the cottage – but that could be innnocent enough, there had certainly been no attempt at hiding it.

'You're fond of photography, I understand?' he said pleasantly.

'I am.' Whittall was on his guard now, very definitely, nothing much to be got out of pressing him further just now.

'A very good hobby,' Kenward said with a smile. 'I keep promising myself I'll take it up one day. If I ever get the time. I don't think I need keep you any longer.' He caught the slight but unmistakable look of relief on Whittall's face. Relief and even more unmistakable, surprise.

When the door had closed behind him Kenward sat twirling a pencil, frowning, biting his lip, pondering over what he had learned about Miss Tillard's money, the dispositions – and intended dispositions – in her will. The codicil greatly increasing the provision for Theresa Onil – but not yet signed. The two sisters, Marion and Pauline, still the principal legatees. His mind darted away to Barratt's woodworking firm, his financial difficulties, that business of Osmond's. Was there any way in which these matters tied up with Lockwood's death? He sighed and stretched. None that he could immediately see.

He sat up abruptly. Barratt hadn't been at that picnic. He was not at work, surely he might have been expected to play a game of golf with Lockwood? Why hadn't he? Probably couldn't stand the sight of him, promptly answered some other part of Kenward's brain. Or the sight of the Pagets, come to that – the very type of auld acquaintance that Barratt probably most dearly wished would be for ever forgot and never under any conceivable circumstances brought to mind. Had Barratt any other more pressing reason for avoiding the picnic? A desire perhaps not to be on the spot when Lockwood began to gasp and choke? . . . Money . . . his mind came round again to Barratt's difficulties, to Miss Tillard's fortune. But no clear line of thought presented itself.

He stood up and walked about the room, with difficulty avoiding bumping into the furniture. One thing was emerging, though, the lack of any real motive for Theresa Onil. Probably able to write her off now. Perfectly sound reason for calling at Oakfield this morning – to ask for assistance to persuade Miss Tillard to go into hospital. And she had received that assistance; and the assistance had proved effective. Pauline Barratt had walked back with Theresa to the bungalow, had talked earnestly to her aunt. And her aunt was at this moment lying in bed in the Chilford hospital.

He had just about agreed to his own proposal to forget Miss Onil when one of the daily women put her head round the door to say he was wanted on the phone. Oh Lord, not the Press again, Kenward said to himself with irritation as he went along the passage, but it was a precise, official voice at the other end of the line.

'In the sandwiches?' Kenward said into the receiver a couple of minutes later, his tone rising slightly in surprise.

'In one sandwich, to be exact,' the voice corrected him. 'The sandwich he took a bite out of, to state the obvious. Very liberally dosed, that sandwich, but no cyanide anywhere else. Not in the other sandwiches or the coffee, or anything else that was collected from the site of the picnic.'

As Kenward went slowly back to the sitting-room with his head bent in thought he had a brief clear vision of Whittall looking at him with that face of distaste. 'Lockwood offered me a sandwich,' Whittall had said, faintly theatrical. Again the inspector felt the tingle run along his scalp. Whittall had faced him across the table at a moment when anyone would have gambled on the coffee. Whittall had been on the golf-course, he'd seen Lockwood raise the beaker to his lips, seen him drink from it, clutch his throat . . . And yet it was the sandwiches he'd shuddered at . . .

'Would you like to stop for a meal on the way? Or wait till we get back to Barbridge?' Jourdan looked ahead at the traffic, a little denser now.

'I'm not very hungry, thank you.' Fiona glanced out at the scatter of suburban bungalows running towards them. 'I'd just as soon wait till I get home.' Till *I* get home, he noted, not till *we* get home. It occurred to him also with some force that Fiona hadn't given him a single direct look since the two detectives had spoken to her. Nor had she addressed to him more than polite impersonal words. About Lockwood's death she had said nothing at all.

It didn't cross his mind that Fiona might have made precisely the same set of observations about himself.

'Well, yes, of course,' Bessie said. 'Monday. My cousin – on my mother's side, that is – he always calls here on a Monday. Round about ten or a quarter past. *You* know him.' She levelled a look at Kenward. 'He has the mobile shop.'

'Oh yes.' Kenward had seen the vehicle hundreds of times over the past twenty years, charging through the country lanes with the cheerful mahogany countenance of its owner peering out through the windscreen. 'And you were away from the kitchen, talking to your cousin – for how long?'

Bessie raised her shoulders. 'Couldn't say exactly. Five minutes perhaps.' That means ten or fifteen, Kenward thought.

'And during that time – '

'During that time Miss Marion, or I should say Mrs Lockwood, carried on with the sandwiches.' Oh, she did, did she, Kenward said to himself, I shall have to go upstairs before much longer and have a word with Miss Marion.

'Did anyone else help Mrs Lockwood with the sandwiches?' he asked.

'I couldn't say, I'm sure. They might have done.' She frowned, remembering something. 'When I was standing talking to my cousin, that Theresa – Miss Tillard's Theresa – I saw her walking by outside, talking to Mrs Lockwood. So I don't really know about the sandwiches now, perhaps Mrs Lockwood didn't carry on doing them all that long.' She inclined her head thoughtfully. 'I'd forgotten about Theresa.'

Kenward sighed. 'And the actual preparation and wrapping of the sandwiches – could we just run over it again? To make absolutely sure you haven't left anything out?'

'That's all right.' Bessie settled herself back in her chair with an air of importance. 'Go ahead, ask me anything you want.'

She was enlarging on her habit of noting down the fads of individual guests when there was a knock at the sitting-room door. One of the constables, eyeing Kenward apologetically.

'It's the lad, sir, the boy who was on the golf-course.'

The inspector uttered a sound of displeasure. 'Tell him to take himself off home. We're not a youth club.'

'He says he's remembered something,' the constable said hesitantly. 'I don't know if he's just trying it on or not. He won't tell me what it is.'

'Oh, for crying out loud!' Kenward got to his feet, quite pleased for all his groaning to be able to stretch his limbs, take his mind off all the fiddling little details of greaseproof paper, who had mustard and who couldn't abide the stuff. 'I'll come and speak to him,' he said grimly. He glanced across at Bessie. 'I'll talk to you again later on if it's necessary. I'm sure you have a lot to see to just now.' He went heavy-footed along the passage.

'It's the sandwiches,' the boy said rapidly as soon as he realized that the inspector was actually prepared to hear what he had to say, hadn't come striding out into the corridor merely to pack him off home with a flea in his ear.

'The sandwiches?' Kenward said sharply. 'What about them?'

'They were changed – switched over – she took the packet from –'

'Hold on!' Kenward held up an authoritative hand. He was seized by a horrid feeling that the lad might get all the threads irretrievably tangled, that it might prove impossible ever to unravel them again. And every hair on his skin proclaimed the feeling that this was it, this was what he'd been looking for. 'Take it easy,' he said gently. 'Quite calmly. Just think exactly what happened, then tell me slowly.'

The boy looked earnestly up into his eyes, he spoke with solemn intensity. 'Mrs Lockwood changed over her sandwiches for the sandwiches in the sportscoat.' Kenward fixed him with a fierce gaze. 'Go on, in detail.' The boy pressed his hands together. 'She was by herself, she was sitting down, reading a book. Then she got up, looked round and walked over to a little pile of things, sweaters, newspapers, the lunch things. She knelt down, then she picked up a sportscoat and put her hand in the pocket. She took out the sandwiches – of course I didn't know then it was the sandwiches, it was a little white paper parcel – and then she took another packet from the anorak she was wearing and put it into the sportscoat pocket. She put the first lot – the ones from the sportscoat – into her own pocket.'

'How quickly was all this done?' Kenward asked with a savage frown of concentration. 'A matter of seconds? The sandwiches whisked out of one pocket and straight into the other?'

The boy raised his shoulders. 'Not as quickly as all that. She handled each of the packets, sort of studied them, she fiddled about a bit with them.' He gave the inspector an anxious look. 'I'm afraid I couldn't quite see what she did to them.' Kenward didn't altogether care for that anxious glance, it held a shadowy hint of the wish to please, to say what the audience wished to hear.

'You are absolutely certain,' he said in a light neutral tone, switching off at the same time all suggestion of intensity from his gaze, 'that Mrs Lockwood did in fact change the two packets over? Is it not possible perhaps that she returned each packet to the coat she originally took it from?'

The lad shook his head emphatically. 'Oh no, she didn't put them back in the original pockets, she switched them over, I'm quite positive about that.' Had his answer, the movement of his head, followed instantly on the question? Or had there been a fractional pause – a split second to weigh up which of two replies would elicit an approving nod? 'Then she went back to where she'd been sitting,' the lad said, unwilling to come to the end of his tale. 'She started reading again.'

'And what time was all this?'

'About a quarter of an hour before the others came back and they all started to eat.'

'Can you describe the coat she took the packet out of?'

'It was a man's sportscoat, a tweed jacket, sort of greenish brown.' Lockwood's jacket, Kenward thought, discarded because of the heat. The other four had gone off to play golf, leaving Marion alone with her novel, or to wander off for a walk if she felt like it. She hadn't in the least minded, apparently, quite liked walking by herself, was addicted to reading light romances, bored to death by golf . . . and of course in the event of wishing to carry out a very personal and private little action such as deliberately slipping a packet of poisoned sandwiches into her husband's jacket, what arrangement could be more convenient?

'How come she didn't see you?' he asked the boy. 'Or did she in fact see you?' If she'd known she was being observed it rather looked as if her conduct was totally innocent.

The boy shook his head. 'She never saw me, she never looked my way at all. I was lying down in some long grass – ' he indicated with economical gestures that he had been lying on his stomach, his elbows on the ground, his chin supported on his fists. 'I wasn't spying on her, or anything like that, I'd been looking for golf-balls for ages, I was tired, I just wanted a rest, I looked at her because there wasn't anything else much to look at.'

Kenward took the boy by the arm and propelled him back to the sitting-room. Just outside the door he halted and looked down at him with a cold hard gaze. 'If there was anything in your story that wasn't one hundred per cent the truth, if you added a little bit or altered a little bit or left a little bit out, now's the time to tell me.'

'I didn't change anything.' The boy's eyes met his, frank, unflinching. 'It happened exactly the way I told you.'

Kenward threw open the door. 'Get this lad's statement down,' he said to Constable Yarrow. He intended to be off up the stairs to have a nice little chat with Mrs L. before many more seconds had elapsed. Probably wisest to speak to Mrs Barratt first about his intention to put one or two matters to her sister – he certainly wasn't going to imply anything in the nature of prolonged or serious questioning.

'I suppose it couldn't wait over till the morning,' Pauline said wearily when he tracked her down in the kitchen where she and Bessie were seeing about dinner in a rather half-hearted way, Pauline moving about like an automaton and Bessie providing a non-stop commentary on everything that had happened, might have happened or in her view ought to have happened during the past twenty-four hours.

'It really is rather urgent,' Kenward said with civil insistence. 'Otherwise of course I wouldn't dream of suggesting such a thing this evening.' Whether Pauline gave or withheld her permission, he intended to walk up those stairs and talk to Mrs Lockwood; the ritual dance of courtesy was a mere nod and bow in the direction of convention. 'I wasn't proposing to stay more than, say, ten minutes with her.'

'All right, then.' Pauline abandoned her show of resistance as she had known all along she must.

There was a small stir of movement from the bedroom when he knocked on the door. 'It's Inspector Kenward,' he said in a clear reassuring tone. 'I'd be grateful if you'd allow me to come in, just for a few minutes, there's something I should like to ask you.' She spoke, said something he couldn't catch. He turned the handle, let himself in, talking easily as he entered. 'I'm very sorry to bother you but I'm afraid there's no help for it.'

The curtains were drawn across the window but the room was far from dark; sunshine drifted in through every gap. He left the door ajar and walked over to the bed.

'Oh, it's you, Inspector.' She tried to struggle into a sitting position, she put up a hand and tried to pat her hair into neatness. 'I'm sorry – ' She began to cry, with a jerky bubbling sound. He watched her for a long moment, permitting himself no trace of compassion, striving with all the discipline at his command to assess her with a totally detached view . . . A widow of a few brief hours, lamenting her dead husband? . . . Or a coldly calculating murderess switching over to the second act of her performance?

'Please try not to distress yourself,' he said at last. 'Is there anything I can get you? Shall I ask them to bring up some tea?'

The crying faltered into silence. She gave a deep sigh, fished in her pocket and drew out a handkerchief, dabbed at her eyes. 'Ask me what you want,' she said, without interest. 'I don't need any tea.'

He pulled up a chair and sat down. 'It's the matter of the packets of sandwiches.' Perhaps he ought to have brought Yarrow with him, perched him over by the door to scribble away as she replied. Then he gave a tiny shake of his head. No, it wouldn't have done, not at this moment.

'What about the sandwiches?' she asked in a dull voice.

'The packet you opened for yourself, you took one sandwich from it and ate about a quarter of it.' The remaining three quarters of that sandwich and the rest of her packet had been gathered up by the police, together with all the other lunch things. 'Where precisely did you get that packet from?'

She frowned. 'From here, of course, from Oakfield, it was one of the packets they make every day.'

'Yes, I know that,' he said patiently. 'What I mean is, did Mrs Meacham hand it to you? Did you pick it up yourself from a number of packets in the kitchen, did you find it on the table in the hall, or where?'

'Oh, I see.' She bent her head, then looked up at him. 'It was in my pocket, the pocket of my anorak, when we sat down to eat I took it out of my own pocket.'

'How did it get into the pocket of your anorak?' At a moment like this his patience was capable of infinite expansion.

She passed a finger across her mouth. 'I left my anorak in the hall, downstairs, over the back of a chair.' She paused. 'When we were ready to go, I picked up the anorak and the sandwiches were in the pocket.'

'You remember that? You felt them there?' She nodded. 'Did you know who put them there?'

'No.' Her voice began to tremble. 'It could have been anyone.' She closed her eyes briefly. 'It could even have been me. If I'd been thinking about something else – I wouldn't remember a little thing like that.'

Yes, he thought, perfectly possible. He sighed, letting it go for the present. He took her in detail over the time she had spent alone on the golf-course before lunch, he went through her own actions and the actions of the others when they returned to join her. She answered quite readily, sometimes with evidence of distress, but never actually breaking down.

And from start to last she uttered not one syllable about switching over the two packets of sandwiches.

Kenward paused, bit his lip. The lad – was it conceivable that he'd actually invented the little episode? Yearned for a share of the limelight?

'I think I would like some tea now,' Marion said in a low tone. 'If you've finished, that is.'

'Yes, certainly, I'll speak to your sister, I'll see it's sent up to you.' He saw again the boy's eyes looking earnestly up at him, striving for accuracy. He leaned forward. 'Why did you change the sandwiches over?' he asked in a light and pleasant tone like a man making conversation at a party.

She jerked her head round sharply, flashed at him a startled look.

'You did change them,' he said, politely insistent. At this moment he would have staked every penny he possessed on the fact that the lad had been speaking the truth. 'You took the packet from your husband's coat and replaced it with the packet from your own.' Still she said nothing, she continued to stare at him. 'Why?' His voice was soft, insinuating. 'Why did you do it?'

'I'd forgotten,' she said in a whisper. 'I'd forgotten all about that.' She began to tremble. Tea, said some portion of Kenward's brain, get her that tea, and then get out and let her sleep.

'The poison was in the sandwiches,' she said in a fierce whisper. 'That's it, isn't it? It wasn't in the coffee at all.'

He stood up, bent over her, looked right down into her face. 'Tell me why you changed the sandwiches,' he said. 'And then I'll go.' He could see the sinews in her neck beginning to jerk in a slow patchy rhythm.

She opened her mouth, she began to speak. 'I – ' Her breath came out in a little sob. She turned her head away from his pinning gaze, she looked over at the masked window, her eyes came back again to his. And suddenly she started to laugh. She let herself slide into the pillows, her head fell back, the laughter crackled up, loud, abandoned, laced with hysteria.

'I wanted the best bits,' she said between helpless gusts. 'I always took the best bits.' She had one hand behind her head now, she was looking up into his face, tears streaming from her eyes, still clutched by irrational mirth. 'I'm greedy!' she cried on a rising note. 'I keep the best bits for myself!' From the direction of the open door he became aware of sound and movement. He half turned his head and glimpsed a face, two faces, concerned and worried eyes. He let out a long sigh and drew himself upright.

When he came back into the ground-floor sitting-room several minutes – and some deeply reproachful moments with Pauline – later, Constable Yarrow was alone. Kenward didn't look at him, he walked over to the table and threw himself into his chair, frowning, his face uneasy, disturbed.

'I let the boy go,' Yarrow said after a few moments. 'I hope that's all right, sir.'

Kenward leaned forward, put his elbows on the table, dropped his head on to his clasped hands. 'I don't think we're looking for the murderer of Stephen Lockwood,' he said, aloud, but addressing himself. He closed his eyes, gave a weary groan. 'I may be wrong but I believe now we're looking for the person who made an unsuccessful murder attempt on Mrs Marion Lockwood.'

Chapter 15

'For the time being,' Kenward said sharply, 'you can forget about Jourdan.' He took a mouthful of scalding coffee, pushed the plate of biscuits towards Ashton. 'You can screw your brains up as much as you like, I'm willing to lay any odds you care to name that you won't come up with any sane reason why Jourdan should want to put Marion Lockwood six feet under ground.' He opened his mouth and poured the coffee straight down, not tasting it, scarcely aware of its fierce heat, conscious of a raging thirst, a mulish determination to lash his flagging brain into fresh activity. 'All Mrs Lockwood's death would achieve for Jourdan would be to leave Stephen Lockwood free to marry Fiona Brooke and keep Jourdan kicking his heels as Lockwood's assistant at Alpha for heaven knows how long. Scarcely objectives Jourdan would wish to achieve.' He leaned forward and seized the coffee-pot, drained it into his cup, nodded down the table at Yarrow who had reached the stage of stealing glances at his watch every two minutes, discovering with increasing depression at each glance just how little the position of the fingers had altered. 'Get some more coffee,' Kenward said abruptly and Yarrow leapt to his feet with a fervent, 'Certainly, sir,' exhilarated at the prospect of actually being able to set his limbs in motion.

'There is, I take it,' Sergeant Trevitt said in the mannered fashion which he had adopted years ago as a piece of private amusement designed to allow him to remain at one and the same time a police detective and completely sane, but which had by now passed into mere habit, 'no doubt whatever that Mrs Lockwood did switch over the two packets of sandwiches? There is, that is to say, some proof of her action, apart from the boy's statement and Mrs Lockwood's admission?'

'Surely the boy's statement is external proof enough,' Ashton said. 'How many items of proof do you want? The boy saw something; when pressed, Mrs Lockwood admitted it. Why would the boy lie? Or why would the woman admit to something she hadn't done?'

'The lad spent hours hanging round here,' Trevitt said. 'Looking for a chance to bed himself down into the case in some way. Then all of a sudden when he really is going to find himself sent about his business, by great good luck he happens to remember a rather striking item of information. I should have thought he would have recalled it without any difficulty when he first came forward to tell his tale. An adolescent lad.' Trevitt shook his head, deprecating the instability, the undisciplined imagination of the breed. 'Can't take everything he says as gospel.'

'And what reason would Mrs Lockwood have,' Kenward said slowly, 'for admitting she switched the sandwiches if in fact she did no such thing?' He held up a hand as Trevitt's mouth opened to answer. 'Don't bother, I can supply the answer myself.' He let out a noisy breath. 'If she had poisoned her husband's sandwiches, of course.' He blew out his cheeks. 'She'd be very happy to make it appear that someone had intended to poison her and had poisoned her husband by mistake.'

'If you want further external proof,' Ashton said suddenly on a lively note, 'surely – the wrappings!' He pushed back his chair, got to his feet under the stimulus of this new thought. 'All the packets are marked, every day, the name of the person they're intended for is written on them in ink.' He put both hands on the table, leaning forward as he spoke. 'Everything was collected from the picnic ground, they'd only just started to eat the sandwiches when Lockwood began to choke. Get the remains of the packets, examine the wrappers, you'll see which of the Lockwoods the cyanide was intended for. You know which packet

Lockwood was eating from, all right then, see what name is marked on the wrapper of that packet.'

'Ye . . . es.' Kenward closed his eyes in concentrated thought, trying to spot a flaw in Ashton's argument, but without success. Constable Yarrow came back into the room with fresh coffee and another plate of biscuits. Trevitt tilted his chair back, watching Yarrow pour out the coffee.

'I don't remember anything being written on Lockwood's packet,' he said, and as he spoke the words he had a sudden memory of picking up Mrs Paget's sandwiches, still in their wrappings, unopened, and on the outside of the greaseproof bag he could see now the name neatly inked in capitals: MRS PAGET. He turned to Ashton. 'When you're given the sandwiches are they always double-wrapped?'

'Yes, I believe they are.' Ashton picked up a marshmallow biscuit. 'They're wrapped in a square of greaseproof paper, then they're put into a greaseproof bag. And the name is written on the outside of the bag.'

Kenward sank a sixth of a pint of strong black coffee without blinking. 'There was no bag for Lockwood's sandwiches. Or for Mrs Lockwood's.' He was quite sure of that. Just the squares of paper.

'There must have been bags,' Ashton said.

'Then where are they now?' Kenward wrinkled his brows. Lockwood might have had a fancy for tidiness, he might have walked off to find a litter-bin, dropped inside it both the missing bags before strolling back to make a start on the last meal he was ever to contemplate. In which case the bags might still be recovered – it was scarcely likely that anyone had emptied the golf-course litter-bins since lunch-time. And then it struck him that if they did indeed discover two discarded bags marked with the appropriate names, there was no way now of knowing which bag had enclosed which set of sandwiches. He seized a bourbon biscuit and bit into it savagely. It was beginning to look as if they might never know now if the poison had been intended for Lockwood or his wife. The entire investigation might have been gummed up by nothing more weighty than the fertile fancy of a boy.

'Pity you let the lad go,' he said sourly to Yarrow.

'We've got his address,' Yarrow said at once. 'He lives here in the village. I could easily – '

Kenward thrust out a hand. 'Oh, leave it for now.' They could get the lad in tomorrow morning. He had no intention of staying up half the night displaying keenness.

'It's just possible,' Trevitt said, 'that Mrs Lockwood might have kept the wrapping from her packet, that is, from the packet she ended up with, whoever it was originally destined for. She might have it in her pocket, for instance.'

'Worth a try,' the inspector said with renewed energy. He'd better find out without delay. If the empty bag was indeed upstairs in the pocket of the blue anorak, Mrs Lockwood might remember it herself before much longer, she might have compelling reasons for making sure no one else discovered its existence. He stretched out a hand and closed his fingers on another biscuit. Was Mrs Barratt likely to let him have another interview with her sister? So soon after the last little performance? He shook his head slowly, hadn't quite completed the movement when there was a knock at the door and Pauline put her head in to say with an air of marked disapproval that Mrs Lockwood was insisting on seeing the inspector again, momentarily giving Kenward the impression that he had jerked himself on to a plane where merely to will a course of action was to set the wheels actually in motion. He got to his feet.

'I imagine you'll want to be present,' he said to Pauline, accepting the inevitable, but she shook her head.

'Marion says not.' Marion had rather particularly and emphatically said not, with the brusque authority of the elder sister which could still spring up sometimes as valid and powerful as if the adult years had been no more than a brief school-holiday dream.

Kenward raised his shoulders. 'If you're sure she's well enough,' he said with an air of concern, able to afford this little gesture now that he was sure he was going to get his interview, and alone at that.

'She seems a good deal better,' Pauline said. Marion had in fact suddenly asked for and eaten a fair-sized supper, had risen from her bed and was now sitting in an easy chair in her room, apparently in command of herself once more.

137

When the inspector had followed Pauline from the room Ashton allowed himself the luxury of a good yawn and stretch. 'I'll have a bit of a walk round,' he said to Trevitt. After all, he could do as he pleased, he wasn't officially attached to the Chilford police, he was supposed to be on holiday – and in a very short space of time he might not be attached to any police force in any capacity at all. 'I won't be long,' he found himself adding all the same a moment later, 'I'll be back before Kenward comes down.' He grinned to himself as he went out into the passage; habit was not it seemed to be so easily broken after all.

He glanced in at the dining-room but it was empty now except for Mrs Meacham straightening the chairs. He crossed the hall, looked round the doors of the ground-floor sitting-rooms. Faces turned to give him an interested, wary regard, re-assessing him now in the light of the knowledge that he wasn't one of them but a copper in civilian clothing, had been mingling unsuspected with the flock for the whole of last week.

Jean was nowhere on the ground floor. She was probably upstairs with the twins. As he came up to the first landing he heard the sound of a door opening, and looking along the corridor he saw Brigid coming out of her room. She pulled the door to with an angry slam, thrust her hands into her pockets, hunched her shoulders and came slouching towards him with a face full of sulky mutiny.

'Yes, she's in there,' she said in reply to his query, tilting her head in the direction of the twins' bedroom. Mike didn't waste time or energy in concerning himself with the reason for her surly mood. If she enjoyed wallowing in bad temper, all right, let her get on with it. Always provided of course that she didn't try to take it out on anyone else.

'Have you come to say good night?' Vicky asked as he let himself into the bedroom. She sat up in bed and stretched out her arms to him.

'I'm just settling them down,' Jean said with a faintly harassed air. 'Don't start exciting them, will you?'

'Why are you still talking business?' Kate demanded from the other bed. 'You shouldn't talk business on holiday.' It had been easy enough to explain away the presence of policemen as being related to Ashton's presence in the house; it seemed quite reasonable to the twins that the local police should wish to consult their father when something difficult arose while he was in the neighbourhood. It hadn't been necessary to specify what that difficult something was, and neither child had noticed that Mr Lockwood was no longer there. Both the Lockwoods had intended to go back to Barbridge in the morning; in the course of the next day or two the children would very probably assume that Stephen had gone and that Marion had decided to stay on with her sister for a little while longer.

'Everything under control?' Mike said in a low voice to Jean, indicating the twins with a movement of his eyes.

'Oh yes, I think so,' she said with assurance. 'No need to worry on their account. They'll be off to sleep in a jiffy.' She stooped and tucked in the covers of Vicky's bed. 'What about you?' She glanced up at Mike. 'Any developments?'

He pulled down the corners of his mouth. 'Nothing conclusive. Scarcely expect it at this stage. You know how it is. Enough lines of inquiry to make your head reel.' He blew out a long breath. 'We'll be calling it a day pretty soon, I should think. Kenward strikes me as a man who likes his sleep.' He spoke in a flat, rather bored tone, he came over and dropped a ritual kiss on her cheek, patted her lightly on the arm. 'See you.' He went off again towards the stairs, the sitting-room, the notes, the coffee and the fancy biscuits.

But he can't kid me, Jean thought as she settled Kate firmly back against the pillows, he's revelling in it. She saw suddenly that this was the first day of the holiday that Mike had actually enjoyed. She paused with her hands on Kate's shoulders and took a long look at the notion.

'What are you thinking about?' Kate asked, staring up with keen interest into her mother's intense gaze. Jean didn't answer, she hadn't in fact heard.

'When you frown like that,' Kate said with authority, 'it usually means you're thinking about something you don't like.' She saw from her mother's look that there was no likelihood of receiving an intelligent reply for another couple of minutes at least, so being of a practical turn of mind she instantly decided to spend the interim in settling once and for all the question of how many silvery stripes there were on the wallpaper between the door and the window. Not counting, of course, the half stripe beside the pelmet.

Ashton went down the stairs with a buoyant step and a strong inclination to whistle. On the last step he halted suddenly and stared ahead. 'Forget about Jourdan,' Kenward had said. 'Jourdan could have had no motive for wishing Marion Lockwood dead.' But what of Fiona Brooke? Ashton thought, pressing his fingers into the polished wood of the banister rail. Surely it would have suited Miss Brooke uncommonly well if Mrs Lockwood were lying now in the mortuary instead of her husband. Ye . . . es, he said to himself, and again, Yes! He set off briskly for the sitting-room, flung open the door and said at once to Trevitt, 'You and I could do a great deal worse tomorrow morning than take a run over to Barbridge.'

Trevitt tilted back his chair and studied with deep interest a long chain he had constructed from paper clips. 'I thought of that,' he said idly. He glanced up at Ashton with expressionless eyes. 'I went so far as to phone Barbridge, told them we'd be on their patch in the morning, asked them to do a little preliminary nosing round.' He gave a faint smile at Ashton's questioning look. 'Kenward'll OK it all right, don't give that a second thought. I'll raise the matter when he comes back, he'll fancy it was his own idea after a couple of minutes.' He let the legs of his chair drop on to the floor, he yawned slightly. 'I get bored sitting about,' he said with an air of derisive apology. 'In sheer desperation I sometimes have to start thinking.'

Chapter 16

Kenward gently closed the door of Mrs Lockwood's room and walked very slowly towards the head of the stairs. He put up a hand and began to massage his left cheek with deep, strong pressure. If she was telling the truth – and it was a gigantic *if* – then her life had been saved by pure and simple greed. She'd selected the most appetising slices of roast pork for her own sandwiches and marked the outside of the paper bag with a tiny cross. As both the Lockwoods liked the same trimmings in their sandwiches, mustard, stuffing and so on, Bessie – or any other helper – would, after consulting the notebook, mark the Lockwoods' two packets indiscriminately with a Mr and Mrs, since they would be aware of no difference between the sandwiches, and Mrs Lockwood would scarcely be anxious to make it plain exactly where the difference lay. When the time came for Marion to pick up her sandwiches from the hall or wherever else they might be left on a particular occasion, she simply chose the packet she had marked with a cross, paying no attention to the Mr and Mrs. And presumably Stephen was satisfied if he saw the word Lockwood on the outside of the bag, he was hardly likely to reject a packet just because it said Mrs instead of Mr. Or it might be that on most – or even all – of the previous occasions Marion's cross had actually coincided with her own inked name. And then again, Stephen Lockwood might never even have troubled to glance at the outside of the packet at all, might simply have opened it and started to eat.

The inspector began to descend the stairs at a snail's pace. Mrs Lockwood had produced a greaseproof bag from the pocket of her anorak without the slightest sign of reluctance or dismay. Kenward had taken it from her, smoothed it out, had read the name: MR LOCKWOOD. And a little to the right of the name, a very small inked cross.

No, she hadn't got the bag that had wrapped her husband's sandwiches. She had put up her hands to her face and said in a muffled voice after a minute or two, 'I'm afraid I can't remember what he did with it.'

'Try to think,' Kenward had said with gentle persistence. 'Did he screw it up and throw it away, put it in his pocket, or walk with it to a litter-bin perhaps?'

Her shoulders moved in the small silence that followed, then she said, 'I'm sorry, I just can't remember.'

'It's all right, don't worry about it,' he'd said. Whittall might remember, or one of the Pagets. They could go through the stuff they'd picked up from the ground, search any near-by litter-bins. And suppose the bag never turned up? They'd be left then with the one remaining bag, the one she'd produced from her pocket, the one marked with her husband's name, and a small cross.

The inspector closed his eyes and groaned. She could have inked in a nice little cross at any time in the last hour or two, sitting at leisure in her room upstairs, safe from intrusive eyes. Or she could have removed the bag from her husband's packet when she switched the sandwiches – if she ever did switch them. When Lockwood took the packet out, its sole wrapping might have been the sheet of greaseproof paper. Come to that, she could have removed both bags at that time, disposed of them in one of several ways after returning to Oakfield, and placed in the pocket of her anorak a third bag which she had taken from the kitchen and carefully marked in order to be able to produce it for official eyes when the time came.

The bags mean nothing, he told himself with dismal confusion as he propelled his feet towards the sitting-room. He stopped and frowned. No – surely if they found a bag in the litter-bin or among the stuff they'd picked up – yes, that would mean something – it would have a name on it. Then he groaned again, more loudly. Mrs Lockwood could have dumped the bag on the ground or in the bin before the others came back to join her for lunch, it could bear whatever markings she had wished it to bear. Finding the bag would prove nothing. And not finding it would prove nothing. He went into the sitting-room and sat heavily down in his chair. Trevitt and Ashton glanced at his face and judged it wisest to remain silent.

'Meacham,' Kenward said at last, feeling a profound distaste for the entire subject of paper bags and greaseproof wrappings, and being more than happy not to address a single further thought to the topic for the immediate future. 'Mrs Lockwood has some reason to suppose Meacham is not what he makes himself out to be.' He saw the look of satisfaction that crossed Ashton's face, the little nod he gave. 'It seems Meacham told her he had been employed by a firm called Hunston's . . . ' He heard his own voice droning on, repeating the details. He felt a vast weariness begin to sweep over him, he felt totally unable to care whether Meacham was a knight in shining armour or a villain of the deepest dye.

'I knew it,' Ashton said with pleasure when Kenward's voice ceased at last. 'Easy enough to check.'

Trevitt turned a calm gaze on Ashton. 'No reason whatever to jump to the conclusion that Meacham was lying. He could have worked at the Larchend branch of Hunston's as he maintained. Mrs Lockwood could have misunderstood the first conversation. And even if he did embroider matters a little, if he made himself out to be in charge of a department when he was merely a counter-hand, what of it? It's not a criminal offence. If every man who glorified his position in order to dazzle his lady-friend were to end up facing a charge there wouldn't be many men walking about free.'

'You wait and see,' Ashton replied with more confidence than he now felt. He could have been wrong. After all, what had he had to go on? Nothing more than the expression in the eyes, a certain air.

'One other thing,' the inspector said, levelling a steady gaze at Ashton. 'It's about your daughter Brigid.' He was not entirely displeased to see the way Ashton's face immediately lost its look of satisfaction. 'It seems you've been having some trouble with her, that you told her she was not to go out in the evenings . . .' Ashton felt a burning tide of humiliation begin to scorch his cheek. 'Mrs Lockwood tells me she had occasion to go into your daughter's room . . .'

'You're scarcely suggesting,' Ashton said when the inspector had stopped speaking, 'that Brigid would feel sufficient animosity towards Mrs Lockwood – '

'I don't know that I'm suggesting anything at all,' Kenward said with massive tolerance. 'Any more than I'm suggesting anything specific about Meacham.'

'The fact that Mrs Lockwood's husband has just eaten a poison sandwich doesn't make the slightest difference to the fact that she's a first-class bitch. Where I go and what I do are nothing in the world to do with her.' Brigid was standing with her back to the fireplace in one of the downstairs sitting-rooms where her father had run her to earth. She had been sprawled in a wing chair listening with closed eyes to the radio, but as soon as Mike came storming in with a 'So there you are, my girl!' she had sprung to her feet and taken up a Joan-of-Arc-at-the-stake stance before the luxuriant mass of pink and white blooms arching from a pottery urn on the summer hearth.

Mercifully there had been no one else in the room, though Mike would have felt quite capable of seizing her by the collar and jerking her to her feet in front of a roomful of witnesses.

'Where you go and what you do are something to do with me,' he said now with a savage frown. The row had been flashing and thundering for four or five minutes. 'When I tell you to stay in your room, you'll stay in your room. To have to sit there in front of Kenward and have him tell me that my own daughter – '

'That's all you think about!' she broke in furiously. 'How you look. How everything affects you. You're supposed to pay some attention to the way things affect me as well, you know.'

'Running round half the night with a load of yobbos. Getting up to God knows what.'

'You think every boy's a yobbo, you don't know the first thing about them. You'd like me to go round in a yashmak with a chaperon.'

And a ruddy good idea! shrieked some primitive portion of his being. Aloud he said with force, 'Telling lies! Stooping to deceit – '

'You're supposed to be a detective!' she cried with scorn. 'You haven't detected much about human beings. If you grind a person down and try and lock them up and never let them go anywhere – what do you expect? Of course they'll tell lies. If they've got any spirit.' She glowered at him, her look dark, stubborn, fiercely individual. And suddenly he saw with a shock of astonishment and recognition that the face opposite him, the face that fifteen years ago had given him its first delicate flower-like smile from among the muslin draperies, had in some mysterious way slowly and imperceptibly transformed itself into a mirror image, and was now his own face, looking back at him.

Such a beautiful, calm, warm evening. Henry walked with a light, buoyant step along the road towards his cottage. On the grassy banks the curdy heads of weeds gleamed in the sweet-smelling twilight.

It had been an unusually long day – it seemed half a lifetime since he had set out for Oakfield in the fresh bright morning. But he felt far from tired. Wide awake, cheerful, stimulated, really rather happy. All day long he had mixed with people on equal terms, and occasionally on terms of superiority. His opinions had been asked and, what was more, listened to. Eyes had looked at him with a lingering gaze, speculation had moved across faces that were turned towards his. He had sat down to dinner at Oakfield. And on one occasion he had leaned forward and addressed Pauline coolly and confidently by her Christian name. She had given no sign of resentment or astonishment, she had in fact given no sign of any reaction at all, she had continued to look down at the table, her fingers still rocking a knife against the edge of a plate.

And furthermore, Henry said to himself with the beginnings of merriment mounting inside him, Detective-Inspector Kenward is becoming rather interested in me. He had a brief clear vision of himself walking easily and briskly along the road as if he were looking down at his own figure from a considerable height. He could see himself quite distinctly, the set of the head, the swing of the shoulders. Henry Whittall, suspect. It gave him a strange exuberant feeling.

Sergeant Trevitt's eyes had barely rested on him. But then Trevitt had never been what you would call brilliant. Henry had known Trevitt in one capacity or another all his life and had never been unduly impressed by him.

But Kenward was different. Kenward was no fool. And Kenward was very definitely beginning to ask himself if Henry Whittall might possibly be a murderer.

He paused, looked about him at the full-fledged trees, threw back his head and let the merriment bubble out in loud and echoing laughter.

'No, don't go round the back. Walk right in through the front door,' Brigid said commandingly into the receiver. 'I'll be on the look-out for you.'

'You're sure it's all right?' Ian asked. 'I don't want to get you into trouble.'

Brigid gave a short dramatic laugh. 'I'm in about as much trouble as I can possibly get into at this moment, you can't very well make my position worse.'

'I must be back here by eleven, you do understand that?' Ian reminded her. 'I can't be late for the show.' But he didn't in the least object to popping over to Westerhill for an hour or two. The combination of Brigid Ashton and a sudden, mysterious death was powerfully attractive. And her father actually lending a hand in the investigation!

'I'll be with you in twenty minutes,' he said. 'Try and lay some coffee on. Plenty of it. Good and strong.'

'I'll take those letters down to the post for you,' Sergeant Trevitt said to his landlady. 'I'd like a breath of air.'

He let himself out into the gossamer darkness and set off up the road at a good pace. He reached the pillar box and dropped the letters in, turned into a side street and strode along with his head down and his hands thrust into his pockets. Still perfectly possible that Lockwood's death had been an accident. Discovering that Marion Lockwood might have allowed him to eat a sandwich intended for herself didn't alter that possibility.

But suppose it wasn't an accident – suppose it was murder. And suppose – and it was only supposition as far as he could see – that Marion Lockwood had been the intended victim, then he couldn't for the life of him see how Henry Whittall could be seriously included in the list of suspects. Whittall had been absolutely potty about Marion donkey's years ago when they were all young, he could have no conceivable reason now for poisoning her.

But Godfrey Barratt . . . ah, what about Barratt? True, he'd been besotted about Marion too in his time. But that was long ago and doubtless seemed to him these days no more than a foolish infatuation of his youth. If her death would solve his pressing financial problems, he might have been more than ready to consider it. Marion could expect a legacy from Miss Tillard, who seemed to be in pretty poor health – she was in any case far from young, she might be expected to close her eyes for good before very much longer. Trevitt came to an abrupt halt; it had suddenly occurred to him that it was quite possible that someone could be actively hurrying Miss Tillard towards that final closing of the eyes. He stood frowning, considering the point. Then he raised his shoulders, dismissing it for the moment, directing his thoughts back to Godfrey Barratt. If

Marion Lockwood had eaten the fatal sandwich instead of her husband, then Miss Tillard's money – or the bulk of it – would come sooner or later to Pauline Barratt, which was pretty much the same thing as saying to Godfrey Barratt; he seemed to be very much the head of his household.

It now seemed that Miss Tillard possessed a fair-sized fortune. And it was not at all unlikely that Barratt could have been helping himself to some of it. Possibly to a substantial portion of it. What if Miss Tillard had died suddenly and Barratt had found himself being called on to account for his part in handling her affairs? What if he had had to explain away the non-existence of sizeable holdings of stock earmarked perhaps as Marion's share? How very much simpler just to sprinkle a little cyanide on Marion's roast pork, silence for ever the mouth that might ask awkward questions.

Trevitt's musings had brought him to a little square with a statue, a circle of lawn, a dozen rose-bushes and a stone bench. He sat down, tilted back his head and stared up at the marble features of some long-dead benefactor of the Chilford citizenry. Pauline Barratt, always a good deal quieter than her sister, more purposeful, more efficient . . . He passed a hand across his face. Might not the same consideration that applied to Barratt apply also to his wife? Was it credible that she was unaware of her husband's monetary difficulties? Would she also not be desperately anxious to hang on to Oakfield, to secure a prosperous future for her sons? Hadn't she always wanted Barratt, even as a gangling schoolgirl? Might she not be prepared to go to extreme lengths to foster his interests now? And if those interests seemed to demand the removal of her sister, had she any particular reason to be all that fond of Marion?

In the distance a church clock struck the hour. He stood up, stretched his arms, emptied his mind Might as well get back, make sure of an early night. He had covered a quarter of a mile when a thought halted him sharply on the edge of the pavement . . . I suppose Miss Tillard is quite safe in that hospital bed? I suppose no one could actually get at her? In the event, that is, of someone wishing to get at her . . .

Is it actually within the bounds of possibility, Mike asked

147

himself with incredulous astonishment, that what my eyes perceive is my daughter Brigid sitting on a sofa two inches away from a long-haired yobbo, both of them swilling coffee as bold as brass? After all he had said! What was the use of opening his mouth at all? He put out a hand and made a helpless gesture, pawing at the air in angry frustration. Then he took a grip on himself, marched into the hall and strode up to the laughing, chatting pair.

'Oh, hello!' Brigid glanced up at him with a bright, challenging look. 'Did you have a nice stroll? How rosy your cheeks are! And how quickly you're breathing! Have you been running? You ought not to run at your age, it might prove fatal.' She turned her head briefly. 'This is Ian Ripley. I believe you've heard me mention him,' she added demurely. 'This kindly, middle-aged gentleman is my father,' she said to Ian, unable to resist giving Mike a bulging grin.

The lad got to his feet. 'I'm delighted to meet you,' he said with every appearance of deep sincerity. 'Brigid's been telling me what she knows about the case.' He had an extraordinarily low-pitched voice with a kind of gravelly edge to it, rather intriguing. 'I can't tell you how interesting it is to me,' he added. He was incredibly thin but in a dynamic hair-spring sort of way. 'I hope you don't mind my coming over like this.'

'Father doesn't mind at all,' Brigid said with a wide, charming smile. 'He simply dotes on young people. He is both worldly-wise and tolerant. A most unusual combination, particularly in the provinces. Have some coffee?' she added to Mike in more everyday tones. 'There's plenty in the pot and it's absolutely scalding.'

'Well, yes, thank you, I will have some.' Mike's irritation seemed to have abruptly subsided. He found himself sitting down in a chair edged forward by Ian. Actually, to be fair, the lad had very reasonable manners. And his hair looked clean and well cared for, and really after all not too excessively long. He found it a trifle difficult to recall just exactly why he had been so fearful for Brigid, so anxious to keep a tight grip on her.

'I presume you can't rule out completely the possibility of accident.' Ian leaned forward and fixed an earnest, questioning eye on Mike.

'He's very interested in law,' Brigid said with a strong dash of pride. 'He's going to read law when he goes to the university next year.'

'Is that so?' Mike felt the ground slipping a little more swiftly from under his feet. 'You never told me,' he added to Brigid, faintly accusing.

She gave him back a long, direct, almost adult look. 'You never asked.'

No, I didn't, did I? he said to himself. I was pretty free with the statements and commands, but plain and simple asking, no, I didn't seem to get around to that. He turned to Ian. 'It's perfectly possible that Lockwood's death was an accident.' No real harm in discussing one or two very superficial and in no way confidential aspects of the case with the lad. And he was deeply pleased to see a smile begin to turn up the corners of Brigid's lips, the expression of – gratitude? – affection? – relief? that came into her eyes.

'If it turns out to have been an accident –' Ian said thoughtfully. He paused and frowned. 'No, I can't see how it could ever be definitely known that it was an accident. I suppose what I mean is, if it is decided that no certain proven alternative to the accident theory exists –' He paused again, jabbed with a finger at the arm of the sofa. 'Then I imagine it would be an open verdict. Not a very satisfactory conclusion for any of the persons involved. Least of all, I should think, for the widow.'

It was no good, he couldn't sleep. A warm night and his brain still active. Kenward abandoned the struggle, opened his eyes and watched the restless images succeed each other in the darkness . . . the picnic spot . . . the kitchen at Oakfield . . . Barratt . . . Whittall . . . Meacham . . . He had a sudden picture of Bessie standing beside her new husband. He let out a fragmentary groan. Oh I hope it's all right for her, he thought without conviction, I hope Meacham doesn't turn out to be just a well-spoken villain.

Another thought reared up at him, driving away the last trace of drowsiness . . . Suppose Meacham did have a record – or some other strong reason for wanting to shut Marion Lockwood's mouth? And suppose it was Meacham who had given the sandwich its deadly flavour, had slipped the packet into her anorak, why then his aim had misfired, she was still alive, Meacham was still at her mercy. Would he realize that she had already opened her mouth about him, had spoken to the police about her suspicions? Good God, he thought with sharp horror, what if Meacham didn't realize it? What if he didn't know Marion had already been interviewed by himself, what if he thought she'd been allowed an interval of peace and recuperation until tomorrow?

He slid out from between the sheets and fumbled for his slippers, careful not to disturb his wife in the other bed. What if Meacham were to open Marion Lockwood's door in the still night, move silently over to where she lay asleep? What if she were to be found tomorrow morning with a knife through her heart – a stocking round her neck – and nothing whatever to say whose hand had eased open her bedroom door? He went noiselessly out into the passage, crept down towards the kitchen and set about making himself a good strong cup of tea.

Come now, he said bracingly to himself as he stood waiting for the kettle to boil, there's no need to get agitated. We took Meacham's fingerprints; if he is an old lag he'll be well aware we didn't take them just to while away the time, so he'll know that strangling Mrs Lockwood in the night wouldn't do him any good, he'll realize we'll know what there is to be known about him tomorrow as soon as we get his official record, he wouldn't have a cat in hell's chance of keeping that information from Bessie, he'd know the game was up the moment Yarrow got a grip on his fingers this afternoon. It's OK. Relax, forget it, drink your tea and go back upstairs, get some sleep, going to be a long hard day tomorrow.

He was pouring the milk into a cup when it struck him that if Meacham actually was a villain and if he had a particle of sense he'd rise from his bed in the night and pack a bag, open the back door of Oakfield and let himself out, vanish back to wherever he'd been before his path crossed Bessie Forrest's . . . In which case, Kenward thought philosophically, we shall have to exert ourselves a trifle in order to snatch him back in again.

He raised the cup to his lips. Ah well, he thought with a shrug, the morning will tell. If Meacham's there to greet us, then he's either as innocent as the babe unborn – or he has some other highly compelling reason for staying on at Oakfield. Some reason I haven't yet been able to think of.

Ashton watched Brigid go along the corridor and let herself into her bedroom. She turned in the doorway and raised a hand, gave him a friendly good-night smile. He opened his own door, closed it with care and stood for a moment listening, then he relaxed. Jean was long ago asleep.

He crossed over to the window, gently parted the curtains, looking down at the shadowy garden, hearing the last sounds of Ian Ripley's motor-bike fading in the distance.

A sharp lad, Ripley, exceptionally sharp. Mike had found himself enlarging on the case a good deal more than he'd intended to. He bit his lip, remembering more than one piece of indiscretion. Didn't do to sit up late talking when you were working on a case, there was always a tendency to say more than you ought. Still, no real damage done. If Ripley was going to take up law as a career, he'd be smart enough to know it wasn't always wise to go round shooting his mouth off . . . Which is something I might do well to remember myself, Mike told himself wryly.

He let the curtains drop back into place, he began to undress. As he was putting his shirt over the back of a chair he was suddenly pierced by a moment's acute terror for Brigid. Oh God, he thought, leaning heavily on the chair, she wasn't in any way involved in the business of the sandwiches – she couldn't – surely –

He put both hands up to his face. Adolescence – a wild, unstable time – suppose she had wanted to give Mrs Lockwood a fright? Play a spiteful joke on her? Not realizing the extreme danger of what she did?

Then panic began to subside. No, of course not, no question of it. The adolescent might be a tricky bird but Brigid simply wasn't as downright stupid as that . . . as malicious . . . as unbalanced . . . No, of course not.

He stood for quite some time looking into the darkness, then very slowly he set about taking off the rest of his clothes.

Chapter 17

Godfrey Barratt had scarcely closed an eye all night. By half past five he could stand it no longer. He slid silently out of bed, dressed with hardly a whisper of sound and very gently went out of the bedroom, into the corridor and down the stairs to the kitchen where he put the kettle on for a cup of tea and made a sketchy sort of toilet while he waited for the kettle to boil.

Not a soul stirring in the house. Twenty minutes, half an hour before Bessie would yawn her way along the passage. He finished his tea and went silently out into the bright new-morning garden, fresh, sweet, stirring with energetic birds. He moved about the beds and borders, tidying, straightening, plucking out defiant weeds, and saw with surprised relief after a fairly tolerable lapse of time that it was almost seven o'clock by his wrist-watch. He went back into the house which was beginning to echo with voices and footsteps, doors opening and closing, the sound of running water.

He let himself into his study and switched on the radio; the news had just begun . . . A bomb incident, a minor train crash, the forthcoming visit of a head of state . . . surely there'll be something about it today, he thought, it's not going to be another twenty-four hours before they announce the meeting . . . and then, mercifully, just when he had all but given up hope, the final item, the Minister and the top men from Osmond's, talks to begin at ten o'clock this morning, impossible to say how long they would take.

He reached over and switched off the radio, leaned back with his eyes closed, his arms hanging loosely over the sides of the chair. He felt worn out, strained almost beyond the point of endurance; it was fully five minutes before he could bring himself to sit up. He pulled himself to his feet, crossed the room and stared into the mirror. Unshaven, bleary-eyed. A fine way for the head of the house to look. And the police due back – when? What time had the inspector said? He couldn't remember, but it was sure to be early. Kenward hadn't in the least struck him as a man who would lie in bed and listen to the grass growing outside.

He let out a long groan, passed his hand across his face and then stood up straight and tall, threw back his shoulders, assumed a look of cheerful casualness, strode over to the door, flung it open and went briskly along the corridor and through the hall.

'Thomas Pickersgill.' Kenward repeated the awkward syllables clearly, steadied the receiver against his left ear and with his right hand made a note of the name.

'Alias Charles Farquhar,' said the detached voice at the other end of the line. 'Also alias Frederick Shelmerdine – I rather like that one – Guy Balfour . . . '

'How many names have you got there?' Kenward asked with a trace of irritability.

'Ten, no, twelve. Do you want them all?'

'Not at this very moment. I'd be interested to know if the name Edgar Meacham's on the list, that's all.'

'Yes, half-way down. Good plausible name. He went a bit mad with one or two. Nigel de la Warr. Can you beat that? Pretty well asking to be clapped into gaol the moment he uttered those sounds at a hotel desk.'

'He very probably was,' Kenward said. 'Got the list of convictions?'

'Yes, all small-time. Want it now?'

'Don't bother, Yarrow can pick it up with the other stuff. Just the gist, let's have the flavour of it.' He jotted down a date or two, the names of a couple of prisons, sums of money, a few incidental details.

'Born in Thetstone,' said the voice, adding an address, a date. 'Married Florence Agnes Green –'

'Married?' Kenward's voice took on a sharper note.

'Yes. Deserted the lady thirty-two years ago . . . ' The voice continued to eject gobbets of information; Kenward frowned down at the floor. Poor Bessie . . . He became aware that the voice had assumed an edge of irritation. 'I said: Do you want the wife contacted?'

'Oh – yes, right away.' Kenward sighed. He didn't in the slightest degree relish having to break the news to Bessie. 'It'll probably be a question of standing trial for bigamy,' he said heavily . . . 'If not for something a good deal graver . . .'

'The other name you gave me,' the voice went on. 'Paget.' Ah yes – Paget; Kenward had forgotten about Paget in his concern over Bessie.

'Anything known?' he asked.

'No, nothing. Army record exactly as stated. Good conduct, did well in point of fact –'

When Kenward rang off a few minutes later he stood looking down at the notes he had made. Should he tell Bessie right away and get it over with? Or see both the Meachams together, watch their reactions to what he had to say in case something of significance might slip out? Was there any point in interviewing Meacham – or Pickersgill – on his own, first, in case by any wild improbable chance there might be some shred of comfort to be discovered for Bessie? He continued to stare at the notes, at the names and dates. He shook his head slowly, sadly. Not much in the way of comfort there. Ah well. Unpleasant duties rarely obliged by getting up and going away. Nothing for it but to press on with it. He squared his shoulders and set his feet reluctantly in motion.

'I had a word with my niece last night. She's a secretary in the design office at Alpha, a sharp girl, not a great deal passes her by.' A tall, heavy man, Sergeant Kimber, shrewd, calm eyes; born and bred in Barbridge.

Trevitt nodded encouragingly. Not a man to pester with questions, Kimber; sit tight and let him talk.

'It seems Lockwood and Fiona Brooke,' Kimber said, 'were pretty thick during the last year. You know how it is in a place like this, you can never really go anywhere without someone spotting you.'

'And Jourdan?' Ashton asked.

Kimber gave a little grunt. 'According to my niece, half the girls in the typing pool have set their caps at Jourdan.' His gaze, intelligent, pleasant, rested on Ashton. 'He's been running after Miss Brooke for quite some time, apparently. They rather think he caught up with her in the last week or so, after Lockwood took himself off on holiday.'

'It must be a great comfort to you to remember how happy you were together.' Wyn Paget had made this kind of utterance on so many occasions in the course of her forty-eight years that she had reached a stage where she more than half believed that her cheering statements were true. She leaned forward and patted Marion's hand. 'Such a dreadful accident.' She shook her head. 'Such an appalling waste.'

Marion took a delicately embroidered handkerchief from her pocket and dabbed at her eyes. 'Yes, indeed, a terrible accident.' She gave Wyn a brave, watery look. In the course of his last interview with her Inspector Kenward had done a little advancing and retreating around the notion of her husband as a model of devotion, but she had simply allowed his words to flow over her. She had made no response except for a couple of gentle nods when he had finished. If he had sat beside her for the rest of the week and lobbed his insinuations at her she wouldn't have opened her mouth and told him how she had seen Fiona Brooke clasped in Stephen's arms. She hadn't the faintest intention of ever mentioning the incident to a living soul. To her unspeakable relief, the picture of the two of them standing locked together was growing less distinct before her eyes. It was beginning to seem possible that in the course of time it would fade completely from her mind, allowing her to remember Stephen as it was right and proper he should be remembered, loyal, loving, upright and true.

'Yes, certainly I was friendly with Mr Lockwood.' Fiona looked down at her hands; she seemed to be examining with keen attention the shape of her fingernails. 'We sometimes had a meal together.' She knows we can't prove any more than that, Ashton thought.

'If I were to suggest to you,' Trevitt said in a pleasant, idle tone, 'that there is a certain amount of gossip to the effect that Stephen Lockwood might have formed the intention of divorcing his wife and marrying you –'

'Then I would suggest to you that a firm like Alpha breeds

gossip.' She spread out her left hand on the surface of her desk, studied the texture of the skin. 'I believe there is also some chatter about myself and Mr Jourdan. Quite possibly about one or two other colleagues I've scarcely spoken to.' Still this difficulty about meeting the eye of her interrogator, Ashton noted. As if in answer to his unspoken observation she raised her head and flicked a glance at him, so rapidly that it was gone before he had time to read it. 'One becomes accustomed to that kind of speculation,' she said with a trace of a smile. 'I would have expected police officers...' To be a little more sophisticated in these matters ... the rest of her sentence formed itself in his mind.

Trevitt changed the subject abruptly, touching now on times and places, exactly how she had spent the time after coming down to breakfast at Oakfield yesterday morning, precisely when she and Jourdan had left Westerhill.

She seemed to relax as his voice ranged over these purely factual matters, as if she felt herself now on safer ground. But she had the opportunity, Ashton thought, she could easily have slipped into the kitchen while the room was deserted, the work of a moment to take down the tin from the shelf, season a sandwich ... She and Jourdan had taken a packed lunch with them on Saturday morning when they had gone for a drive along the coast; she had had a chance then to see the way in which the picnic food was prepared, to have a good look round the kitchen.

But she would scarcely be able to go straight up to a crowded shelf and pick out the one tin containing cyanide ... or would she? He closed his eyes for a moment, trying to conjure up a picture of the tin. It had originally held drinking chocolate; on the pale blue label someone had pencilled the word CYANIDE in large capitals. Suppose Fiona had been standing in the kitchen on the Saturday morning, chatting to Bessie, telling her what time she and Jourdan expected to be back, for instance, or asking about places of interest in the neighbourhood. She could have been studying the shelves as she talked, without any purpose whatever, simply allowing her eyes to wander at random from incipient boredom. She could have seen the tin with its heavy lettering, could have been arrested by the uncompromising syllables: CYANIDE. Bessie might have been called from the kitchen, Fiona might have reached up and taken down the tin, removed the lid and glanced inside, replaced the tin on the shelf, all out of nothing more than idle curiosity.

But by Monday morning a plan might have formed in her mind, she could have remembered the tin – or the very existence of the tin might have been the chance factor that set in motion a certain train of thought in her brain.

Had she done it? He sat back and looked at her with a casual-seeming scrutiny. She was very pale but then she had been very pale when he had first seen her, on the evening she had come to Oakfield. It was probably her natural colouring, it seemed to accord well enough with her smooth black hair and green-grey eyes. She certainly didn't appear to have been in any way laid low by shock. Here she was, at work this morning – but then she'd most likely have dragged herself to work this morning even if she had been half dead, she would scarcely wish to advertise to the entire firm how much she'd been affected by Lockwood's death.

I suppose she *was* badly affected by his death? he suddenly asked himself with a feeling of shock, of having been abruptly catapulted from one mental position to another totally un-suspected. Did it after all suit her book for Lockwood to vanish so swiftly from the scene? Lockwood was the person who had died, had it after all been Lockwood who had been the intended victim? He felt confusion rush across his brain, he couldn't work it out, sitting there in the little office; he had to let it go, make a mental note to worry at it during the drive back to Oakfield.

He became aware that Trevitt was getting to his feet, that the interview was at an end.

'We have your private address,' Trevitt said, looking down at his notebook. 'And your phone number. I take it you'll be avail-able if we should wish to get in touch with you again for any reason?'

She remained seated, tilted her head back so that she would have been looking up into Trevitt's face except that her eyes were half closed, her gaze was directed down at the neat pile of papers on her desk.

'I'm not thinking of going away,' she said clearly. 'If that's what you mean.'

Trevitt gave a sharp nod. In the doorway he turned, spoke over his shoulder. 'The inquest's this afternoon. In Chilford. It'll be opened and adjourned in all probability. I don't know if you thought of attending. If you'd be interested.'

She put up a hand to her face. A tiny sound escaped her lips. Ashton looked at her without subterfuge. She had thought their visit over, she had fed out her resources inch by inch, she had just managed to keep going; when she had tilted back her head and spoken to Trevitt it had been with the very last shred of her emotional stamina. And when he had turned at the door and levelled at her one final dart it had been too much, there had been nothing left. Ashton felt a wave of compassion sweep over him, a feeling of deep revulsion for a profession in which inescapably one human being was called on to push another to the limits of endurance.

She shook her head, trying to indicate: No, I am not interested in attending the inquest. She began to cry, silently, painfully, she dropped her head on to her hands.

There was no change in the expression on Trevitt's face. He stood watching her for a moment, then he took a step back towards the desk. Oh for God's sake, leave her alone! Ashton wanted to cry out. But he said nothing, stood waiting for it to be over.

'Something you would like to tell us?' Trevitt said gently. 'Something you would like to add to what you've already said? Some little change perhaps in your statement?'

She kept her face buried in her hands. She shook her head with strong, almost frenzied movements. Every line of her body willed them to go. Trevitt jerked a look at Ashton but Mike wouldn't meet his eye, wouldn't ally himself to the scene by so much as a conspiracy of glances. Trevitt raised his shoulders in a dismissive shrug, turned again to the door. Without a backward look Ashton followed him out of the room. Neither man spoke until they were out of the building and half-way across the car park.

'Oh, I fancy Miss Fiona Brooke,' Trevitt said with deep pleasure and Ashton knew beyond a doubt that he wasn't referring to her charms as a woman.

'You've nothing to go on,' he said. 'Nothing concrete.' Nothing as solid, for instance, as a fingerprint. A jumble of blurred prints on the lid of the tin in the kitchen. Only two recognizable prints, one belonging to Bessie Meacham and the other to Pauline Barratt. Both of them would have had good reason to handle the tin in the days when it had held drinking chocolate, there was no proof whatever that they had handled it since.

Trevitt halted by the car. 'Instinct,' he said, still with that elated look. 'A hunch. Worth a lot of so-called evidence.' He opened the car door. 'A woman's crime,' he said with authority. 'Poison. The weapon of the weak.' He stopped abruptly and gave Ashton a startled glance. He lowered himself into the driving seat, sat staring out through the windscreen. And Ashton knew as clearly as if Trevitt had told him, that at the moment of speaking his final words it was Brigid's face that had risen up before his mind.

Chapter 18

'I must say I think I'm getting to be rather good at making coffee.' Brigid poured the scalding liquid into the cups in a long bubbling stream. 'Here you are.' Black for Ian, always black in the mornings while he was trying to come to grips with the new day after being up till all hours at the Sweet Potato. Cream and sugar, plenty of sugar, for Bessie, who had as usual been up since cock-crow.

The pair at the table were deep in discussion. They took their coffee from her with abstracted looks, stretching out groping hands and drawing the saucers towards them across the table, forgetting even to murmur routine thanks.

'And it has been your invariable custom to wrap the sandwiches first in a sheet of greaseproof paper, fold it, pleat the top, then insert it into a greaseproof bag?' Ian was leaning forward with his elbows on the table, his head sunk between his hunched shoulders, so close to Bessie that their foreheads almost touched; he was frowning fiercely into her eyes.

'I can show you the very greaseproof paper,' Bessie said in a strongly dramatic tone. 'Hanging up there.' Without turning her head she jerked a thumb in the direction of a sheaf dangling by a loop of string from a nail on the edge of a shelf. 'And the greaseproof bags.' She stabbed a forceful finger at a drawer in the dresser.

'And you then took a ball-point pen –'

'Or it might be one of them fibre-tipped,' Bessie interrupted, inflamed by now with the terrible passion for exact detail that appeared to have seized everyone who had held a conversation with her since lunch-time yesterday.

'Ball-point or fibre-tipped.' Ian winged a single baffled thought at the twin notions, unable for the moment to assess any deep significance either way, having regretfully to let it go . . . for the present, anyway. 'And you wrote on the outside of each bag –'

I don't know which of them is worse, Brigid said to herself, springing to her feet with an impatient movement. She began a tour of the kitchen, opening drawers, looking into cupboards. She came on a tin full of freshly-baked Garibaldi biscuits and ate half a dozen while she continued her prowl.

As she passed the kitchen window she glanced out and saw the inquiring face of the lad from the village, the one who had been on the golf-course. She raised her hand and gestured towards the back door, glad to have someone to talk to.

'Inspector Kenward wanted to speak to me again,' the lad said with considerable importance as she led him into the kitchen. 'He spent quite a long time talking to me this morning.'

'Would you like some coffee?' Brigid reached up to the shelf for a beaker.

'Oh yes, please. I had to go over what I saw at the golf-course again, every bit of it. Inspector Kenward kept trying to make me change my story.' He gave a proud, pleased movement of his head. 'But I wouldn't. Not a single word. I couldn't. Because it was the truth I told him in the first place.'

Brigid let out a huge noisy sigh. 'Do you want some of these currant biscuits?' They were gathering up the last superb crumbs when Ian leaned back in his chair and allowed his eyes to rove about the room. His gaze suddenly focused on the lad. 'Who're you?' he asked sharply.

The boy looked at him with swelling pride. 'I was at the golf-course when Mr Lockwood died. I'm the one – '

Ian jumped up, knocking his chair over. 'I want to talk to you.'

Brigid had only just time to cram the lid on and whisk the tin back to where she'd found it before Bessie came out of her trance and the sternly practical light of every day returned to her eyes.

'I suppose Bessie has to know.' Meacham had begun to frame the words as a question tinged with the last microscopic vestige of optimism but in the moment of actually speaking them they turned hopelessly and finally into a statement of fact. He sat looking at Kenward with a still face, his hands loosely clasped.

All part of his professional equipment, the inspector reminded himself sternly, brusquely dismissing a foolish inclination to pity; he knows well enough how to play the lost and lonely lad. He raised his shoulders fractionally. 'You know as well as I do,' he said in a voice stripped of feeling, 'what the form is.'

Meacham gave one small nod and remained motionless like a man waiting for the executioner. And then Yarrow stuck his head in at the door to summon Kenward to the phone. He stood up with a sensation of relief. A few minutes gained before he had to send for Bessie and wipe the smile off her face, possibly for ever. He sighed deeply as he thumped his feet irritably down on the polished floor. Why the hell did I ever become a copper? he asked himself for the thousandth time. Appalling hours, ludicrous pay, shot at from all sides, permanently savaged by frustration, handed all the lousiest jobs by the community – opening your mouth to announce disaster to the widowed, the fatherless, the abandoned, deserted, betrayed, deceived . . .

He picked up the receiver, resigned to yet another thumb in the eye from life. 'Kenward here.' He began to listen, staring gloomily down at his feet.

'Your inquiry about Florence Agnes Pickersgill,' said the official voice. Kenward jerked himself up straight.

'Yes? She's been contacted? She's willing to give evidence?'

'I fear not,' said the voice, bland, detached. 'It seems the lady is dead. Found by a neighbour, apparently. Lying at the foot of a stepladder with her neck broken.'

'As a matter of fact I would like to go,' Jean Ashton said with a frank avowal of curiosity in her tone. The inquest on Stephen Lockwood was to be held at three o'clock. 'But of course it's impossible with the twins.' She gave a regretful shake of her head.

'I tell you what,' Mike said. 'Meet me afterwards, say half-past three, could be a bit earlier or later, hard to be exact. We can all have tea together, you and me and the twins. You can wait in the teashop, I'll join you there, then it won't matter if I'm a few minutes late. I'll ask Bessie, she's sure to know a decent café in that area.'

'Right.' Jean looked pleased. Always glad of an opportunity to dress herself up and present herself in a public place, even if it was only a teashop in a seaside town. She glanced at her watch. 'I think I'll find the twins now and take them out for a walk along the beach before lunch.' She looked at her husband without any very great expectation. 'I suppose there's no chance of your coming along too?'

'I'm afraid not.' He'd just come back from Barbridge, hadn't even got as far as reporting to Kenward, had encountered Jean on the terrace. He nodded towards Trevitt waiting a few yards away. 'I'll be busy for some time yet. You go off and enjoy yourself.'

How silent the bungalow was now! Theresa Onil felt the stillness wind itself about her as she sorted through a box of papers. In the hall the phone rang suddenly and she got to her feet with a feeling of relief.

Mrs Barratt, asking if there was any news of Miss Tillard. 'I'm going along to the hospital about tea-time,' Pauline said. 'I'll ask if they'll let me see her. I shall be in Chilford then, of course, because of the inquest.' She paused briefly. 'I don't know if you'd be interested in coming too? I could pick you up at about twenty to three.'

'You're very kind,' Theresa said. 'But there's no need to trouble you. I'm not interested in attending the inquest. I can't really think of any reason why I should be.'

'In my own mind,' Ian Ripley said with immense earnestness, 'I call my theory Retaining Control of the Sandwiches.'

'Indeed?' Mike said politely. He managed to sneak a look at his watch. Ten to two. He'd slipped out into the garden for a breath of air before the rest of the day bulldozed its way towards him; Ian had materialized before him at the bend of a path, overflowing with ideas. A few yards away Brigid stood plucking leaves from a bush, stripping the leaves into skeletons, flinging at the pair of them from time to time a glance powerfully suggestive of barely-controlled impatience.

'If the murderer was even reasonably intelligent – ' Ian began when Mike interrupted him.

'It has not been established that there was a murder.'

'Assuming that there was a murder,' Ian began again, drawing a deep breath, 'and that the murderer was even reasonably intelligent, then he – I will refer to the murderer as he, although it could just as easily have been a woman – then he must have been at the picnic in order to retain control of the sandwiches.'

Mike frowned. 'I can't quite see – '

'Only one sandwich was laced with cyanide – '

Mike frowned even more heavily. 'And how, pray, did you come by that piece of information?' Surely he hadn't told the lad every damn thing he knew or suspected?

Ian sighed and waved his hands, unwilling to waste time particularizing about Mrs Meacham, Brigid, the schoolboy, the various chatty constables about the place. 'The murderer simply could not afford to let the wrong person pick out the fatal sandwich. All that that would achieve would be a totally pointless death and an end to his chance of being able to have a second go at his intended victim.'

'Ye . . . es.' Mike was beginning to grow intrigued, his attention was deflected from pinpointing the source of Ian's facts.

'Therefore the murderer must have been at the picnic, unless – ' Ian paused for emphasis – 'unless there was absolute

163

certainty, and I do mean absolute certainty, that the poisoned sandwich could be eaten only by the victim. To give you an example, suppose for instance the sandwiches were very strongly flavoured with garlic and it was a known fact that everyone at the picnic except the intended victim loathed and detested garlic, while the victim loved the stuff, then I would call that a total certainty.'

'Provided always,' Mike said immediately, 'that the garlicky sandwich was known in advance to be a garlicky sandwich. Otherwise it might only disclose its nature at the first bite and that would be too late as far as the biter was concerned.'

'Good point,' Ian said with surprised approval. 'I had rather overlooked that. But I don't think it invalidates my theory.' He sent a swift mental look over his brainchild; it still seemed pretty good. 'It is known with certainty that the roast pork sandwiches made up yesterday for both Mr and Mrs Lockwood were identical, same flavouring and trimmings. Therefore the murderer could not rely on the poisoned sandwich being eaten only by the victim, so he must, according to my theory, have been present at the picnic, which rules out a number of people I am quite sure the police suspect. Mr Barratt for instance, and Mrs Barratt, Mr and Mrs Meacham –'

'Hold on!' Mike said abruptly. 'I think you're forgetting that the poisoned sandwich was in fact eaten by the wrong person.'

'Aha!' Ian said at once in triumph. 'I was coming to that.'

'When you formulated your theory,' Mike went on, continuing his own train of thought, 'you were, I suppose, assuming ideal conditions for the murder and in point of fact these ideal conditions could not have been fulfilled, because the plan misfired and the wrong person got the cyanide.'

Ian shook his head violently. 'You will keep assuming that the wrong person got the poison. I maintain that the person who got it was the person who was intended to get it. I stick to my theory of an intelligent murderer who must retain control of the sandwiches, who must be present at the picnic. Ask yourself what actually happened. What happened was that Stephen Lockwood died. And the sandwich that killed him was directed into his hands by his wife. She murdered him and she intended to murder him.'

Mike stared at him, frowning, sinking his teeth into his top lip.

'No other person,' Ian said with force, 'could know for certain which of the two Lockwoods would eat the poisoned sandwich that had been made up to please the taste of both of them. But Marion Lockwood could be certain, she actually went over to his coat on the golf-course, she put the sandwiches into his pocket. She had no idea anyone was watching her.' He studied Ashton's face, saw that he had made an impression. He drove home his point. 'All considerations about the wrappings are of no consequence. Mrs Lockwood could have added or subtracted wrappings pretty well as she chose, she could have omitted or altered or substituted or destroyed one or other or both sets of wrappings. The sandwiches are the important fact and she directed the poisoned sandwich into her husband's hands.'

Footsteps came along the path behind them. 'Here's Sergeant Trevitt,' Ian said with a fierce sense of disappointment, knowing that Ashton was about to be snatched away; he could have talked to him for a great deal longer, expounding and elaborating on his theory.

'We ought to be thinking of getting along,' Trevitt said as he came up to them. 'Kenward's about ready.'

'Yes. Right.' Mike gave a last long considering look at Ian.

'You'll think about what I said?' Ian's voice had taken on a trace of hesitancy, he was suddenly just a youngster again, addressing elders. 'There could be something in it.' He felt abruptly, savagely, deflated, his compelling ideas reduced to a tangle of nonsense.

'I'll certainly think about it,' Mike said. 'Smart lad, that,' he said to Trevitt as they walked towards the house. 'Some rather interesting ideas.'

The inquest was formally opened and adjourned for a month at the request of the police, a predictable piece of procedure which occupied very little time but which nevertheless drew a sizeable crowd of curious citizens and holidaymakers.

When it was over Kenward came down the steps with a silent, occupied air. Bessie Meacham . . . he couldn't escape the thought . . . if she could by a little sprinkling of the fingers have caused Marion Lockwood to vanish from the earth . . . and if Miss Tillard were to vanish shortly afterwards . . . by a highly convenient coincidence? . . . Or a carefully planned sequence of events? . . . then Pauline Barratt would have inherited a very healthy sum of money . . . the Barratts would have been able to remain in prosperous occupation of Oakfield . . . and Edgar and Bessie Meacham would have been secure in their comfortable berth . . .

'I'll be off to join my wife, then,' said Ashton's voice just behind him. 'If that's all right with you?'

'What? Oh yes, certainly. Good of you to give us your time at all,' Kenward said in an abstracted fashion. Ashton pushed his way through the knots of onlookers and crossed the busy road. All the way to the café he was accompanied by the image of Fiona Brooke huddled over her desk, her shoulders shaking in terrible silent sobs . . . a beautiful girl grieving for the death of love? Or a woman shattered by the knowledge that she had tried to kill an inconvenient wife and had succeeded instead in killing her lover?

He found the tea-room, pushed open the door, attempted to thrust from his mind the whirligig of thoughts.

Jean was already seated at a table by the window, with the twins one on each side of her, expectantly watching the door; all three of them looked exceedingly spick and span. Kate jumped up as she caught sight of him, and waved an excited hand. She was immediately pressed back into her seat by her mother, shushed into good behaviour. But she managed to beam a bright, inquiring, welcoming look at her father as he approached the table.

'Where have you been?' she demanded before he had time to pull out a chair. She was beginning to grow a trifle mystified by the absences and disappearances he was suddenly indulging in.

He bent down and dropped a kiss on her cheek. 'Are you hungry? Are you going to have ice-cream and lots of fancy cakes?' At once she forgot her unanswered question, she smiled up at him delightedly. 'Here, have a look at this, see what you'd like.' He picked up a menu from a near-by empty table and put it in her hands.

'Nothing in the way of surprises, I suppose?' Jean said as he finally sat down. 'Everything go as expected?'

'Yes.' He felt all at once rather tired, he would be glad of some tea.

'I'm not at all sure the whole thing wasn't a pure accident,' Jean said suddenly. He shook his head at her without speaking, wearily indicating the waitress advancing towards them, the necessity for discretion. 'I'll order, don't you bother,' Jean said, recognizing the fatigue that assailed him.

He gave her a grateful look. 'Just tea for me, nothing to eat.' He sat back and half closed his eyes, let his mind drift, hearing the sounds of the tea-room begin to diminish, assume a dreamlike quality. Some little time later he felt a small hand press into his arm.

'Wake up, Daddy, drink your tea.'

He opened his eyes and smiled at Vicky. 'I wasn't asleep, just having a little rest.' He sat up, feeling quite refreshed, really a good deal more wide-awake and energetic.

'Amazing what five minutes will do,' he said cheerfully to Jean. He picked up his cup and began to drink his tea, freshly made, strong, excellent. 'A very good cup of tea.' He smiled across the table at his wife, looked idly about the room. Not too crowded, a bit on the early side yet for afternoon tea. A clean, bright place, they might come here again.

'What are you doing?' Jean's voice said sharply. He turned his head. She was looking with amused bafflement at Kate who had removed the plastic top of the salt cellar and was carefully tipping the salt into her left palm. On her hands she wore the pale beige gloves her mother had laid down on the cloth when they had taken their seats at the table. Something seemed to lay hold on Mike's brain, he felt its chilling touch spread out beneath his scalp.

Kate raised her eyes and shot her mother a mischievous, pursy smile, then she bent her head to her task again.

'You have to wear gloves for putting salt on,' Vicky said importantly. 'Kate told me.'

'It seems a very odd custom to me.' Jean smiled with holiday tolerance. Mike watched in frozen fascination as Kate leaned forward and took a cucumber sandwich from the plate in the middle of the table, carefully removed the top piece of bread with her gloved right hand and then dipped her fingers into her cupped palm, took a pinch of salt and sprinkled it over the cucumber. She repeated the dipping and sprinkling three or four times, then shook her palm over the watery slices, making sure no salt remained on her glove. She replaced the covering bread, pressed it firmly into position and sat back, delighted at the absorbed attention of the others.

'That's the way to do it,' Vicky said admiringly. 'Kate knows. Kate knows everything.'

'Not absolutely everything,' Kate said. 'A very great deal, but not everything.'

Jean began to laugh, she glanced over at Mike and abruptly ceased laughing. 'What's the matter? Aren't you feeling well?' Mike had put an elbow on the table, was supporting his forehead in his hand. 'Are you ill?' Jean asked, her voice rising. He drew a deep breath, let his arm drop from the table. His face looked tired and pale.

'Did you do that yesterday?' he said to Kate in a voice that strove after ease and lightness. 'Yesterday morning. Did you put salt on someone's sandwiches?'

He was aware of Jean's face, her brows drawn sharply together. 'Oh no!' she said under her breath. He didn't look at her, he kept his eyes fixed on Kate with a pleasant, casual expression, striving to preserve the fragile web of her attention, her concentration, to gather up the facts – if facts there were – before they slipped away and became irretrievably lost among fantasies and imaginings.

She lifted the sandwich to her lips, took a bite and pulled a face, but continued to chew with a wry, amused grimace, 'It's dreadfully salty,' she said when she had swallowed the mouthful. 'I'm not going to eat any more of that sandwich, if you don't mind. It isn't a bit nice.'

'He must be a very silly man,' Vicky said, looking over at Kate for confirmation. 'Don't you think he must be a terribly silly man?'

168

'Who, dear?' Mike said in a low clear voice, almost afraid to speak. He felt the sweat break out on his forehead. Of all the impossibly tricky customers to question, young children stood head and shoulders above the rest, darting eel-like through patterns of logic, argument, probability.

'I don't know if he's a silly man or not,' Kate said tolerantly. She burst into a peal of laughter. 'Perhaps he just likes salt.'

'Who likes salt, dear?' Jean asked her in a matter-of-fact tone. 'Someone we know?'

'Oh yes, you know him.' Kate glanced across at her sister. 'They do know him, don't they, Vicky?'

Vicky nodded energetically. 'Yes, of course they do. Why don't you have another sandwich?' she suggested. 'Without putting any salt on it this time. They're quite nice, I had one.'

'I think I will.' Kate reached out to the plate, remembered her gloves, began to giggle, drew back her hand to remove the gloves.

'Who is it we know who's so fond of salt?' Jean said with a smile.

'Oh, you do keep on asking questions!' Kate blinked her eyes fiercely, tugged impatiently at the fingers of the gloves. At the other side of the room a waitress came through the curtained archway. She was carrying a tray with two glass dishes and Mike knew without a doubt that she was bringing the ice-cream Jean had ordered for the twins. He had the strongest feeling that if the woman came right up to their table, if she set down the tray and spoke to the twins, then it would shear through for ever the gossamer thread of memory.

'You should answer your mother's questions,' he said lightly, 'then she wouldn't have to keep on asking them.'

Kate turned and gave him a cheekily confident grin. 'Or,' she said, deeply amused by the brilliance of her own wit, 'she could stop asking me lots of questions and then I needn't bother to answer them.' She threw back her head and laughed delightedly. Across the table Vicky burst into spluttering mirth. Within thirty seconds he saw that both children had totally forgotten why they were laughing, they continued to explode with merriment from sheer pleasure at themselves, the jolly afternoon, the ecstatic feeling of being swamped by amusement.

He looked at Jean, his eyes registering the end of the episode, resigned to failure. She made a little wryly humorous grimace back at him.

'Later, perhaps?' she said very softly. And at that moment she realized beyond a shadow of doubt that there was no question whatever of his leaving the force and joining Guardcash, that the possibility had never really existed.

Mike raised his shoulders, let them drop again. The waitress reached the table, set down the glass dishes with precise movements.

'There we are!' she said cheerfully. 'Just what the doctor ordered!'

Kate began to giggle again. 'The doctor didn't order them,' Vicky said in an argumentative tone. 'We did.' Both girls began to shake with laughter. The waitress smiled down at them.

'Nice to be young.' She patted the top of Vicky's head.

When she had gone Kate dug her spoon into the ice-cream and took a delicious mouthful. 'Oh, it really is nice!' she said to her mother. 'You should have ordered one for yourself.' She flicked a glance at Vicky. 'I bet he's so fond of salt that he'd even put it on ice-cream.'

'Oh no, he wouldn't,' Vicky said. 'Not even Mr Lockwood would put salt on ice-cream.'

'Why particularly Mr Lockwood?' Mike could scarcely breathe, he heard the words come out as if someone else were speaking them. 'Why would it be Mr Lockwood who would put salt – or not put salt – on his ice-cream?' Oh let them answer me, he prayed, let them not dissolve again into giggles and fancies.

Kate dug her spoon in again. 'Because of course,' she said with loud emphasis, 'Mr Lockwood puts such a terrible lot of salt on his sandwiches.'

Chapter 19

Ashton held firmly on to Kate's hand as he walked a few paces behind Jean to where she had left the car. Vicky skipped along beside her mother, humming a tune to herself. Over the rest of her ice-cream Kate had let fall sufficient fragments of fact for Mike to be certain that whatever had been seen had been witnessed only by Kate, that any remarks of Vicky's were based entirely on what Kate had told her and so served only to blur the outline of actuality. He was concerned now to separate the pair, somehow persuade Kate to tell her story before the details dimmed, avoid alarming her in any way – and, even more difficult, get her to talk in front of Kenward or Trevitt without implanting in her mind the notion that what she had to tell was so important that she would inevitably be led to exaggerate, invent, embroider.

Completely out of the question to have made a serious start on the business sitting there in the tea-room; he had unobtrusively encouraged them to finish the meal as quickly as possible. When they reached the car he indicated to Jean by a movement of his head that she should take her place in the driving-seat with Vicky beside her. He opened the rear door for Kate and climbed in after her.

'Hang on a minute,' he said to Jean. He closed his eyes, tried to remember where the other two men would be at this moment. Kenward had said something about going into the Chilford police station. Had he intended that Trevitt should go with him? Was Kenward going back to Oakfield again today? If so, when? How long would his business at the station take him?

Mike bit his lip, he couldn't really remember, couldn't be sure, had only been half listening as he walked beside Kenward up the steps into the courtroom. What should he do? Call into the station, pick up one or other of the two men, take him back to Oakfield? What explanation could he offer? A few sentences spun from the lips of a giggling child? He had a vision of Kenward's eyes; sardonic, wearily amused, looking back at him.

Should he take Kate by the hand and march her into the Chilford station, sit her down in an interview room with Trevitt opposite, put a constable in the corner to take down every airy word? Utterly impossible.

'All right,' he said to Jean. 'Let's go. Back to Oakfield.'

They were turning in through the entrance gates when he saw the car coming down the drive towards them. A police driver at the wheel, a passenger in the rear, sitting well back.

'Pull over,' Mike said to Jean. 'That may be Trevitt.' As soon as she had halted the car he flung open the door and sprang out, held up a hand. The police car drew up a few yards away, Trevitt stuck his face out of the window.

'What's up? D'you want me?'

Mike walked across, opened Trevitt's door and bent down to speak. A few minutes later Mike came back to his own car and resumed his seat beside Kate who had fallen into a light doze during the short journey. Jean set the car in motion again. Vicky knelt on the passenger seat and peered out through the rear window at the police car going out through the gates, vanishing, and then reappearing a few moments later and proceeding up the drive again, towards the house.

'Why is that car coming back?' she asked as she stepped out on to the gravel. 'Have they forgotten something?' But no one answered. Jean took her hand and with a nod to Mike led her towards the front door through which subdued – or suppressed – protests could be heard coming for a minute or two afterwards.

'Are we back?' Kate sat up and yawned. 'What time is it? Did I go to sleep?' She allowed her father to draw her out of the car.

Trevitt came quietly up to them as they crossed the terrace. Mike had expected him to do his best to vanish into the background, out of Kate's immediate consciousness, but instead he spoke instantly and jovially to the child.

'Hello there.' He dropped into a half-kneeling position beside her and began to chat to her about her holiday, the beach, how she had spent the afternoon.

'I heard such a strange thing about Mr Lockwood,' Mike heard him say after a few minutes. 'I wonder if you know what it was?'

She narrowed her eyes at him. 'Was it about the salt?' she asked in a conspiratorial whisper.

He nodded. 'That was it. I'd like to hear about it properly from you. I have an idea you know what really happened. Will you tell me?'

'Mm!' She gave a single jerky nod. 'Of course I will!'

'We'll go inside,' he said casually. 'We'll find somewhere comfortable to sit down.' He rose to his full height and took her hand. They walked together into the house, Mike going in after them with a distinct feeling of having been abruptly relegated to a very small part in what was going on.

Trevitt settled himself into the corner of a sofa in one of the sitting-rooms. With a pleased wriggle of her shoulders Kate sank back into the cushions beside him. Mike seated himself a little distance away, behind them; he opened his notebook with a very odd sensation . . . taking down the words of his own child!

'How did you happen to see Mr Lockwood putting all that extra salt on his sandwiches?' Trevitt asked in a cosy conversational tone.

'It wasn't on all his sandwiches,' she corrected him. 'Just on one sandwich, the top one. I was in his bedroom – ' She saw the look of surprise on Trevitt's face. Her cheeks grew rather pink. '*Actually*,' she said in a frowning whisper, 'I'm not supposed to go running into other people's bedrooms but sometimes it just can't be helped.'

'Exactly what I always say myself,' Trevitt agreed stoutly. 'It could happen to anyone.'

Kate looked pleased and relieved. 'Well, we were playing hide-and-seek, Vicky and me, and I ran very quietly into the room and hid in the corner, behind the curtain. It's a sort of place where you can hang coats and things if you like, only Mr and Mrs Lockwood didn't have anything hanging there so there was plenty of room for me. I was waiting to see if Vicky would discover me and then I heard someone come into the room and close the door. Well, actually, *lock* the door. Of course

I knew it wasn't Vicky from the way he walked, and any-way Vicky would never lock the door, so I was a little bit scared in case I might be found out and I just peeped out through the crack in the curtain.' She mimed the actions as she spoke.

'And you could see who it was who'd come into the room?'

'Oh yes, I could see him very well. It was Mr Lockwood. He had a jacket on and he took a bag out of the pocket and put it down on the table. He opened the bag and took out the sand-wiches. They were wrapped up in a piece of paper. We always have them like that, they give them to us for our lunch. He took the top bit of bread off the first sandwich and put it down on the table. Then he stood up and picked up the chair he'd been sitting on.' Her eyes opened wide. 'I was really getting rather frightened, I didn't know *what* he was going to do.'

'What did he do?'

'He took the chair over to the big wardrobe and he stood on the chair and put his hand on top of the wardrobe. He fiddled about a bit and when he climbed down again I could see he was wearing a pair of blue gloves on his hands.'

'Were they the sort of blue gloves ladies wear?'

'Well, not exactly. They were blue rubber gloves, the sort Mrs Meacham wears in the kitchen. He took the chair back to the table and sat down again. He opened his hand and there was a sort of screwed-up bit of paper in it and he opened that and it had some salt in it. He pinched up the salt in his fingers and put it all over the sandwich. He shook every little bit of salt that was left on to the meat, he didn't leave any of it in the paper. Then he put the piece of bread back on the meat and pressed it down very hard. He wrapped the sandwiches up in the paper and put them in the bag and put the bag back in his pocket.'

'And all this time he was wearing the gloves?'

She nodded vigorously. 'And then he went over to the dressing-table and took two white tissues from Mrs Lockwood's box and he came back and put the paper that had had the salt in it inside the tissues. He'd never put the piece of paper down anywhere, he'd kept it in his hand the whole time. He wrapped up the paper very tight inside the tissues so it was just a little rolled-up ball in his hand. Then he took off his gloves and went over to the wardrobe and stood on the chair and put the gloves back on top of the wardrobe. He got down and carried the chair back and then he looked round the room – ' she hunched her shoulders. 'Ooh, I didn't dare to breathe! And he unlocked the door and went out and closed the door behind him.' She laughed. 'I was terrified in case he locked the door again and I couldn't get out, but he didn't. I know where he went then, because I heard him.'

'Where was that?'

'He went into the lavatory next door and pulled the flush. Do you know what I think?'

'No.'

'I think he just went in and dropped the rolled-up tissues in the lavatory and pulled the flush right away, because that was what it sounded like. I waited a little bit because I could hear him talking to Daddy.' She didn't shoot a glance at Ashton sitting a few feet away; it seemed to Trevitt that she had totally forgotten her father's presence. 'Daddy was asking Mr Lockwood if he'd seen Vicky and me. And then it all went quiet for a little bit. I heard Mr Lockwood go downstairs and Daddy went off along the corridor and then I heard him talking to Vicky and he took her along into our bedroom, so after a minute or two I sneaked out and went into our room as well.'

'That was very interesting,' Trevitt said appreciatively. 'You have a very good memory.'

'It's quite easy, really,' she said helpfully. 'What you have to do, is you sort of think about it and you can see it all happening in front of you and you don't really have to remember, you just say what it is you can see and people always say what an astounding memory that child has, but really it isn't astounding at all, it's just thinking about it.'

'I must try that next time,' Trevitt said. 'I'd like people to say what an astounding memory that man has. It would make a pleasant change. What they usually say is what a fearful clot that man is.'

'I'm sure you'll find it'll work,' Kate said earnestly. 'It always works for me. And I don't think you're a clot. Well, not a *fearful* clot.'

'Thanks ever so much,' Trevitt said. 'Consider me a friend for life. Shall we go and find Vicky now?'

Kate jumped up. 'Yes, she must be getting very bored without me. Of course she has Mummy to talk to, but that's not the same as having me, is it?'

'It certainly is not,' Trevitt said. 'I should very definitely say it's not the same thing at all.'

A few minutes later he joined Mike in the hall. They went up the stairs side by side, slowly, thoughtfully.

'It is, I suppose, just within the bounds of possibility,' Trevitt said in a light, objective tone, 'that your daughter Kate could have made the whole thing up?'

'I don't know,' Mike said heavily. 'I simply don't know.' Could she have pieced it together from half-heard, half-understood fragments? Children often heard a good deal more than one fancied they did. He thought of all the wagging tongues at Oakfield, the schoolboy, Ian Ripley, Brigid, Bessie Meacham. His mood slipped into dejection. 'It's quite on the cards that we're just wasting our time.'

Trevitt continued to walk on. 'We'll soon see,' he said pleasantly. 'Expect nothing, then you'll never be disappointed. I dare say some perspicacious Chinaman said that at some time or other.' They reached the door of the Lockwoods' room. He tapped on the panel, there was no reply. He tried the handle, the door wasn't locked. They went inside and stood looking round.

A table, a chair beside it, a box of white tissues on the dressing-table, a curtained alcove in the corner. 'Proves nothing,' Trevitt said. 'Dare say she's been in and out of this room half a dozen times, whether she's supposed to keep out or not.' He picked up the chair and carried it over to the large mahogany wardrobe, he flicked a glance at Mike.

'You a betting man? What's the odds there's a pair of blue rubber gloves on top of this wardrobe?'

Mike raised his shoulders without speaking. 'Do you know,' Trevitt said, 'I rather fancy I'm going to find those gloves.' He stood on the chair and looked on top of the wardrobe. There was nothing there. He stood on tiptoe and peered into the little well in the centre, he stretched out his hand and ran it over the

176

wood although he could see quite clearly that there was nothing there at all.

'Could have slipped down behind the wardrobe,' he said as he got down from the chair. He went over and looked along the space between the wardrobe and the wall, a good eight inches or so in depth, no trouble at all to see anything. If there had been anything there to see.

'Ah well,' he said cheerfully as he came back into the middle of the room again. 'It made a pleasant diversion. When your daughter's a bit older she might try her hand at writing fiction. She'll probably be a howling success.'

They went down the stairs, saying very little. I wish to God I was at home in Perrymount, Mike thought, I wish I'd never set foot in Oakfield. As they crossed the hall Trevitt said, 'I rather fancy a glass of very cold milk from the fridge. I wonder if I could persuade Mrs Meacham –'

'I'm sure she wouldn't mind.' One thing, Mike added to himself, she can't very well drop cyanide into a bottle of milk by accident. He followed Trevitt into the kitchen. Bessie was standing by the stove, peering into saucepans. She got Sergeant Trevitt his milk without wasting many words.

'Thank you.' Trevitt raised the glass to his lips, took a long drink. 'Oh, that's good, can't beat a glass of ice-cold milk on a warm day.'

There was a rap on the kitchen door. 'By the way, Bessie, I've just remembered,' said a pleasant country voice from the passage. Half a face manifested itself round the door. 'Oh, I'm ever so sorry. I didn't know as there was anyone –' The face vanished again.

'Come in, do!' Bessie said.

'There's no need,' said the voice. 'If you've got company. It'll wait.'

Bessie clicked her tongue. 'Come in, Daisy Martingale, when you're bid!' The woman edged into the room, stood just inside the door. 'It's only the police,' Bessie said. 'Not proper company.' In response to these reassuring words Mrs Martingale gave a single agitated nod. 'You've given a rub over Mr Godfrey's study, I hope?' Bessie said.

'Yes, of course I have.'

12

'Just one moment,' Sergeant Trevitt said, causing Mrs Martingale to grow briefly an alarmed two inches in height. 'Am I to understand that this lady works at Oakfield?'

'Yes, of course she does,' Bessie said. 'She's worked here off and on for years. In the season mostly.'

'Monday mornings, Tuesday evenings, Wednesday afternoons –' Mrs Martingale began a nervous litany.

'Oh yes!' Ashton said suddenly, remembering her name on the list. He'd totally forgotten her existence. He took a step forward and murmured in Trevitt's ear. Mrs Martingale began to pluck imaginary pieces of cotton from her skirt.

'She was over at her daughter's all yesterday afternoon and evening,' Bessie said. 'Her daughter's first baby. Twenty-five miles away, her daughter lives.'

'That's right,' Mrs Martingale said rapidly. 'I stayed the night with my daughter, only got back home at four o'clock today. I wouldn't have come back then but for having to think of my job.' She smiled. 'Ever such a nice little boy she had. Six pounds seven ounces, not too big and not too –'

'Very glad to hear it,' Trevitt said. 'I'm sure we both offer you our heartiest congratulations.'

She gave a little nod, looked pleased and relieved, cast about in her mind for an equally courteous rejoinder.

'I was ever so sorry to hear about poor Mr Lockwood's terrible accident. I never thought when I seen him there in the hall yesterday morning as it was the very last time –'

'You saw him in the hall then?' Trevitt said in an idle tone. 'What time would that be, do you happen to remember?'

'Oh yes, I remember well enough.' Confident now, on her home ground. 'On account of I was waiting to do the hall. I'd finished in the downstairs sitting-rooms, started work early on purpose. Wanting to get off early, you understand – with Mrs Barratt's permission of course – seeing as I had to catch the bus over to my daughter's.'

'And that would be?' Trevitt said with a relaxed air. 'What sort of time?'

'It was when they were going off to the golf-club.' Trevitt became absolutely motionless. 'They're always in and round the hall at that time of the morning, they pick up their flasks and sandwiches and so on. It'd be somewhere about a quarter to eleven. In the usual way I wait till they've all gone, I leave the hall till after, but yesterday, on account of my daughter, I wanted to finish early.'

Trevitt nodded. 'Quite so. Did Mr Lockwood happen to speak to you?'

'Oh no, he never saw me. I keep out of the way when there's guests about, as is only fitting. I was in that little sitting-room on the right as you come in, I was waiting till they'd all gone, I had the door a little tiny bit open, just so as I could glance out, you understand. I wasn't wasting my time,' she added defensively. 'I gave the furniture a bit of a rub, just kept looking out. If I'd have known it was the last time – ' She thrust a hand into her pocket, pulled out a handkerchief and blew her nose. 'Poor man, what a nasty thing to happen. To think I actually saw him pick up the very flask – '

'It wasn't in – ' Bessie began but Trevitt slanted at her a look of such withering ferocity that the rest of the sentence perished instantly on her lips.

'If only I'd known about the flask,' Mrs Martingale lamented. 'If only I could have stopped him.' She heaved a vast sigh. 'But there, we're all in the hands of the Lord.'

'So you actually saw him pick up the flask,' Trevitt said with an air of respectful admiration. She nodded. 'Just the one flask?' he said easily. 'Cast your mind back. Take your time. Try to remember exactly what it was you saw.'

She frowned, bit her lip, let out a long breath. 'Yes, that's right. Just the one flask.'

'And his sandwiches?' Trevitt let the words fall lightly. 'Did he pick those up at the same time?'

'Well yes, of course, he'd need to take his sandwiches.'

'Just the one packet?'

'Well, yes. Everyone just gets given the one packet.'

'He didn't, for instance, pick up his wife's packet at the same time?'

She shook her head at once, emphatically. 'Oh no, he wouldn't need to do that.'

'Why not?'

'Because he'd already put them in her pocket.'

179

It was very quiet in the kitchen. In the corner the fridge sighed and complained. 'You're quite certain?' Trevitt said in a gentle, almost caressing tone.

'Oh yes. He came into the hall – from upstairs if you follow me – he looked round, I suppose he was looking for his wife, then he picked up her anorak, that blue one she wears, it was over the back of a chair and he took the sandwiches out of his pocket – ' She paused, frowned, looked at Trevitt with slight surprise. 'Yes, that's right, he did take them out of his pocket, I don't know how he came to have them there.' She raised her shoulders briefly. 'Anyway, he put them in the pocket of her anorak. Then he dropped the anorak back over the chair and went over to the table and took his flask and sandwiches and went outside.'

'And Mrs Lockwood? Did you see her round about that time?'

'Yes. She came into the house – from the terrace, that is – a few minutes later. She just went over to the table and picked up her flask and she went to the chair and took her anorak and went out again.'

'I see,' Trevitt said. 'Thank you very much.'

'What was it you just remembered?' Ashton asked.

Mrs Martingale looked puzzled. 'How do you mean?'

'When you knocked at the door just now you said: By the way, Bessie, I've just remembered.'

'Oh yes, I know what it was. Slipped my mind.' She turned to Bessie with a little air of triumph. 'It's your gloves.' Trevitt's head came sharply round. 'Your blue rubber gloves,' Mrs Martingale went on. 'As you were hunting for yesterday morning. I meant to tell you, but what with getting off so quick – '

'You mean you've found them?' Bessie interrupted.

'Yes, it was ever so funny.'

'I left them down there,' Bessie said with force, jerking her head at the cupboard under the sink. 'Where I always leave them. A perfectly good pair of rubber gloves, almost brand new. And yesterday morning when I come to pick them up, they're not there!' She threw a dramatic glance at Ashton. 'Things just don't up and walk, not by themselves they don't.'

'Where did you find them?' Ashton asked casually.

'That's what I keep trying to tell you,' Mrs Martingale said. 'Ever so strange. In number six, you'd never guess where. Right on top of the wardrobe!'

'On top of the wardrobe?' Bessie cried in loud disbelief. 'Whatever would they be doing up there?'

'I'm sure I couldn't say. But believe me or believe me not, that's where I found them. There was this cobweb over in the corner by the window so of course I goes and gets the long cobweb broom to flick it down and I must have pushed a bit too hard for the head flew off the broom, you know how those things are, ever such flimsy little heads they have, fall off as soon as look at you, and you have to go to all the bother of clipping them on again. It fell off on to the top of the wardrobe and I had to stand up on a chair to get it down and while I was up there I saw this pair of blue rubber gloves in the well on the top of the wardrobe and I said to myself, Well I never, those'll be Mrs Meacham's gloves as she was going on about –'

'That'll do, then,' Bessie said sharply. 'And where are my gloves now, I'd like to know?'

'I left them in the broom cupboard, along of my things.'

'Then you go up and fetch them,' Bessie commanded.

Trevitt put up a hand. 'Actually, if you don't mind, I'd like to go and get them.' Bessie looked astonished. 'Might be of some interest to us,' Trevitt said. 'I'd just as soon you didn't handle them for the present.' Microscopic traces of cyanide on the gloves, without a doubt.

'My gloves?' Bessie said on a high note. 'Of interest to the police?'

Trevitt nodded, then he turned to Mrs Martingale. 'By the way, number six, whose bedroom is that?' Just to make sure.

She screwed up her eyes in thought and then clapped a hand to her cheek. 'Well, I never! Number six – that's poor Mr Lockwood's room – that was. Mr and Mrs Lockwood, I should say. However did Bessie's gloves come to land up there?'

Ashton came into the sitting-room with a tray of coffee, he set it carefully down. 'I just heard a news flash.' He jerked his head in the direction of the kitchen radio. 'They're going to mount a rescue operation for Osmond's, the Government are not going to let it go bust.'

Kenward inclined his head thoughtfully. 'And a good thing too. I imagine Barratt will sleep soundly tonight.'

Mike poured the coffee. 'Mrs Meacham burst into tears when she heard the flash.' He handed a cup to the inspector. 'She put her head in her hands and sobbed. I was rather taken aback.'

'Never a shallow woman,' Kenward said, looking back at his roving days. 'Plenty of good honest emotion in Bessie Meacham. Or I suppose I should say Bessie Pickersgill.' He lifted the cup to his lips. Turned out after all she was actually married to her new husband, all perfectly legal. That other wife of his – a prize shrew from what Kenward had been able to make out, couldn't really blame the fellow for taking to his heels – she'd been dead and buried, unbeknown to Meacham, a good twelve months before he slipped a ring on Bessie's finger. Overreached herself spring-cleaning, it seemed, fell off a step-ladder and broke her neck. An obsessively house-proud woman, apparently, under the impression that folk existed for the benefit of the dwellings they inhabited. Kenward stared reflectively into the steaming depths of his coffee . . . They who live by the mop and duster shall perish by the mop and duster . . . He sighed and shook his head.

Trevitt took a mouthful of coffee; he tilted his head and gazed up at the ceiling. 'I wonder if there was a moment,' he said with detached inquiry, 'when Lockwood realized that he'd taken a bite of the poisoned sandwich, that instead of killing his wife he'd succeeded in killing himself?'

Kenward drew a long breath. 'Could have been.' He felt tired, relaxed, at peace. 'Cyanide isn't quite as instantaneous in its effect as folk seem to think, doesn't act in a split second. He had time to take a drink of his coffee before he began to choke, he wouldn't have died for a minute or so after that. I doubt if he was capable of much rational thought, though, not the way he'd be just then.' He shook his head slowly. 'I suppose he thought his wife's death would pass for an accident. And if not, then there were plenty of folk about who might have had good reason for wanting to say good-bye to Mrs Lockwood. And there was nothing to connect him directly with the preparation of the sandwiches.'

'He could have gone down to the kitchen in the middle of the night,' Trevitt said. 'Stuffed the gloves into the pocket of his dressing-gown, tipped the cyanide into an old envelope or a piece of paper, gone back upstairs and hidden them on top of the wardrobe.'

'Do you know,' Kenward said suddenly, 'Lockwood offered Henry Whittall a sandwich. The top sandwich. If Whittall had taken it, he would have dropped down dead.'

'Then how could Lockwood be sure that his wife wouldn't do the same thing?' Trevitt said. 'How could he know she wouldn't offer the sandwich to one of the others?'

Mike frowned, working it out. 'He knew she wouldn't offer it to either of the Pagets because they all had sandwiches from Oakfield, they all had roast pork with slight variations in trimmings, there would have been no point whatever in any of the Oakfield contingent offering sandwiches to each other.'

'And Whittall was the only outsider,' Kenward mused. 'The only one with non-Oakfield sandwiches, the only one therefore that any of the others might be inclined to offer a sandwich to.' He paused, remembering Whittall sitting opposite him, giving that little shudder of distaste. 'But Lockwood knew for certain that Whittall wouldn't accept one of the Oakfield sandwiches.'

'How could he possibly know that?' Trevitt asked.

I wouldn't dream of eating dead flesh, Whittall had said, Never have done and never will do. 'He was a vegetarian,' Kenward said. 'And Lockwood would know that. Lockwood and he were at school together.'

Trevitt looked puzzled. 'Then why *did* he offer Whittall a sandwich? Knowing he wouldn't accept it?'

The inspector's eyes regarded the picnic, the way it must have been. 'A kind of exuberance, I fancy, a flourish, the cherry on top of the bun.' A man might easily feel like that in the last few minutes, about to commit a murder . . . He imagined Lockwood, keyed up, defiant, elated, taking a sandwich from the packet in his hand, scarcely looking at it, scarcely even aware of his own actions, talking most probably, smiling, laughing, taking a bite, chewing, swallowing, reaching over for the coffee, raising the beaker to his lips . . . and a moment or two later that single splintering second of fear, the instant horror-stricken realization, the gasping, choking, great tearing breaths. There would have been no further coherent thought. His last emotion on earth must have been that massive appalled surprise.

More about Penguins
and Pelicans

Michael Innes

A Night of Errors

Inspector Hyland was quickly on the phone to Appleby about the identity of the corpse:

'Sir Oliver Dromio – quite one of our local big-wigs. And a beautiful murder. Hit on the head – they think perhaps with the butt-end of a revolver – and then burnt to a cinder in his own fireplace.'

It was to be a confusing night, where identities were to be consumed and revealed in flames.

'The intellectual, the phantasmagoric, the exhilarating Mr Innes' – *Church Times*

and
Death at the President's Lodging
Death at the Chase
Lament for a Maker
Operation Pax

Patricia Highsmith

Strangers on a Train

'Bruno slammed his palms together. "Hey! Cheeses what an idea! We murder for each other, see? I kill your wife and you kill my father! We meet on a train, see, and nobody knows we know each other! Perfect alibis! Catch?" '

From this moment, almost against his conscious will, Guy Haines is trapped in a nightmare of shared guilt and an insidious merging of personalities.

'Miss Highsmith . . . is a writer who has created a world of her own – a world claustrophobic and irrational which we enter each time with a sense of personal danger' – Graham Greene

Ripley Underground

To avoid charges of forgery, the Buckmaster Gallery must produce the British artist, Derwatt. But he, unfortunately, is dead.

Tom Ripley is the only man who can perform the miraculous – but Tom cannot afford another scandal, and will stop at nothing, including murder, to avoid discovery.

and

The Talented Mr Ripley
Ripley's Game
Deep Water

Raymond Chandler

Farewell, My Lovely

'The dialogue crackles, the killer kills, the action covers a great deal of ground and hard knocks at terrific speed' – *Spectator*

The High Window

'Very tough, very tense, enormously lively' – *Observer*

The Lady in the Lake

'It is most efficiently written : the story travels at exhilarating speed. It is a brilliant who-dun-it' – Desmond MacCarthy in the *Sunday Times*

The Long Good-bye

'Chandler is the most brilliant author now writing this kind of story' – Somerset Maugham

Playback

Chandler's last great thriller.

The Big Sleep

'A book to be read at a sitting' – *Sunday Times*

Pearls are a Nuisance

'Full of life and character : as tense as a tiger springing into action' – *Daily Telegraph*

Killer in the Rain

A collection of early Chandler stories.

and

The Little Sister
Smart-Aleck Kill
Trouble is My Business

Margery Allingham

'Miss Allingham has a strong, though well-controlled, sense of humour, a power of suggesting character with a few touches and an excellent English style. She has also a sense of the fantastic and is never dull' – *The Times Literary Supplement*

'Margery Allingham stands out like a shining light. Everything she writes has a definitive shape . . . each book has its own separate and distinctive background' – Agatha Christie

Margery Allingham books published in Penguins

The Crime at Black Dudley
Police at the Funeral
Sweet Danger
The Tiger in the Smoke
Mr Campion and Others
More Work for the Undertaker
Mystery Mile
Traitor's Purse

Emma Lathen

Banking on Death

URGENT MEMO
TO: All connoisseurs of the unusual whodunit.
FROM: John Thatcher, Senior Vice-President of the
        Sloan Guaranty Trust.

Looking into a routine account recently I discovered
murder – no less! After a succession of encounters with
what I can only call *extraordinary* people, I even
discovered the murderer! Unfortunately I must admit
that my pride in my achievement is not unqualified.
Absurd as it may seem, I found myself *involved* with
these people; I found, indeed, that I was moved,
frightened, even exhilarated by the whole affair. For those
interested, I attach a full account of the matter.

Also by Emma Lathen

Come to Dust
The Longer the Thread
Murder Makes the Wheels Go Round
Death Shall Overcome
Accounting for Murder

Nicolas Freeling

'My whole idea,' states one of Freeling's characters, 'was to write about Europe in a European idiom. Something that has a European flavour and inflection.' If this was also Nicolas Freeling's intention, what a triumphant start he has made to his un-American activities! Here are characters that are subtle rather than tough; dialogue that echoes real life; settings (in the Low Countries) exactly inventoried; and, in Van der Valk, the Dutch inspector, a detective as human and unorthodox as Maigret himself.

'Has established himself as the most interesting new crime writer for some years' – Maurice Richardson in the *Observer*

Because of the Cats
Criminal Conversation
Double-Barrel
The Dresden Green
Gun Before Butter
The King of the Rainy Country
A Long Silence
Love in Amsterdam
Over the High Side
Strike Out Where Not Applicable
Tsing-Boum